IMPOSTURE

IMPOSTURE

Benjamin Markovits

W. W. NORTON & COMPANY
New York • London

Copyright © 2007 by Benjamin Markovits
First American edition 2007

Manufacturing by Courier Westford
Production manager: Anna Oler

Library of Congress Cataloging-in-Publication Data

Markovits, Benjamin.
Imposture / Benjamin Markovits. — 1st American ed.
p. cm.
ISBN 978-0-393-32973-5 (pbk.) .
1. Byron, George Gordon Byron, Baron, 1788–1824—Fiction. 2. Impostors
and imposture—Fiction. 3. Young women—England—London—Fiction.
4. London (England)—Fiction. I. Title.
PS3613.A7543I47 2007
813'.6—dc22   2007004948

W. W. Norton & Company, Inc.
500 Fifth Avenue, New York, N.Y. 10110
www.wwnorton.com

W. W. Norton & Company Ltd.
Castle House, 75/76 Wells Street, London W1T 3QT

1 2 3 4 5 6 7 8 9 0

He felt his fisted grip on the world being prised loose finger by finger until the last easing away seemed an almost welcome and deliberate release.

The Physician (unfinished), by J. W. Polidori, 1819

PROLOGUE

SOME YEARS AGO I TAUGHT at a private school in New York. One of my colleagues there was an English teacher called Peter Pattieson; I had a dim sense, as I met him, of having heard the name somewhere before. Mr Pattieson kept up an air of considerable mystery around the school halls. He was unhealthily thin, with a sparse billowing beard and tall head of hair; if you looked closely you could almost see beneath it the face and head of a childish, smooth-skinned man. I was too young at the time to guess the age of anyone of Peter's generation. He might have been forty, for all I could tell; he might have been deep into his sixties. I didn't at first have much chance of a close observation. Over a decade before my arrival, he had decided to stop talking – to everyone, that is, outside of the kids in his classrooms.

There were a number of rumours about him. That he used to pitch for a minor-league baseball team; that he once played Hamlet at the National Theatre in London; that he almost became the drummer for the Ramones. He had overdosed the night before their first gig, or so the story went; by the time he recovered, he had been cruelly and casually replaced. Whichever of these were true (maybe all of them were), nobody could doubt that the shore on which he washed up had been beaten in its day by a sea of drugs. With English teachers, you can always spot the hedonists. The ones who teach Bellow are not; the ones who teach Pynchon are. The ones who teach Wordsworth and Tennyson are not; the ones who teach Coleridge and Blake, obviously, are. Mr Pattieson taught Pynchon and Huxley and Dowson and Beddoes and Byron: he couldn't have announced his past any clearer if he'd worn a tie-dyed bandana, black shades, and a handlebar moustache to class. (What he wore, in fact, was an unwashed white shirt with a black jacket, covered in pipe ash.) His students, needless to say, adored him. Members of the cult of Pattieson were easy to recognize: the boys with their wispy whiskers and dirty, unfashionably formal clothes; the girls wearing black make-up and white foundation, collared shirts and velvet cardigans.

He was, as I've mentioned, a hard man to get to know. If you said something friendly to him in the hallways, he might volunteer a grunt in response. The grunt, I noticed at once, had something of an Irish depth to it, but whether he'd grown up in Ireland, or simply in Irish New York, I couldn't have said. The school was full of Irish New Yorkers, many of whom had never left the Tri-state area; their voices seemed to hum a little between the pull of different accents. If you asked Peter a question directly, something that needed an answer, he'd nod or shake his head. Demanding more than a yes or no from him earned you only a solid stare from eyes that rather bulged under the thick lenses of his glasses. At lunchtime, between classes, and sometimes (when I woke early), in the morning before assembly, I'd see him standing in the driveway just outside the school – smoking on the grounds was forbidden for student and teacher alike – with a pipe in his mouth and heavy earphones on. A walk-man, at least ten years out of date, jutted from the front pocket of his jacket. I remember, once, as I passed him, catching the tones of Fauré's *Requiem* coming out of his ears; another time, I was amused to hear the cheerful rising beat of 'In the Summertime'.

One of the privileges of the first-year teachers was that we were allowed to sit in, whenever we had a free period, on the classes of our more experienced colleagues. Towards the

x

end of the spring semester, I finally drummed up the courage to sit in on Peter's. I left him a note in his box (according to the protocol). There was nothing he could do about it that didn't involve some kind of a conversation with me – which was, as I'd practically reckoned on, the one thing he'd stop short at. It was one of those April New York days when the snows blow suddenly in. The heating had been shut off for the week of fine weather preceding; nobody, it seemed, could get it to come back on. The classroom was freezing; though the warmth of our bodies was just sufficient to steam up the windows. Sometimes, as a run of drips cleared a path in a misted pane, we caught a glimpse of snowflakes, as often as not whirling upwards in a gust of wind. Peter, I remember, kept his overcoat on: it gave him a Gothic dignity that rather suited the topic of discussion.

I don't know what I'd expected from him: some sort of transformation, I suppose. Perhaps, that behind closed doors, his clubbable self would emerge: secretive, naturally, but warm and generous and expansive, if only, from the contrast, to prove how much the world was the loser by his constant suppression of his own personality. Well, there was no transformation. Of course, he couldn't keep quiet in class, but his voice, when I heard it, seemed only in some hard-to-name way the natural eruption of his general silence: mumbling; reluctant; low; compelling. He stared as he always stared; his arms, as always, hung frozen by his side. It made sense, I saw that at once; he was silent because it suited him. That was the real personality. What the classroom brought out in him was only the conscience of duty: he talked because he had to, for once, and somehow the force of that obligation made itself felt. What surprised me, from the teacher's point of view, was how persuasive that force proved to be: his dirty, dishevelled kids slouched forward in their chairs, hoping, from their quiet attention, to catch every word.

The class was a senior elective on Byron – Peter had reached that stage in his stubbornness, or his career, when he could teach whatever he liked. I'd come to the school straight from a masters degree at Oxford, on the Romantics. It was the magic of Oxford, to an American ear, just the name of it, I think, that got me the job. In any case, Byron had been the subject of my thesis; I had picked Pattieson's class partly in the hope of showing off to him, a little, my professional expertise. I didn't often get the chance; and there was something in Peter's disciplined solitude that I found very seductive. Young men are often, I believe, only confident from their desire for praise; their confidence, at least the outward show of it, begins to wane as they wean themselves from the praise. At least, that's how it was with me. I wanted Peter to admire me; I wanted him to talk to me.

Most of the classrooms in that school, including my own, were set up like seminars around a very expensive cherry-wood table. We fancied ourselves as being almost collegiate; that was the tone we took to justify, among other things, the fees we took. Peter, however, had refused his expensive cherry-wood table and the cherry-wood chairs that went with it. His class was arranged, as it always had been, in institutional rows of narrow desks, which faced the teacher, who stood at a chalkboard. I took my place at the back where I could stretch my legs and observe all the greasy haircuts of the students in front of me. I was hardly, in the scale of things, much older than they were, and began to feel the force of my alignment. I belonged clearly to the ranks of brazen, uncertain boys and girls whose lives, regardless of the disaffection they pretended to, were all before them; rather than to the lecturing loneliness of a teacher who, whatever else was mysterious about him, had clearly come to terms with the fact that the best of his life lay behind him.

The lesson, as it happens, was on a story called *The Vampyre*, which had been written, Mr Pattieson said, in the same burst of inspiration that produced Mary Shelley's *Frankenstein*: they were begun in the same country villa, overlooking Lake Geneva, during the same bout of miserable weather, in the summer of 1816. Lord Byron and his occasional lover Clare Clairmont, Mr and Mrs Shelley, and Byron's doctor, a young man by the name of Polidori, had been holed up together for a week. To relieve the boredom, they began to recite ghost stories to each other, and it was only a matter of time, among so many writers, before they attempted their own. *Frankenstein* appeared in 1818, to a considerable sensation; and the following year a rumour went around the booksellers of London that Lord Byron was about to make his own contribution to the contest. Though the question of an imposture was obviously in the air, nobody had much interest in the answer. The scandal of Byron's separation, just three years old, had not died but faded into softer recollection. Rumour alone would have been enough to sell his books. Only John Murray, Byron's old publisher and friend, had much stake in insisting that it wasn't true.

What came out in the end, anonymously, in April 1819, was the little pamphlet that Mr Pattieson began to distribute among the class. I turned it over in my hands. The Gothic frontispiece, the play on fonts, the thickening of the ink around the date, all suggested the painstaking copy of an original issue – though dog-ears and soda-stains revealed the generations of students who had thumbed our booklets before us. Mr Pattieson recounted, for my sake perhaps, the tenets of New Historicism. (It was the kind of high school where such terms belonged to the general currency of ideas.) What mattered to Pattieson about a work of literature, more than anything else, was the history of its publication. *The Vampyre* had first appeared in Henry Colburn's *New Monthly Magazine*. It had sold as only Byron could sell, five thousand issues in a day: this fact alone seemed to give the poet away.

In a canny editorial, Colburn had hesitantly announced its authorship. Pattieson read it out. He wanted us, particularly, to note how skilfully the publisher had hinted at what he didn't dare to name: 'We received the following tale in the course of last autumn from a Friend travelling on the continent – in the company of an Individual, the stamp of whose Genius it is impossible to mistake.' Peter's reading voice was like his lecturing voice, only lower still, and still more enslaved to the rhythms. It took me a second to realize that he'd broken out of it: a delay, I think, that proves how little, to a man like Pattieson, the English language has changed in the past two centuries. He spoke Romantic like a mother tongue. Colburn, he continued, had touched on something that had always titillated Byron's public: the idea that the poet's best work would lie just outside the edge of what he dared to publish himself. The suggestion was that the present story had been stolen from him: it had the fascination of something overheard. Anonymity seemed the real proof of authenticity.

Mr Pattieson called on us to read in turn (it allowed him to retreat into silence) and yes, my heart did flutter a little when my own chance came. *The Vampyre* told the story of a young man, Aubrey, making his way into society. (Among the heap of manuscripts that came to me on Peter's death, I discovered one of the original pamphlets, which is now lying beside me on my desk.) Aubrey is taken under the wing of a prominent aristocrat named Lord Ruthven, who invites his protégé to accompany him on a tour of the continent. They set off and begin to see the world. A band of brigands stops their path outside of Athens. Fighting them off, Ruthven receives a fatal wound; and he begs his young friend to conceal, for the space of one year, all news of his death. Aubrey swears to it, and buries his companion under a pile of rocks among the dry foothills of the city, before continuing his travels alone.

This, I remember, is where my own reading took over.

When Aubrey at last returns to England, he is astonished to find his mentor, brilliantly alive, restored to his place at the heart of society. But the young man is bound by his oath and keeps silent, even when Ruthven begins to court his sister, the darling of Aubrey's youth, his constant playmate. Horrified, Aubrey succumbs to madness and awakes to reason only on the morning of their wedding, when he threatens his former protector with exposure. Ruthven retorts that if the marriage is put off, Miss Aubrey will be 'dishonoured. – Women are frail!' (It was my last line, and I gave it not a hiss but a deep austerity of intonation. The soul of a *vampyre* is his respectability; I wanted to show Peter that I knew it.) The tie is solemnized, and the bride and bridegroom leave for their honeymoon in Brighton. Aubrey, heartbroken, reveals what he knows to his sister's guardians, who promptly institute a search. But Ruthven has fled; and they discover, instead, that Aubrey's sister has 'already glutted the thirst of a Vampyre'.

Well, that was the story; and we sat for a minute in something like stunned amusement when it was over. The reviews – Pattieson broke our silence at last – had for the most part been critical. 'But,' as he said, 'it was their business to be.' Translations were almost instantly begun, into French and German. Goethe declared it to be a masterpiece. An opera, several dramas, and a novel grew out of it. In John Murray's backroom, poets and politicians debated its authenticity. 'The feeling, on the whole,' Peter added, in that soft Irish cadence which gives to any literary discussion a kind of native authority, 'was that Byron's most singular characteristic, his ability to please – in other words, his lucky instinct for the mood of the times, the way of the world – couldn't be shammed; that the reception of the book was sufficient proof of its author's genius.'

That was the question Pattieson finally put to us. Had Byron written it? 'You've been studying him for four months now,' he said. 'You should be able to recognize the way he writes; it's like learning to spot your lover by her walk. How long does it take to acquire the trick of that? A day, a week?' Yes, that was the way he talked. It was the kind of thing he used to say – the kind of thing, which, if anyone else had said it, would have roused the girls against him. But Peter could get away with anything like that; the girls loved him. He passed around a few samples of Byron's prose, for points of comparison: one of his letters from Venice to Thomas Moore, the preface to the first two cantos of *Don Juan*. And for the second half of that double period, the class, as teachers sometimes dream of saying, practically taught itself. Peter sat in his grey overcoat beneath the grey chalkboard in stony silence. He had got what he'd wanted, what he'd worked for: a return to it. It was a lesson to me, at the time, of how much a teacher can quietly accomplish by simply asking the right question. Even when the heating came on again, with a stertorous succession of clanks, his students gave only a brief sarcastic cheer; before coming back, quickly, respectfully, to 'discussing amongst themselves' the problem he'd set them.

I remember thinking, even at the time, that the subject might have had a more than simply academic appeal to a man like Peter. Of course, he was an old, or rather a New, romantic; and vampyrism was in some respects only the nineteenth-century metaphor for drug-abuse. Both proceeded from an appetite for life that couldn't be satisfied, whose limit was really the approach of death. Byron himself, famously, died a martyr to it – to his hunger for experience. But the larger questions, of anonymity, of authenticity, must also have played their part in a history as mysteriously vague as Peter Pattieson's. He had the air, among all his other airs, of a man to whom justice had not been done – whose gifts had time and again failed of their recognition. That Peter himself was complicit in that failure, I couldn't doubt; but he must have taken a private and perverse pleasure in setting us the task of distinguishing between the prose of Lord Byron, the most celebrated poet of his age, and the work of some anonymous nineteenth-century impostor. How much, Peter was subtly asking, can you tell about a life, from the living of it?

Towards the end of that class – and the students, by the way, decided at last that Byron *had* written the ghost story – I finally remembered where I had heard Peter's name before. I really should have spotted it earlier. It was something of a relief: a word at the tip of my tongue had tripped free at last. But I was sensible, too, of a sly and secret appeal to my vanity: I had gotten the joke. That appeal (imaginary, of course) still had its force. His secret seemed too small to be given away; in any case, I had determined to keep it to myself. Or rather, I was willing to wait until a more intimate opportunity arose, *to let him know I knew.* I hoped, with a funny sort of humility, that it might be my ticket to a conversation.

The year was almost over before that chance came up. I had been kept late at school. One of my students had said she was having trouble with an essay, only it turned out to be trouble of a different nature, and I had needed all of my youthful professional tact to emerge from the conference unscathed. It was a warm, enveloping Friday afternoon, at the close of May. From the football field, I heard the shouts of a game of Frisbee. The chestnut trees lining the drive up the hill had filled out beautifully; the view of the city below them was smothered in green. And the sound of the leaves, restlessly layered, almost made up for the absence of cool in the breeze. As I walked down the hill to the subway stop, I saw Peter standing at the gates and beginning to stuff his pipe. For once, his headphones lay loosely around his neck; the trees were music enough. I had my line ready – I had been steadily rehearsing it from a copy of *Old Mortality* I found in the English staff room. 'Most readers,' I said to him; it took all my courage to keep my voice up, while he kept his head down, 'must have witnessed with delight the joyous burst which attends the dismissing of a village-school on a fine summer evening.' He stared at me now, as I continued my little recitation: 'The buoyant spirit of childhood, repressed with so much difficulty during the tedious hours of discipline, may then be seen to explode, as it were, in shout, and song, and frolic, as the little urchins join in groups on their playground, and arrange their matches of sport for the evening.'

Peter picked up the speech, at last, in his reluctant brogue. 'But there is one individual who partakes of the relief afforded by the moment of dismission, whose feelings are not so obvious to the eye of the spectator, or so apt to receive his sympathy. I mean the teacher himself' – but he broke off then to smile at me, with something like the weightlessness of relief. It was rather a gruesome smile, I must say, exaggerated by the spread of his moustache and beard across his cheeks, and hardly improved by the fact of its rarity. But it was better than anger, which is what I had partly been fearing. 'You have found me out,' he said.

'Well, I won't give you away.'

I left the school at the end of that year, as it happens; that final week encompassed the period of our friendship. A chance had come up for me to live cheaply in England and write; which is what I had wanted to do, and I took it. I had made warm friendships among my various colleagues, and stayed in touch with several of them; though I can't say that Pattieson's is one of the connections I kept up. He wasn't the corresponding kind. When I heard of his death (from an overdose of arthritis medication), many years later, the regret I felt had more to do, if I must be honest, with the prospects of friendship now finally resigned, than the life wilfully lost. I had assumed at the time that his was the sort of privacy which included, among its secrets, several inti-mate lovers and friends; but none that I heard of ever emerged at the funeral, and I myself was too far away, too much preoccupied with a new life, to make the journey. A few weeks later, I came home to find a post office slip on the entrance mat. 'THIS DELIVERY ARRIVED WHILE YOU WERE OUT,' it said in block letters. A note in the contents box read 'from the estate of' followed by an illegible scrawl. I thought of Peter at once; and the next thing I felt was the guilt of my neglect; but the package had been too large to fit through the letter-slot, and I remember indulging a little the annoyance I suffered at having to walk, twenty minutes each way, to the post office depot to pick it up.

His real name, of course, wasn't Pattieson; the covering letter from the lawyer who handled his estate began with that admission. It was Sullivan. The glamour of imposture, which is what I had credited him with, couldn't survive the dry legal tone of correction. It seemed but a sad deception – for a grown man to resort to such games; and now that he's dead I don't mind giving him away. Pattieson, as I had finally recalled, was none other than Walter Scott's modest, imaginary schoolmaster, the supposed writer, as far as the joke went, of the *Waverley* novels, whose name supplied the gap left by Scott's anonymity. It struck me as just the kind of fiction a lonely old schoolteacher *would* indulge in, to cheer up his insignificance. I remember, afterwards, doing the maths. He was sixty-three when he died, which meant he was fifty-five when I knew him; at that point he'd been teaching at the school for about fifteen years. At forty, then, or thereabouts, the lure of deception, however pointless and private, had proved too great for him; the game presumably began when he applied for the job. I had a sudden sense of the overwhelming force, which most of us hardly keep at bay, of the desire to tell lies. No doubt his were part of a more general retreat – which included, it occurred to me, his refusal to speak a single word to his colleagues. Which included in the end, I suppose, his death. English masters, of course, often want to be writers. It seems a cruel sort of punishment that they spend their lives teaching the works of the great men who were.

XIX

Well, Pattieson, or Sullivan – I don't know which name to go by; *Peter*, I think, is the simplest and best – was a writer, too, in his way. The package, which formed the sum of my inheritance, contained a number of manuscripts, both finished and not, at the heart of which lay a succession of novels on the life of Lord Byron – written largely in what you might call the style of the times: of Byron's times, that is. Whether he sent them to me because I had *found him out*; or whether, as I think more likely, he had seen my reviews occasionally in the pages of various journals, and supposed me capable of putting his work forward, I'll never know. I have been reliably informed, in either case, that the gift of them entailed the right of publishing them; which is what I eventually set out to do. This, then, is the history behind the following tale, as they used to call them; which is doubly relevant, in that the story itself builds on the lecture he gave on *The Vampyre*, which I was lucky enough, years ago now, to have heard. He has taken liberties, of course, with the facts, as no doubt he is entitled to do. One would hardly, given his history, expect from him the simplest veracity; and there's a joke, a little one, he couldn't refrain from making, about the extent of Byron's influence – I mean, paternity. I don't suppose, at this late date, that the Rossettis will mind accepting into their genealogy a drop of the Vampyre's blood.

A word on the text. Friends of mine have remarked on what an odd thing it seems for a high-school English teacher from New York to write a story in a style nearly two hundred years old. Apart from everything else, there's the danger of anachronism, over each particular; not to mention the general danger (to take the word literally) involved in writing *against time*. Well, I suppose we all write against time; and for my part, I have never been so wedded to the age I live in to think of any deviation from its tone as a serious infidelity. But that Peter himself must have been conscious of this charge, one of our remembered conversations makes clear. At lunch one day, towards the end of that endless week that precedes the breaking-up of class, we went for a walk together through the neighbourhood of the school, as we both used, singly, to do. Among the grey gabled homes of Riverdale – I've always thought it a shame that the ugliness of American gothic is so often the language of wealth and glamour in Connecticut and New York – we discussed Keats's two *Hyperions*. In particular, his last triumphant stab at immortality, the second, allegorical fragment known as *The Fall of Hyperion*, which he eventually abandoned – from the fear, he once wrote, of its being too old-fashioned, too Miltonic, that is. Peter told the story (I let him tell it, though I had heard it before), of Hunt and Shelley's conversation about the poem. Hunt had wondered how a little Cockney apothecary who didn't speak a word of ancient Greek could make an epic of their mythology. I can still hear Peter mumbling the famous reply – through the soft mass of his beard, which was both the emblem and the instrument of his general reluctance to expose his face to the world. 'And Shelley, whom envy never touched,' Peter had said, 'gave as a reason, that Keats *was* a Greek.' I think on that note I can finally let him tell his own story.

BENJAMIN MARKOVITS
London, 2006

publisher himself had gone out, and the door was locked, that the gentleman whom our tale concerns approached the shop – in spite of his youth, with the support of a walking stick. His free hand held a copy of the *New Monthly*, as if he had only come to return what was no longer wanted. Even so, he continued to read from it, with a kind of reluctant satisfaction, given away by the murmur in his lips. As he reached Colburn's door, he attempted to fold the magazine into the hand that held his walking stick – awkwardly enough. The paper was dropped and picked up again; afterwards, he stood for a minute frozen, as if to gather his thoughts, while staring at the name on the brass plate.

He wore his dark hair in curls, which fell loosely across his forehead in such a way as to hide the recession of his hairline. His features, on the whole, were very fine: eyes, black and large; a cleft of stubbornness in the chin; a sensual protrusion of his lips. His strong, straight nose and small, womanish ears suggested internal contradictions. In fact, he was somewhat womanish all round, in figure and pose; his boyhood seemed never to have escaped into manhood. Even the sharp broad lines of his jaw implied a certain delicacy: a precision that could not bear rough handling. When he was angry and puffed up, as now, they comically took on the appearance of a full mouth – an effect brought into clear relief by his high stiff white collar and coal-black coat.

It was the dress of a dandy; but the costly tailoring seemed to have slackened over time, and spoke less of the exactions of taste, than of the compromises a man is forced to make with his own bad luck: the clinging to, the keeping up. In any case, the fashion had changed. He looked at least five years out of date – a prodigal returning only to find that his threadbare suit, carefully, proudly preserved, has long since fallen out of style. He was the sort of young man who inspires wherever he goes a vision of his untidy bedroom. One supposed he hadn't any money for a coal fire; one imagined the draughts. The walking stick favoured his left ankle; an old injury, perhaps, which, from the perversity of blood, had become inflamed in the spring chill.

The London sky had been thickening all day; clouds had piled up over Soho. Their shadow fell over Great Marlborough Street and under cover of it, the first rain fell, fat drops still rare enough to be counted. As if rehearsing a speech, he began to mutter at the red front door: 'You had no business publishing that story. It was written for the pleasure of friends. It had a private significance I don't want publicly guessed at.' But a sense of foolishness seemed to quiet him, or prick him to courage – all the more urgently, as he was beginning to get wet. He leant his stick against the door-jamb; then, with one hand, spread the magazine above his head. With the other, he knocked. Gently, at first, and then with a growing and rhythmic insistence, whose music, after a minute, seemed to become its real function, and a source of relief.

'Is no one in? I want to see him, too . . . You will ruin the paper.' A woman, leaning suggestively under her umbrella, appeared at his elbow. She was looking at the plaque on the door – *Henry Colburn, Bookseller*. The brass glowed sullenly in the dark afternoon.

He said without thinking, 'I don't mind ruining it; I wrote it.'

She paused a moment and gave him an underlook. 'My Lord, I hardly knew you.' She tilted her umbrella back behind her head to let the light come through to his face. 'You've grown so dark and thin.'

He examined her in turn. A pinched, pretty countenance, sharp-nosed, and somewhat pale, the colour of ash-wood – rather brown than white. Her bottom lip pushed out stubbornly, pinkly. One wanted to take it in hand and pull; a chastisement which, one might suppose, had its sensual undertone. A worn wet bonnet was as faded as her hair. There was a terrible gentility of crow's feet around her eyes: she seemed the kind of young woman who equated decency

3

with worrying. But she had a fine figure, if small-hipped – and then, the indescribable, threadbare *youth* of her stopped one's heart. She couldn't be more than eighteen or nineteen (light kindling burns quickest) and her face already wore the screwed-up look of concentrated loneliness, its brave front.

'We met,' she said, after another pause, in a low tone, 'at the Duchess of Devonshire's ball. Many years ago now. You wore green tails and yellow boots; and were much admired. I . . . I was in a spangled dress; we danced one waltz and . . . sat out another together.' Then, blushing at the recollection, she added, conspiratorially, 'I had understood . . . I had understood you were abroad.' She touched a hand to her throat. 'Miss Esmond – I mean, Eliza. I'm staying for the season at Lady Walmsley's.'

For a moment, he didn't answer, and then with a smile of inward humour, he bent intimately towards her. 'I was, of course, very much; but, as you see . . . Returning on the quiet, for several reasons. I hope you'll do me the honour of – keeping my silence. I can't think where it would be more prettily kept.'

'Of course,' she murmured, 'of course.' She stood in the dry shadow of her umbrella, unhappily apart, as if untouched by a common affliction. The rain fell simpering around her, and made up, a little, for the silence that grew between them.

Her discovery seemed to have unsettled her. She couldn't move, and the young man managed to get rid of her at last only by offering his own copy of the magazine, such as it was: the ink had begun to run, and stained her fingers as she took it, with the gentleness of reverence, from his hand. She promised, of course, to return it; which brought out, inevitably, the secret of his address, in Lincoln's Inn. Finally satisfied, she walked away, though as she turned the corner onto Regent Street, she cast her gaze back on him once more. He was, by this time, thoroughly drenched. His hair

4

hung flatly and darkly over his temples. Even his coat dripped from the hems into the puddle in which his shoes stood. She could hear him, too, with his fist raised, banging steadily and hopelessly against the large red door.

CHAPTER TWO

H E HAD NEVER BEEN to the Duchess of Devonshire's ball; but it seemed, for an instant, only natural that he should have: such pleasures, such admiration, were clearly only his real deserts. Such a fine young man he was. He had a sudden, giddy sense that the world is what you make of it, the way you tell it. Then one of his inspirations . . . well, that was mischievous. But it cheered him briefly, not only from the success of his imposture, but the fact that it was just the kind of prank he used to play in his hot youth – before, that is, the settling in of his circumstances that marked the end of it. He consoled his conscience: he hadn't set out to deceive Miss Esmond, especially as she seemed to him somewhat fleshless prey. Still, her nervous, vibrant hesitations appealed to him.

Even so, he was glad at last to be rid of her. There was something awful about the pretence. The tax it made upon his face, the muscles of his smile, the subtler strain it put upon his own self-image. He watched her stepping in and out of the rain-shadow of the house fronts, her umbrella set at an angle against the wind; and doubted he should see her again. Probably for the best; though he imagined, as she walked, taking her waist in hand between his thumb and forefinger. Soon he was blind from the rain in his eyes, and before she reached the corner of Regent Street, he had turned again to begin his assault on the door. For a minute, the only thing he felt was the banging in his hand and heart.

Well, there was no use getting completely drenched; Colburn wasn't in, or wasn't answering. This was just the kind of inconsequent reversal that he tended to treat as final. He was apt to 'stick' when nothing good could come of 'sticking'; and liable to give in, just when something might. But the girl had somehow heartened him, her silly delusion. A coffee-house across the road had a view of the door. He hadn't any money, but when he saw a young man in a knee-length coat slip out of the seat in the bay, he ducked in to take his place. The room was thick with the stench of wet wool; the low continuous echoes of conversation seemed equally oppressive. But no one noticed him; the lukewarm dregs of a cup of coffee remained, and he could cradle his hands around the mug. A mash of coal fire was just hot enough to warm the soaking clothes against his skin. He shivered whenever these touched his leg, and began to drink. The coffee had a spike of rum in it; as it ran through his blood, he reflected on the succession of good luck and bad that had brought him, cold and dripping, to haunt Colburn's door.

It was only three years ago that Lord Byron had engaged him as his travelling physician. The poet, when they met, himself remarked on the similarity between them. Byron had palmed his cheek gently and said, 'I like to admire myself . . . in a youthful mirror.' He put his own hand to his face. No wonder the poor girl was taken in; and as his trousers began to stiffen in the heat from the fire, he repeated the line to himself. It offered surprising comfort, suggesting as it did larger connotations to a life that had become cramped with insignificance. A strange phrase, though. It seemed, like a smoothing hand, to rub away his features and replace them with a reflective sheen – in which Lord Byron, dimly, appeared. All that it left of *himself* was the impressionability of glass, the rosiness of youth.

John Polidori had just turned nineteen when he first came down to London from Edinburgh. He was the youngest medical student ever to take his degree. Grand and inevitable good fortune awaited him. That was his faith, his consolation, as he began to kick his heels at home. He was just 'looking out for a position' – a line which, as he soon discovered, he had every opportunity to repeat. After one month, he sometimes added, 'It was only a question of finding something suitable; one didn't want to snatch at first chances.' After two, he professed himself, with a charming modesty, 'Ready for anything'. After three, he used to explain, in a degree of detail that he himself suspected of becoming tedious, the difficulties a young doctor could expect to face, in setting up a practice. After four, he kept silent; he had started to smell of disappointment.

His father's nose, in fact, used to wrinkle with distaste every time his son descended late to breakfast, or went up early for his afternoon nap. It didn't help that his favourite sister, Frances, was getting married; Polidori couldn't bear the thought of her leaving home before him. As the oldest son, he was desperate to 'make good an escape' – that was the phrase Frances had used for her own. She was about to marry a man named Rossetti, another émigré. Rossetti was handsome enough and well-connected, perhaps; at least, he had just been appointed consul in Milan. Yet he seemed to Polidori a little flighty, or rather, gifted with a grace that suggested if not inconstancy then the lightness of touch that produces it. He was the wrong husband for her. What Frances wanted . . . well, the prospect of her marriage had astonished Polidori into a sense of his own loneliness.

John and Frances were the first- and second-born in a gaggle of eight. They used to play at mother and father together – used to kiss, as they had seen their parents kiss, chastely, before going up to sleep. Polidori remembered the blinding of her curls against his face. She was two years his junior, but now he felt that Frances had outgrown him; she was playing mother to him, too. He sometimes heard her singing on the stairs outside his room, as if unconsciously; though he guessed it was only to rouse him out of bed in the

morning, whenever he was lying in. Still, he found the
sound of her almost unbearably moving, her fine arch
Italian voice, and stayed in bed only to keep her singing:

> Sleep is a reconciling,
> A rest that peace begets.
> Doth not the sun rise smiling
> When fair at even he sets?

When he did rise up, it was not without tears: his childhood
was over, she was singing the funeral dirge. (They had
seemed to him then the first tears of manhood; but as he
stared now at Colburn's door, through the steam gathering
on the glass, they struck him rather as the last of his youth.)

Finally, a 'break in the weather' came. That's how he put it
to himself, as if the sense of failure he had been enduring
were only the darkness of a rainy season. He had received a
summons from his mentor, Dr Taylor, a leading figure in
Norwich's radical societies. Polidori was ready to jump at
any excuse for a diversion. Norwich, at least, offered a
respite from his own idleness; and he returned from his
eventful visit as late as he could, only a week before the
wedding. He was bursting with 'news'. Yes, something had
finally happened, as he'd known it would. Sweaty with
sleeplessness from his coach-ride, he sought out his father,
Gaetano, straight away. The house, as Mother phrased it,
'had been thrown up and down' by the confusion of 'last
minutes'; and the old man used to take what he called 'a
cold, *quiet* bath' before breakfasting *en famille*.

Dr Taylor had passed on to his protégé a remarkable offer.
Lord Byron, it seemed, wanted a physician; and a mutual
friend had asked Taylor for a recommendation. Polidori,
who was not without literary aspirations, had followed the
story in the papers; his mentor had indulged his own sweet
tooth for more private scandal. The poet's wife, in bidding
for a separation, had hoped to prove him mad. There was

gossip, of course; though so far the name of Byron's sister had escaped the smear of press-ink. And stories of his lordship's Harrow and Cambridge days had been successfully hushed up. Then there were the more distant rumours of what Byron himself supposedly dismissed as his 'genial gift for adaptation' – a necessary facility for any traveller – the spirit to take a place, and its people, *as they come* – which he had indulged freely, especially in Turkey. In any case, he was looking to go abroad again and wanted a young man, a doctor, to accompany him.

Some of this Polidori communicated, while averting his eyes from his naked father; he was faintly dispirited already by the contrast in their cleanliness. The old man's skin had taken on a blue shadow under the shock of the cold, and his hair lay in sleek lines down his neck. His temples were fair and bald, and his jowls hung silkily with the smooth additions of age. When he rose out of the water at last, a steady drip depended from his shrunken member; the wet percussion of it was a constant reminder of where not to look. 'I have been blessed by many sisters,' Polidori thought, involuntarily. A habitual complaint, a part of the family idiom: *poor, put-upon, cosseted Polly* (as the family called him) *and all his girls.*

There was Frances, of course, with her dirty Italian complexion, her brother's cleft chin, and a hooked, boyish nose. Tremulous thin lips were the only outward evidence of her soft heart. When she was ten, he had teased her into following him up the large awkward arms of an oak tree, which overlooked one of the ponds of Hampstead. She had followed him anywhere then. But her hands, in the end, proved too small to grip around the branches, and she had fallen, lightly, suddenly, onto a root below – unharmed, as it happened, except for a little cut stretching out the corner of her eye, from the tip of a leafy twig, as she fell past it. It bled heavily into her vision. She screamed and screamed. He had never known such shame and heartbreak. Now all that remained of the scar was a hot red line that came out whenever she was happy or angry. But she had long ceased to follow him anywhere; and more and more he himself felt the pull of her comings and goings.

But there were others, too, three sisters more. The youngest of these, Esmé, with a fat blunt face like the palm of a hand, had herself reached the 'following' age. Red curls fell to her shoulder; freckles thick as clover surrounded her eyes. She had greeted Polidori clamorously on his return from Norwich, and now trailed him downstairs. She was greedy for him and wanted always to know what he thought, what he carried in his hand; what pleased him; how he planned to fill the time. Her satisfaction, his restlessness – stuck at home, at his age! – played curiously off each other. If only he found such comfort in his person as Esmé did. What did he offer the little girl that he denied himself? She slapped her naked soles on the broad wet stones, crying 'Tell me, tell *me*' from time to time, and splashing whenever she could. Polidori felt the burden of his age. As the eldest child, great things were expected of him. But his recent idleness had disappointed his father; and consequently perhaps, Polly still trusted too thoroughly in him. He wanted to please.

Gaetano looked squarely at his son. 'I am not sure,' he began, not in the tone of uncertainty, but rather, with the false hesitation of someone softening bad news. His accent had retained the sourness, the refinement of his native Tuscany, the musty thinness of cognac. 'I am not sure . . . his Lordship would prove a . . . beneficial example to you. You are' – and here he looked down himself, ashamed either of his doubts or the intensity of the sentiment – 'a wonderful boy, of great natural talents, but easily led astray. Easily seduced . . . by enthusiasm. Lord Byron has not impressed in me a confidence in the stability of his character.' (The arrogance of this plain old man!) 'His influence would be pernicious.'

Somehow Polly had been expecting this; in spite of his father's love, and such indisputable good luck, somehow . . . He began to make his case, but Esmé was tired of being ignored. 'Ding dong bell,' she cried out, 'ding dong bell', touching her father's little piece this way and that with her pink hand. Her laughter was like the sudden stopping of a horse on loose stones. Polly picked his sister up in his arms, where she wriggled abominably; his father gave him a look over her wild head. As if to say, better she were yours, at your age, than mine, at mine. His thin lips flattened to a line. Polly said only, 'But you must see – you must see – the great honour –' and stopped short. His father stepped heavily out of his bath.

The wonder of it was that Gaetano, of all people, should have understood the allure of Lord Byron's companionship. He had served, in his own youth, as a secretary to the great Italian dramatist Conte Vittorio Alfieri. Gaetano always spoke the name with the relish of an emigrant tasting, after a long absence, the bread of his home again. Other, even grander, names inevitably followed it. Alfieri's mistress had been the Countess of Albany; a title that brought out, in Gaetano's pronunciation, the worst of his English snobbery. And she herself had been the widow of 'no less august a personage, than Charles Stuart, the Young Pretender'. It was on the strength of these connections that Gaetano had retired to London and set up a profitable business, as a translator and Italian instructor. Alfieri's influence had been the making of him.

In fact, Polly's news did put Gaetano in mind 'of those youthful associations'. And he recounted over breakfast, 'for its instructional value', the story of his eventual dismissal. Polly had heard it before and Frances shot her brother an amused look, which Gaetano saw and pointedly ignored. He was the kind of father unembarrassed by repetition; repetition, in fact, was the gavel of his authority. 'The Count,' he said, filling his mouth with a slippery forkful of fried onions, 'recovering from an illness and consequently low-spirited, begged me to keep them company in the evenings. At one point, the Countess (from what private quarrel who can guess?) asked Alfieri why my youthful thighs were rounded while his own were flat. "Stuff and nonsense," Alfieri replied, wrinkling his nose, resentful of that illness – age – from which none recover. They passed on to some indifferent talk. But from that time I no more had the honour of being one of the exalted party.' '*I no more had the honour*, etc,' his children, who had heard the line before, began to echo him. But Gaetano persisted, adding more sharply now, to press home his point, 'Neither could I complain of this. I myself felt that the question had been unseemly – more in character for a drab than for a discreet and modest lady.'

Gaetano wore his prudishness, in the broadest sense, as a kind of distinction. The world was better left untouched; it stained one so. And he had, in general, refused to handle it – aside from his tireless fertility, from the dirty business of making and raising eight children. He hadn't entirely renounced the world, only that part of it lying outside his own powers to chastise and create. Nor could he suppress the pleasure he took in this little triumph over the great man, though it was only the inevitable, and ordinary, triumph of youth over age: of plump legs over bony. Lord Byron's offer to his oldest boy had reminded Gaetano of the company he had forfeited in his own youth. And Polly, in fact, read into the old man's disapproval only the ordinary, and inevitable, envy a father feels for his son.

After all, Gaetano had always wanted him to write, to preserve the name of Polidori in the aspic of literature. To go, as he said, one better than himself, an honourable translator. He had pushed his son to take up medicine precisely because it seemed a useful career for a man of letters, on several counts. And Polidori had consented. Yet here was a chance to further both ambitions: the greatest poet of his age wanted a physician. But Gaetano still urged him to decline the offer. In the weeks to come, their argument persisted: a quiet war, whose isolated shots grew occasionally into skirmishes.

Polly, for once, stood up to his father. He accepted the poet's invitation to tea and arrived at Piccadilly Terrace as nervous as a schoolgirl. It was Lord Byron's sister, Augusta, who greeted him first: a lively woman, plump and ungainly with the imminence of childbirth. Her mobility of expression largely concealed the dullness of her sleeping face. There was something about her nose, flattened at the tip, that suggested the bullying hand of stupidity pressed against her, unless it was only the fleshy accretions of her pregnancy. Stroking the hair off Polidori's forehead, she examined the two young men, side by side. 'You might almost be brothers,' she said, teasing the pair of them with the motherly, sensual touch of her warm palms. They smelt of cloves. Byron's stomach had been upset by nerves, and 'Goose' (as he called her) had been brewing a concoction to quiet them.

His apartments at Piccadilly Terrace were cluttered already with the preparations for departure. Polly, in fact, sat down on a box of animal feed, as he guessed by the stable odours rising from it. The couches were covered suggestively in his Lordship's clothes. Byron said, 'What do you think of him, Goose?' lying back amidst his own tangled *accoutrements*. And she looked at Polidori with a look not so much cunning as having the joy of cunning in it. 'I think he'll do, at a pinch.' She seemed happier, easier, than either of the men. The duns, as Byron said, 'like crows, were always clamouring at dusk.' One felt their presence; a crowding in, that gave to the air in the room a decided pressure. Something must shortly erupt. But his lordship's manner, in the shadow of farewells, seemed almost painfully sweet. Taking Polly's cheek in his hand, Lord Byron agreed with his sister. 'I like to admire myself . . . in a youthful mirror,' he said, as the young man bent his head to kiss the poet's fingers. It was a kind of parting gift, an act of persuasion: who could resist him?

Polidori turned home that night in high spirits. He had left the brother and sister entwined upon a low couch. The image of them, of their quiet freedoms, stuck in his thoughts and acquired over time the slow, bright heat of contained fire. His father was waiting for him in the study. He attempted, in the strongest terms, to dissuade his son from going. The tenderness of his paternal concern had soured into anger, almost into indifference. 'Lord Byron will be the end of you,' he predicted coldly. 'A fresh pot fired too quickly cracks at once. You will not survive the heat of his *amour propre*.' Polidori, still standing, refused to be abashed. 'His Lordship has treated me,' he said to Gaetano, 'more than generously, as his equal, his friend.' He mentioned Augusta's flattering remark, not without qualification: hoping to appeal to his father's family pride. 'Of course, my youth lends more colour to my countenance. To my hair: curls and lustre. And besides all that, I am perhaps as much as a tiptoe taller.' He blushed as he spoke but managed to keep back the tears; it cost him a great deal to defy his father. Rebellion made him childish again.

And then, on the eve of Frances's wedding, Polly almost relented. (He remembered it now, with the bitterness of the coffee on his tongue: the chance, not taken, to yield to an ordinary life.) Father and son decided to leave the house to the women. They sauntered arm in arm through the streets of Piccadilly, both somewhat chastened by the thought of losing Frances to that smooth-skinned man. Polly recounted one of the games the two of them had played as children. He would offer Frances his hand, and she would pretend to bite it: just closing her lips and teeth across his knuckles, until he abruptly withdrew, his fingers wet from the touch of her mouth. Then they repeated the act. And each time, looking up at him black-eyed, she bit down harder and harder on his flesh; until her teeth reached bone and he

15

cried out and spent on her the fruits of his bad temper. 'This, too,' he said, 'was a part of the game: my anger afterwards.'

Gaetano, as they made the rounds of St James's Square, elaborated on the true reason for his reluctance. He said that he understood something of the burden great men thrust upon their companions; something of the patience, the simplicity of character and the easy confidence one needed to carry the weight of their arrogance. He himself had suffered, terribly, in his youth, at Alfieri's hands, at the unanswerable claims of the poet's self-love. Those evenings he spent with the Count and Contessa offered, of course, wonderful compensations, but he felt, in their presence, the blood drain from him, his life-blood thinning away. 'Fui terzo tra cotanto senno,' he declared, in a voice he specially reserved for quoting Dante: 'I was third, amid such company.'

And he feared his son possessed something of his own sensitivities; indeed, to a still more painful degree. That he might not survive the contact of 'so fiery a comet' as Lord Byron. That just those qualities for which a proud father entertained such hopes – Polly's honour, his fine-feeling, his appetite for life – would expose him to the full force of impossible comparisons. This was his phrase: 'impossible comparisons'. 'Fui terzo tra cotanto senno,' he repeated; even at his most vulnerable, a pompous bully.

Polly promised him, as they crossed into Piccadilly on a mild night just muffled in the light cotton of a spring haze, that he would write to Lord Byron at once and decline the offer. His father embraced him quaintly. His full-sailed belly pressed against his son, as he held one hand against his own heart, while the other reached to touch the young man's shoulder. But by the next evening, Polly had changed his mind. He had seen, at the ceremony, the wince of his sister's scar grow red with happiness. He had watched Rossetti stretch his pale hand towards Frances for a ring. He had wondered, addressing his sister in his thoughts, and smiling a little, 'Why do you not bite him? Why do you not bite him?' – rather unhappily, too. On Monday morning he set off for Lord Byron's apartment, hoping to intercept the post. He found his lordship at home, writing letters. 'You've changed your mind again, I suppose?' the poet said looking up, not unkindly. Polly enjoyed the feeling that his lordship had taken the measure of him already. He nodded, smiling too, to save his voice.

Within a week, he had made his preparations. Byron was leaving in the morning for Dover. They were taking two carriages. One was a rather grand contrivance, fashioned after Napoleon's model. It would carry Byron and his friend Scrope Davies, a small, thin-faced man, dressed in unhappy perfection. To fool the bailiffs, Polidori and Hobhouse – another friend, fatter and more serious and sillier at once – would set off first, in Scrope's calèche. His lordship asked the young doctor to appear at dawn; he wanted to make a good start. It was a fine thin April morning. Polly arrived while the poet was in bed. His sister answered the door in her rounded négligé; she said that Byron complained of a headache, he had only just come in from dancing. There were biscuits and soda-water in the drawing room, in case Mr Polidori had not yet breakfasted. 'Goose' returned to Byron's room. He heard his laughter, a low, sweet sound that suggested the kindness of melancholy, forced good spirits. Somewhere Frances lay in that young man's arms.

Polly broke a biscuit and tried to eat it. It was too dry, it would not go down. He was all dust and nerves. The room lay in the disrepair of departure. A Harrison clock ticked audibly, like a throat that will not swallow. There were several cases, of clothes and books. A broken vase lay shivered on the marble hearthstone; yellow tulips scattered confusedly, rumpled here and there by the weight of the shards. The slick of wet had spread already to the floor and stained it. French doors gave onto a balcony and he stepped out. The watery blue of sky was just deepening with day. A sheet of sunshine, like cotton drying on a line, lay fluttering on the paving stones. The world was all before him: he turned to look up the street, but took little in. Only a girl, her back to a wall, shivering in the young dawn. Her cheeks hollowed by shadows; her aspect pinched. The greed or hunger in her glance made him look away. His prospects seemed too wide for the view at hand: the narrow corridor of buildings, the growing rumours of traffic from Piccadilly. The wind blew unevenly, of sweet and sour mixed; the stench of sewage just rising from the gutter, and the fresher tonic of the spring. He held his hair out of his eyes then turned inside again, to contemplate his new life on a grander, imagined scale.

CHAPTER THREE

ELIZA ESMOND HAD NEVER BEEN to the Duchess of Devonshire's ball.

Her sister, Beatrice, was known as the beauty of the family. She had that cast of girlish features – a small weak chin, high cheeks almost bruised by the bones beneath her eyes, the eyes themselves large and light, windows, it seemed, giving onto a clear bright expanse of soul – which touch men's hearts without exciting pity. Eliza herself, pretty enough, just shaded their response towards the latter. She had a look of innocence abused, and worse still, too long preserved: consequently soured. Rather sensual in its way, like all frustration.

Their father, Nathaniel Esmond, was a clerk at the naval registry; a man with high ambitions; an awkward poet who had turned lately to writing romances in order to make money, though neither his verse nor prose had seen the light of print. Beatrice, by five years the elder, had assumed the part of baby-sister. She had adopted a very practical unworldliness. She knew just what she wanted from the world, or rather, just what she could reliably take. The weight of filial duties – the burdens of living up to a passionate, ineffectual father – had never afflicted her. She happily ceded that portion of her inheritance to Eliza and married at the first opportunity.

Anthony Simons, a lieutenant, was not particularly handsome. Beakish, weak-chested, bow-legged, he nevertheless held himself upright on close feet with still hands: a physical containment that suggested the controlled pressure of his interior life. He had a keen eye for the pleasures of the world and a gambler's sense of the odds of enjoying them. Beatrice struck him as the best he could get in the way of beauty, a willing and inventive sexual partner, and a useful social prop. They married for love, it was said. Not quite true: rather, for an intimate sense of shared ambitions, which wasn't quite the same as fortune-hunting. To her father's surprise, Simons quickly reached the rank of captain, fought at Tarragona with the courage of calculation, and made a small fortune in prizes.

In the aftermath of Waterloo, Captain Simons and his wife managed to establish themselves in the London scene, which had conceived a passion for all things military. Beatrice's beauty won her the attentions of the men, and her husband's careful tolerance preserved them from utter disappointment. After the scandal of Lord Byron's separation, several of his acquaintance 'cut' him. When he attended the Duchess of Devonshire's ball, on the eve of his departure for Dover, Beatrice reserved for him several dances – though only once, indeed, did they step onto the floor, while she ably obscured the awkwardness of his left foot by pressing herself against his hip. The rest of the night they gossiped in the corner. Beatrice rightly presumed that in the years to come she would rather be envied than despised for her show of faith and favour. She was also a sufficiently innocent flirt to take real pleasure in the company of beautiful men.

Eliza was staying at her sister's house in Piccadilly. Their little girl was ill, and Beatrice wouldn't trust her to the nanny. Eliza had slept on the floor beside her niece; and at four in the morning, the mother herself came in, not unlovingly, to wake and thank her sister – and boast of her triumph. She confessed she was 'too gossipy to sleep', and linking her arm in Eliza's, led her to the guest room. The captain, as his wife called him, was already 'snoring with the gods', and sometimes the sisters shared a bed. In spite of their differences, the daughters of a widower inevitably look to each other for certain motherly comforts.

There she undressed in a heap and climbed under the covers. In the heat of the ballroom, she whispered, Lord Byron had smelt not unpleasantly of overripe figs. His colour was excellent, like fresh butter, streaked here and there with redcurrant. Eliza could hardly contain her jealousy, and complained that Beatrice thought of nothing but her stomach. Beatrice confessed that *he* certainly gave her an appetite, and laughed – just hiding her teeth, which were not very good, with a jewelled forefinger, even in her sister's presence.

'I said to him,' she said to Eliza, 'that if he'd only married me, I shouldn't have minded who else he brought to our bed.'

'You didn't dare,' Eliza reproached her, not without admiration. She lay on her side, her chin propped up on her elbow. The older woman stretched out on her back; her face, still flushed from dancing, just beneath her sister's. The soft fine hairs of her skin shifted in Eliza's breath. How young Beatrice looked, in spite of her twenty-two years, in spite of her recent motherhood. She had the shape of someone still forming, the unripe figure that suggests the lines it will grow into. Eliza, by contrast, looked as if she were already retracting, at sixteen. Her figure was good, but spare rather than green. The bone of her collar pronounced how little she could live on, how much she could do without. Her smell was dry, too, like dead petals, while Beatrice filled her bed in the stewed richness of spent energies. Eliza stroked her hair away from her forehead, then wiped the sweat of it against her own cheek; after all, *his* might have touched Bea's perspiringly. 'You didn't dare,' she repeated.

'I dare anything,' her sister said. Byron had confided his plans to her: he was leaving in the morning. For the continent – he didn't know if he should ever return. 'I have a premonition,' he had declared to her, 'that I shall die in Greece; or the divorce courts. The sun, however, shines brighter in the former.' He had offered to accompany her home. She had demurred. Perhaps she would see him off, very early, before the bailiffs came? His bedroom window gave on to the street, and he hated a dry farewell . . .

'I thought your sister had the leaving of you,' Beatrice had said, mimicking her own voice now, its arch twitter, for Eliza's benefit. Then he'd bent down to her ear and whispered something – Beatrice dared not repeat it even in the quiet of her own bed. Eliza, suddenly the young girl, the little sister, ached to be told. Show me what it is like to live among men. She feared already how much she would never learn about the world first-hand. Her personal history was books, the list of what she had read. But Beatrice only sighed and sat up: she had heard her daughter crying in the night. It amazed Eliza, how easily her sister changed shapes.

At dawn, Eliza awoke in a fever. She dressed quickly to pre-empt second thoughts and stole through the house into the street. The chill of the summer morning dried her sleepy eyes; she blinked and shivered. The city slept magnificently around her. The rising sun prepared in secret for the day: a strange inhuman exhibition, in which the grandeur lay rather behind-the-scenes than in the public performance. Across Piccadilly and down Jermyn Street; her footfalls had a guilty softness.

She had lived her life in her head: in books; in poetry and Romances. She still read and corrected her father's work, and had recently, as his eyes failed, begun to serve as his amanuensis. She had lived her life in her father's head. And often blushed at the insights thus formally offered into his thoughts: a world both threadbare and bitterly passionate. His work had led her at last into more promiscuous readings. She had read, at first reluctantly and then with growing hunger, Byron's *Pilgrimage*; devoured Scott's *Waverley*, Byron's *The Corsair* and *Lara* – fallen in love again, again. Her appreciation for the richness of life had been ushered in not by the contrast between her own thoughts and the complexity of the world, but by the contrast between her father's imagination and the imaginations of Lord Byron and Sir Walter Scott. As she hurried among the shortening shadows towards Piccadilly Terrace, she had the feeling – not that she would for the first time enter the world – but that the prison of her thoughts had been immeasurably expanded. She had stepped onto a larger interior stage.

She stopped outside his door, across the street, and pressed her back to the wall. The sun cast a slanting line of light over the cobbles: a knife cutting a yellow wedge off the thick dark. She stood in the shadows and saw the bright fist of a lamp behind the curtains.

These shifted in the morning wind; the French windows had already been opened. A small balcony gave onto the street. A young man stepped out on its ledge. He wore a white cravat beneath a high collar, and a dark coat. His face, consequently, looked rather squeezed out: it perched atop them. His hair fell over his brow and he held it away. For a minute he stood there, glancing up and down the street. She would have cried out to him – 'I've come, look, I've come after all', hoping that her sisterly resemblance might persuade him – but his eyes passed over her lightly, and she didn't dare offer an interruption he had chosen to ignore.

He seemed to her, at a distance of perhaps twenty paces, if not happy then restless – and as happy as restlessness can make a man who will shortly find an avenue to relieve it. The sheer fact of his presence amazed her, his physical translation from the name on a frontispiece into a face. 'So this is Lord Byron,' she thought. The lines ran quietly through her head:

> Apart he stalk'd in joyless reverie,
> And from his native land resolv'd to go,
> And visit scorching climes beyond the sea;
> With pleasure drugg'd, he almost long'd for
>   woe . . . .

He was astonishingly handsome, a picture of suppressed vitality. The world was all before him. His gaze coloured the narrow view, the long, high corridor of the street, as distinctly as the sunshine that brightened his cheek. The way he turned abruptly back indoors struck her almost as a casual display of power. She saw him blow the lamp out in his hand, and the curtains grow both lighter and duller at its extinction.

She was very much in love – very tired and blissfully unhappy, footsore, her trailing skirts roughened at the hems – by the time she reached her father's cottage in Somers Town, near Camden.

CHAPTER FOUR

L ORD BYRON'S OLD ROOMS, as it happened, lay but a
fifteen minutes' walk from Polidori's seat in the bay-
window. The rain at last gave way to the quieter grey
of dusk. For an hour almost he had been brazening the
uncomfortable stare of one of the waiters, a narrow-faced
bony young man, with an extra inch of nose, who made his
impatience felt by leaning over to light the candle at
Polidori's table. In the shine of it, Polly glanced at his own
reflection in the window. – It seemed like more than three
years ago.

Gaetano, of course, had been proved right from the first.
The damage was done. And now Colburn had published his
story, in a fog of anonymity, through which he had just
raised the flag of Byron's name. God knows how Colburn
had got his hands on it. It was another one of Polidori's
muddles; which, if he let it, might easily develop into one of
his scrapes. He hadn't decided yet whether or not to let it;
that was the truth his reflection gave ruefully back. Because
of his shyness, it cost him terrible pains to act; and when he
did, he was liable to overdo it. But everyone was always trying to put him down! Polidori guessed that this feeling grew
out of unreasonable vanity; also, that it might more or less
fit the case. It required a certain violence for him to break
free – of his own inhibitions, as much as anything else.

Lord Byron had once said to him (and Polidori could
almost, in the hum of the coffee-house, hear the poet's thin
musical voice), 'It is odd, but agitation of any kind gives a
rebound to my spirits. It sets me up for a time.' Polidori was

still in the habit of keeping up, years after the fact, his end of any conversation with the poet. Now he silently answered him, 'This is the difference between us. My struggles leave me desperate afterwards.' Or not quite desperate, perhaps. Polidori had no gift for misery. He tended to make himself ridiculous, which struck him in any case as much worse. Absurdity afflicted him instead: Sorrow's cousin once removed, its poor relation. For an example of which, he thought with a smile, one need look no further than that afternoon: his fruitless attack on Colburn's red door; the pointless little lie he'd been tricked into; his thorough drenching.

That smile brought him up short; it served to remind him, oddly enough, that his own life was no laughing matter. He had tired his father's patience and his godfather's purse. His rooms at Lincoln's Inn were a miserable pair of empty boxes. He hadn't the means to furnish them; he was already dallying with debt and wanted money to begin a pupillage (his latest scheme) in the law. The clerks and legal apprentices he had seen, quietly crowding the halls and stairways of his residence, had given him the idea of joining their profession. They seemed to be agreeably solitary types. He had every confidence of fitting in with them; and they had, moreover, mostly their own industry to depend on for the advancement of their careers. Medicine had not suited him; he had not suited it. It was too sociable a profession. Lord Byron had been used to joking, to his face, that none of Polidori's patients could ever want a better doctor: they were all dead. Polidori, depending on his mood, had either laughed or furiously blushed. Perhaps he preferred them that way, he once answered. Sometimes it *did* seem a great joke to him, that his blundering, bludgeoning youth should kill whatever he touched: a sign of his outsized vitality, of his uncontrolled force. Sometimes it seemed to him evidence of a deeply felt intuition, that he lived outside the world, at the wrong end of things. His touch was negative; it created absence. The letter of the law might just agree with him; he had half a mind to study inheritance questions. At least the principal clients were already dead.

Meanwhile, an inclination to take up cards again had begun to tease its way into his thoughts. Faro had proved his great solace at Edinburgh. At seventeen, childish, lonely, he had been given his first taste of the company of men. Gambling had the virtue, if no other, of making for clear relations with them, and presenting him with something to talk about. Polidori felt, perhaps too vividly, the joy of his mathematical turn of mind. But he also had an impulsive nature, and the combination tended to produce thick streaks of luck, both good and bad. His father, after a run of particularly heavy losses, had made up the debts on one condition: that his son give up the habit for ever. Polidori had sworn to; but he had lately had his sense renewed of how little any promise he made to his father might be worth in practice. Even so, Polly had thus far resisted trying to revive his fortune at the card tables. Giving in to that temptation seemed to him a decisive, a final step.

At least, for once, he was innocent – of what? of plagiarism? Was there a word for what he might stand accused of: for passing off his own work as someone else's? Not that it mattered whether he was guilty or not. Polidori knew by now (he had learned it from Byron) that one needs a pose, a posture, to get what one wants. What he wanted . . . the phrase streamed off into conjecture, until he brought it to a sharper point. What would he settle for? And the answer came back, with dispiriting modesty: his most basic reward, his fee. He was ready, perhaps, to sell his larger claims: to immortality. A line ran through his head, offhand, insistent, that might serve. 'I forgot that damned *Vampyre* as soon as I wrote it; but the least you can do is pay me . . .' Byron had such a persuasive manner. Whatever he felt, very rich in colour, seemed to stain everything around him, everyone. Whenever Polidori uttered a word, one heard the soft echo of inattention.

And yet, at last, something he'd written was being given, in its way, his due. Another strange vision from that strange week had been published. First, of course, there was *Frankenstein*, and now *The Vampyre*. Who would have guessed, amidst such famous company, that only the doctor, and the poet's young wife, would *come good*? Lord Byron and Shelley both silent, in this respect. None of their summer party could remember who first suggested the game of writing ghost stories. Polidori fancied it was himself; though invention had failed him from the beginning, and only a nudge, and a hint, from Lord Byron had got him started at all. He vividly remembered taking three mornings to write it, lying at the feet of Mrs Shelley. She 'had run', as she said, 'into the doldrums' of her own story; and to fill the uninspiring hours, began to sketch him, first in pencil, afterwards touching up the grey lines with spreading colour. He wished he had the picture still; it might brighten his room – yet how faithfully every moment of that year remained with him! The waters of Lake Geneva had sent a wet wind through the balcony doors. The height of summer; you could hardly smell the mountains in the air. He remembered the solitude of composition, its self-communion, all the sweeter for the company of friends. (Why shouldn't he call them *friends*? None of them were there to contradict him.)

He rubbed, with a squeaking thumb, the mist off a window pane. He had been keeping an eye on anyone making his way along Great Marlborough Street. It was attuned to catch, amidst the tireless uneven stream of people, the slowness of an approach. Then he felt it, suddenly: the thrill of authorship, rising up in him. Not even anonymity could quench it. He had seen the story pirated around Covent Garden. He had seen men sitting on the street-kerbs, among the remains of the vegetable market, to devour what he had written as soon as they had it in their hands. Byron used to boast that his *Corsair* had sold ten thousand copies in a day. He had said to Polly one night, coming home late, that what he loved about fame most was 'that little calm at the centre of attention'. One of his more winning moods, vain but loving, too, when he needed company. When he wasn't writing, Byron couldn't bear to be alone late at night; and Polly couldn't resist the temptation to comfort him – no one ever could. Now Polidori wondered wryly how many copies he had sold himself. It was only Byron's *name* that counted. Anybody might do anything with that name, there was no other difference between them . . . It amazed him sometimes, the persistence of his vanity. Maybe he wasn't entirely without hope.

Presently, a broad-shouldered figure in a long coat stopped outside Colburn's door. He stood there a moment uncertainly – Polidori, through the gloom, could just make out his searching hand against the red – until, with a brisk step, he pushed his way in. Polly picked up his stick and ran after him into the street.

Colburn himself answered the door in something of a hurry. He was about to step out again; he had only gone in for a minute. He hadn't another to spare. Polly suffered strangely from a sense of his own good looks; their feminine niceness. Colburn was a rough-faced gentleman, much abused by time, broad-shouldered, thick-haired. Handsome in a massy way, like a prominent crop of rock, very much in the weather – as Lord Byron himself might have said, 'rather sublime than the alternative'. Polly stared past the publisher's shoulder into the shop-room, a high, panelled chamber tiled with black and white squares. Shelves deep with books cast a comfortable gloom. Terrible, the effect of riches upon him. He couldn't help feeling their contrast in circumstances: money sometimes seemed to him almost to possess the force of logic. Still, he summoned as much indignation as he had within him. The pressure of it put a squeak in his voice, but he managed to get out his complaint. 'I think you might stop for a minute, after all. You see, I wrote *The Vampyre.*'

Colburn gave him a hard look. 'You'd better come in,' he said at last, 'though I'm only changing to go out. I suppose you can watch me.'

Polidori followed him into the shop. A small door at the back, hidden between the shelves, opened onto a kind of store-room; Colburn ducked his head beneath the door-frame. Inside, columns of pamphlets and books lay stacked between armchairs, haphazardly placed. A table in the middle was covered in copies of *The Vampyre*; Polidori began to suffer from a sense of the weakness of his claim. What had been made of it was clearly larger, grander than his own week's idleness of composition. A fire, freshly laid with coal, was beginning to burn its way through the black heaps. At the back of the room a staircase, decorated curiously enough by pairs of shoes, led into more private apartments, and Polidori followed Colburn up its steps.

The publisher, meanwhile, had been keeping the conversation to himself. There was no shirking about him; no dressing-up of facts. He hadn't any intention of testing Polidori's claim. The fact was that he'd taken the authorship on faith, from a man he didn't care to give away, except to say that his character was such, one couldn't reliably count on it either for truths or lies. Well, he was perfectly equal to the fact that that faith might have been misplaced. In any case, he had decided (within the time it took them to mount the stairs) to offer Polidori thirty pounds, on one condition: that he wouldn't kick up a fuss about the authorship. Colburn looked round over his shoulder then, to fix his eye on the young man. They had just reached the door of his dressing room. Colburn's unembarrassed pursuit of a fortune, by literary means, afforded him a kind of winning frankness. There was no cant about him; he dealt unsentimentally with money. (This was new in Polly's experience of patronage.) 'Thirty pounds is perfectly reasonable; one could hardly give more. Without the suggestion of Byron's name, after all, *The Vampyre* would be worthless. Come, shall we say thirty pounds? Consider it something from nothing.'

He broke off his gaze and turned in. In a rallying tone, he added, 'The tale is flying off the presses. The last thing anyone (including its author, I suppose) would want, is to cast a shadow over its authenticity. Of course, Doctor Polidori can see that.' The 'Doctor', perhaps, was a respectful touch; but it had the intention of subtly including him in the expression of Colburn's point of view. In fact, what Polidori *saw* was the publisher's back, as he entered the dressing room. Polly was unsure of his invitation, and keenly felt the indignity either of waiting outside, or of waiting within. This may have been what suddenly decided him to 'kick up a fuss'. He followed Colburn inside.

Polidori refused to 'see it'. Thirty pounds was the price of a legal apprenticeship; it might be the making of him. But 'he would rather throw away his life than his honour, his title to immortality,' etc. There was a certain chasing, beseeching quality to these effusions; Colburn let him have his shout. He began to dress and interrupted 'the doctor' at last only to ask him to press hard against the fresh cravat around his neck, to keep the knot in place. Polidori complied, but found it difficult to carry on talking with his finger on another man's neck. He recalled once helping Byron into his costume on the night of a carnival, a memory that carried with it the force of original confusions. Under its influence he fell into a silence, which was broken at last only when Colburn selected a scent. Polidori sniffed the air once or twice, closing his eyes to the puffed mist, to answer his asked-for preference. Then he followed him out again, in the awkward shuffle-step of a man keeping pace at another man's back heel – down the stairs again and through the store-room into the shop.

The publisher opened the door for Polidori; then, at the

threshold, took the young doctor by the elbow. The rain had loosened again and fell in thick lines. Colburn had to shout above it, but Polly was standing in it: the circling spray dampened the hems of his trousers. These had stiffened in the heat of the coffee-house; he felt them now soak and sag. He hated wet ankles. 'I tell you what,' Colburn said. 'I'm dining at Long's. We'll talk over a bottle of champagne. See what we can do for you.'

The table at Long's was almost full. Polly had to perch on a chair angled into an unused doorway. He imagined Lord Byron smiling at him and, internally, acknowledged his joke: yes, they had painted him into a corner. He struggled to keep up his end of the conversation. Colburn's acquaintance were older, more forceful men, engaged in business of various descriptions. Polidori's charms, such as they were, depended on the charity of women. His refinements wilted in the strong steady climate of masculine company. Speechlessly, with something like vengeance, he began to drink. The champagne was excellent; cold and clear as a bell, with a tone as sharp as if the bell had been vigorously struck. And he consoled himself, secretly building up courage, with the thought of refusing to pay for it. He could hardly stretch out his leg without knocking a knee; he was practically coiled with rage. By the time the bill came he was drunk and hot for a fight; but Colburn, handsomely, never let the question come up. He quietly settled their share of it. Polly felt the wind go out of his sails; and the taste of gratitude in his mouth, as he stuttered out thanks, sickened even himself.

Supper was followed by a 'third of a daffy' at Tom Belcher's; and, afterwards, descending to one of the Hells in Covent Garden, they ended up at the faro tables. Polly found his tongue at last. 'I used to have rather a weakness for faro,' he confidentially declared, to no one in particular. He was forced to repeat himself, somewhat louder: 'I used to have rather a weakness,' etc. until Colburn, finally, took him up. 'Should you like a hand or two?' Polly, somewhat chastened

32

with fear, shook his head. He dutifully sat out the first game; but, as the run of cards unfolded, he could not refrain from dispensing a bit of advice. 'Come,' someone said, 'I should like the benefit of that young man's experience; only, it is wasted in speculation.' The *young man*, drunk on grape and grain, permitted himself an indulgence – a hand or two only. He leaned a little heavily towards Colburn; might he perhaps beg a small advance . . . 'Call it a debt paid,' Colburn replied with a smile. 'Shall we say, thirty pounds? I believe you understand me.' Polly, silently, agreed. 'He's sharp, is Captain Sharp,' a waiter warned him, nodding at Colburn. 'Don't let him take you for a Flat.'

By the end of the night, he'd lost half his stake and had the sense, returning home at last in the damp uncertain dawn, that he was capable of gambling away anything at all. There was nothing that couldn't be wagered: his life, his soul.

He remembered later, being too cold to sleep, that strange encounter with the pinch-faced girl. Another worry, which afflicted him more than it ought: that Miss Eliza Esmond, the guest of Lady Walmsley, might visit him in his rooms and discover his imposture. Why had he played the fool? A sign of how unhappy he was – the brief surge of pleasure at her mistake. He did not like to think of the disappointment she would feel at seeing through his pretence. 'I had taken you for a gentleman, but now I find that you merely played the part, to seduce an innocent girl, whose only sin was her sensibility,' etc. He remembered her voice quite vividly. It was reedy, but fine and clear, like the ring of a tin tongue in a silver bell. He lay in bed and foresaw not her anger, but his own deepening shame. The truth of his life seemed so much the worse for the contrast he set up, for the shock of her discovery. He must be coming down with a head-cold. Otherwise, why would that word 'seduce', uttered, as he imagined it, in the heat of her outrage, roll so feverishly around his thoughts?

He awoke at noon to find a note under his door – from his godfather, a pursy-lipped Catholic named Deagostini, who was rather devoted to his 'charities'. Deagostini had written to say that he could not in all conscience pay for the young man's pupillage. There were so many more deserving candidates for his *largesse*. Besides which, to be frank, he was tired of what he called Polidori's 'waxing and waning'. Taking up the law did not strike him as a good idea at all; and he bristled at what had been Polidori's attempts at persuasion: 'I must intrude upon your judgement with a few observations prompted to me by my humble conception founded upon forty-five years' experience both of myself and of many others to my knowledge . . .' Polidori understood exactly what was meant: Deagostini liked the objects of his pity to do as they were told. Well, Polly was too proud for such stooping; he had not fawned on Lord Byron, and saw no reason to prostrate himself before a glorified grain merchant.

His sense of righteous indignation put him, strangely enough, in better spirits. That afternoon, in the restless hopefulness of unemployment, Polly turned once more to his travel-papers; it was time he brought them into shape. Murray had at one point offered him five hundred pounds for a memoir of Byron. When Byron dismissed him, at the end of that famous summer, Polidori had returned home and approached Murray with his journals. They strolled through St James's Park together, arm in arm; it had been a dry summer, and the leaves were brown on the trees. Murray cosily hinted at the good such a publication could do for a young man's career; he looked forward to a long relationship. Afterwards, they repaired to Murray's set of offices on Albemarle Street. A glass of whisky and soda in an easy chair; the rough, snug pleasure of a good cigar. Murray bade him farewell with a firm hand, the MS pressed between his elbow and rib. He promised to read it at once, a quick response. Indeed, a week later, he respectfully declined the journals, and was never heard from again.

The bad news had seemed to Polly at the time in keeping with his growing self-suspicions: that he came naturally at everything from the wrong end; that he killed whatever he touched. But Colburn's *rough good-nature* – that was Polly's phrase for it; abuse tended to awake in him a sense of trust, a desire to please – inspired him to make a second trial of the journals. It gave him, at least, something to work for; and he spent the next day in a fever of revisions. The hard work itself struck him as the outward evidence of some internal spring of renewal; what couldn't be doubted was the fact of the rising within him. A few mornings later, Polly slipped the manuscript under the large red door on Great Marlborough Street. Walking away, he felt a strange elation. This, he told himself, was the great blessing of literary labours. One had always a second chance at fame. *The Vampyre*, after all, as he reminded himself, with the pleasant modesty of self-congratulation, had been doing rather well; maybe his luck was turning.

CHAPTER FIVE

ELIZA LAY IN HER BED under the eaves in an absolute ferment. If she sat up she knocked her head, an external constriction that had begun to feel innate. Wherever she turned, inside or out, there were walls obstructing. Sleep seemed impossible: her eyes felt as wide and bright as the moon. In the nightshine, high trees shifted, this way, that, like a thought lazily repeated. She was conscious of green spaces storeys of air below, the backs of gardens walled away from the dirty road. *He* had touched her hand. His own copy of *The Vampyre* lay on her nightstand; she had read it again before sleep; and now, of course, could not sleep. It amazed her, of course it did, that he could take an interest in her; but she had heard his appetites were promiscuous. It satisfied her, at this early stage, that whatever womanly virtues she possessed he desired in quantity. Though she had only the dimmest sense of them: a smell? the pull of her dress, as she walked, between her legs? the lure of her bottom lip? Whatever they were, *hers* had hardly been tested or tasted. Even so, a quiet sense of her own importance had never left her; an arrogance which had twisted this way and that to survive, and grown only stronger. She was confident she could persuade him to love her.

Beatrice had recommended her to Lady Walmsley, a tall stooped woman, heavy-headed as a picked tulip. Eyes large as eggs stood on end. Her powdered hair cast a cloud about her: she seemed, intimately, to inhale only herself, her careful preservation. And moved to deliberate rhythms; her lightest gesture required an answer afterwards, a slow return of weight. She was nobody's fool. Her conversation, placidly agreeable, made everyone else agree. Her son, amiable, fattening, childish with filial piety, had nevertheless died bravely at Waterloo. And she had welcomed his widow, Mrs Violet, rather forcibly to the family hearth. Mrs Violet was a stupidly beautiful creature, hardly human, her prettiness weightless and ineffectual. The worst she could do was cut – fine paper-cuts, that hurt more than they bled. She disliked playing the widow, and practically refused the name Webster. 'Mrs Violet' had been agreed on as a kind of compromise; and to Eliza's ear, it just suited her. The name had a cold, a threatening beauty. Lady Walmsley did not trust her daughter-in-law with the education of the twins. And Mrs Violet did not trust Eliza, who was taken in, under no strict terms, as a something between a guest and a governess, and consequently, as nothing at all.

The house in Mayfair overlooked bright terraces across a lozenge of green park that grew dark and rich in wet weather; a comfort to the eye, a filling-in. Eliza took great pleasure in these views. Her father's cottage backed onto the miserable new canal, still dirty from construction. The prospects it offered were various degrees of brown. She lingered often on the landing of the stairs, pressing her face against the cold broad windows, to enjoy her larger outlook; but never felt confident enough to assume the run of the drawing room. She had once been asked, in the first week of her stay, 'owing to the state of the parlour', to make use of the servant's entrance, through the side door, into the gardens, and round the back. Lady Walmsley apologized in puffs of genial powder. 'Only you see,' she said, shaking her head lightly, 'one must follow fashions.' They were having the tiles replaced by parquet. Mrs Violet looked on; her bright little smile just loose enough one might slip a letter knife between her lips. Eliza understood, and never again entered by the front door, except in general company.

She had come in November, in an early snowfall. Beatrice's coachman held the umbrella above her sister's head, leaving her own neck free to the air, and together they skittered up the tufted steps. Introductions had already been made. Her sister only wished to see Eliza 'settled'; she was great friends with Lady Walmsley; she had danced several times with her son. He was a wonderful dancer, with dry hands – so rare in young men these days, and a great comfort to a girl. Well, a woman could understand the trouble one took with one's lace. Such a shame, what a waste it was: she had absolutely wept for weeks on end to hear the news. For days. And so many unpleasant young men returning, who trod on one's toes, absolutely untouched. They installed Eliza in a long, low room under the eaves, until more suitable accommodation could be found. At the dark end of the year; and now it was nearly summer, and she had not shifted from the narrow bed under the slant of the roof. It amazed her how quickly, how painlessly indeed, she had learned her place in the world.

The children were her only consolation (until now), though they were brutish enough in their way, little Hopewell and little Caroline, shortened to Hope and Care in their grandmother's affection. Foul to each other and false to everyone else; they were not unloving, at least, in the pinch of tears. What a large cold house it was to be so small in. They had guessed, almost at once, the station of their instructress, and made her feel it whenever they could. Even so, no one could comfort them better; and it often amused Eliza to observe in their pink faces the wrinkles of conflicting calculations. No, but she loved them still. There was no one else in the world who ever touched her, whose weight she felt, day to day, pressing against her arms, her breast, her lap. She felt the absence of them like an ache when Lady Walmsley took them to the country for Easter; though they were cold to her on their return, proper and superior, 'quite grown up' she called it to their faces, to show

38

she didn't mind. And she had, as she put it to herself, to 'wait them out' – until the inevitable miseries of childhood brought them to her breast again.

Not that she didn't have her own uses for them. The nursery was the only room in which she felt assured of her place. It overlooked the narrow alley between the houses, a dark high corridor that caught a distant slant of light in the late afternoon. She often sat on a very small chair in the window when the twins were asleep and read by the glow reflecting off the stuccoed walls: *Marmion*, Little's *Anacreon*, *The Bride of Abydos*. Her mouth moving to the insistence of the couplets, her pulled-out lower lip clinging lightly to the top. This was loneliness to her at its sweetest, and even the threat, constantly suggested, of the children's waking only sharpened her pleasure in the privacy. It was there she fled to, after meeting, as she supposed, Lord Byron himself at Colburn's door.

He had looked thinner than she'd remembered or imagined him; and yet that discrepancy fed only her appetite for giving sympathy. She began, in thought at least, to fatten him up. It was only restlessness, one could see it in his nervous hands, that kept him from eating; and she supposed herself, fearfully, happily, equal to the task of making him rest. His eyes, she saw them suddenly again, were so dark one could hardly believe any light passed into them; and, indeed, there was something blind about his face. It had the dignity of the blind: the staring indifference of someone who could not see himself. That was the real curse of sightlessness, that it took from one the possibility of seeing one's clear reflection; and she imagined that fame, perversely, had a similar effect. Well, she hoped to teach him, lovingly, to see himself again as she could see him . . . Though as for that, her vision might prove rather sharp: he seemed to her handsome and helpless, too fine, almost, in feature and manner, for anything like the weight of ordinary happiness. She would never forget the sight of him, drenched, banging his fist on the door.

In sympathy, she rubbed her own fingers, and was pleased to note that the stain of ink from his hands was still on them – quite dry, thankfully. She wondered how long the mark would endure. And while Polly himself, at that moment, held his finger against Colburn's neck, she sat on a child's stool with her knees raised high against her chin and a book spread across them. She imagined his voice as she read from it: high and musical, with just (she smiled as she thought of them) those little precisions of a foreigner. His travels had not left him untouched.

> It is the hour when from the boughs
> The nightingale's high note is heard;
> It is the hour when lovers' vows
> Seem sweet in every whisper'd word . . .

Well, the hour was nearly tea-time, but it would have to serve.

In the days to come, she was almost wholly preoccupied by her 'next move'. Of course, he couldn't visit her at Lady Walmsley's. In the first place, they were sure to see through any pretence of imposture he put on, and recognize him for what he was: the greatest, most beautiful, most scandalous poet of his age. Then the *devourings* would begin. Lady Walmsley, large-headed lioness, had a way of claiming all the pretty young men for herself. Mrs Violet had often remarked upon it, the sole subject on which she chose to confide in lowly Eliza. And whatever her ladyship left over, Mrs Violet herself was certain to consume. The poor governess, her station in life painfully exposed, would hardly warrant so much as a hello, hardly a kiss of the hand. He would see her for what she was, a drudge. Her only claim to romance was the hunger with which she regarded it. She was the child of books: the orphan of them, rather, for they made cold parents.

No, it would not do, she could not invite him to Lady

Walmsley's. And she hardly dared yet visit him in his rooms. A decisive step, it seemed to her, a declaration of intent: you can do what you like with me. The thought of how far his inclination might take them inspired in her shivers of delicious apprehension; but she was willing, still, to postpone the trial. If all else failed, of course, she could throw herself on his mercy; hoping that he might take up her offer in a warmer spirit. But these were early days, and among the milder thrills in prospect, the simple uncertainty of the weeks ahead would prove a wonderful occupation for her thoughts, the food of privacy.

In the end, the *next step*, a second meeting, almost fell into her lap; she had only to seize the occasion. What she wanted was to carry on an *intrigue*. What she needed was the privacy of crowds and an excuse for dressing up.

Lady Walmsley had invited the Simons to share their box at the theatre. Massinger's *Old Debts* had lately been revived. And Beatrice had, just on the Friday morning, cried off. She was, as she said, absolutely swimming through the thick of a summer cold and didn't mean to spoil the evening by coughing, sneezing, fainting and expiring. Besides, she felt so muzzle-headed, she could hardly hear a word anyone said: it was no good gossiping at her, and it would look bad if she pretended to listen to the play. So unlikely. Perhaps Eliza could make up her place in the party; what a fool she was for such nonsense in any case. And if she stopped in before at Binghamton Row, Beatrice could dress the poor creature herself. She would personally vouch for her respectability: Eliza wanted only a sister's touch, after all, to look human.

Lady Walmsley called her in to the sitting room. She had breakfasted on buttered toast and the crumbs of it lay scattered across the slope of her bosoms. In spite of her grand manner, she had the air of a fine piece of statue left in the rain; the pigeons had got at her. The deep red of the Chinese wallpaper lent its colour to her cheeks, already sufficiently rouged. Eliza saw the powder-filled cracks in her skin, grotesquely magnified from time to time by the old woman's wandering lorgnette. She had a habit of waving it uncertainly before her eyes, enlarging their washed-out blue. She addressed Eliza with kindly irony. 'Beatrice has told us how clever and literary you are; quite the *blue*.' Lady Walmsley looked forward for once to hearing a *critical* view. It was shameful, she said, but she always went to the theatre simply for pleasure. And then she added, just lowering her chin to signal a change in tone: Eliza was fortunate – a little cough – in her choice of sisters. 'Beatrice speaks very highly of you. Very fortunate indeed.' Then she subtly introduced the subject of a change in dress: perhaps if she wished to thank her before the theatre . . . Eliza was welcome to the gig.

Mrs Violet, who had been crocheting in the window, said, 'You are a lucky girl, aren't you, Eliza. Such a treat you have in store tonight. A real treat.' Her pretty face, in the light, had the deep gleam of porcelain, a sealed glow. Widowhood had sharpened her, refined her beauty: one had the sense of a cast of features setting. A perfect glaze. (She obscurely resented Eliza. It was much wiser, she often told the young woman, never to marry; Eliza had hit upon the safest plan. One suffered so terribly for love, as she had found. She positively envied Eliza her spinsterhood . . .) A play, she added, might be just the thing. She'd noticed – 'hadn't she only yesterday remarked upon it, Lady Walmsley?' – what a sour-face poor Eliza had become. Stomping around the house, running into everything; quite distracted. She'd always been the fool of her imagination, but this was something worse, and beginning to upset the children. She was growing into a regular gorgon. Burying one's nose in a book never did anyone's looks any good. Not that it mattered any more . . .

'Yes, thank you; a great treat,' Eliza mumbled. And indeed, it struck her as just that. Her life wanted only a little dressing-up: her sister's finery, a gossiping crowd, the heat of the stage. Lord B himself had at one time, she knew, presided over the board at Drury Lane. Perhaps she could just get off a note to him?

CHAPTER SIX

A WEEK HAD PASSED, and not a word from Colburn. Colburn's thirty pounds, half of it gambled away, had nevertheless relieved Polidori of his most pressing debts, without offering any prospects for his future. He could eat again, a little. He sent his best set of clothes, Lord Byron's cast-offs (worn daily after the demise of his everyday suit) to the tailors for mending. But he was beginning to grow anxious over Colburn's silence; and to quiet his conjectures (how long should it take a busy man to read through two-hundred-odd pages of manuscript?), he began to write again. That is, he began to attempt to write. He had spent most of the week in his rooms, waiting for something to turn up, considering the disorder of his life – helpless before it, almost comforted by it. There seemed nothing he could do to escape it. He decided to record it, in its largest sense: the waste of his life.

Sometimes he counted over all the people he had killed. Lord Byron's line ran through his head: *Polidori's patients could never want a better doctor. They were all dead.* Well, he was used to corpses. At Edinburgh the students had paid anyone with a stomach for the digging a pound for each dozen cadavers. Most often the sextons themselves, hardened to the business and with casual access to the graveyard, took up the offers. But when his gambling debts first piled up, Polidori tried his hand at the work himself. He discovered, to his own surprise, how easily he could do without sentiment. Sentiment was the true obstacle; squeamishness was quickly overcome. One dead man looked much like another. People distinguished themselves in their gestures. Though indeed some of these survived, or appeared to survive, in spite of the rigor mortis.

His mentor Dr Taylor had once invited him to assist at a surgery. Polidori was staying with him in Norwich at the time, a few weeks before his sister's wedding. The surgery involved a delicate procedure upon a boy of fifteen, who had fallen under a horse. The case itself had attracted a certain celebrity. Various local interests were at stake in his life. Men from the local wool-factory, it was alleged, had chased the young gentleman, the son of the factory owner, into the path of the horse – in protest at the introduction of mechanical looms. A weaver named Ben Wilson was being held responsible. He was, among other things, a radical dissenter, whose pamphleteering had long been a thorn in the side of the boy's father. The Luddite riots in Manchester were still fresh in memory. Everyone had suffered in them, but the loom-breakers had suffered the most: they'd been hanged for it. Wilson claimed, with bitter irony, to having been 'framed' for the crime. The question of blame had set the town on its head, and the only satisfactory answer seemed to lie in the lad's survival. A heavy hoof had pressed against a rib and broken it; the fractures threatened to puncture the child's heart. Medically, socially, legally, it was a very neat tangle, as Dr Taylor put it, something of a radical himself.

It was the week in which Polidori had first heard the news of Lord Byron's offer. Taylor had summoned Polly to Norwich to discuss 'his future'. He saw no reason not to carry on that conversation in the middle of their little experiment on the boy's life. There was money to be made, he said, from the company of greatness; it was only a question of appealing 'to interested parties'. John Murray, for example, Byron's publisher, might be expected to pay handsomely for a travelling journal. Meanwhile, they had cut a square of skin from the boy's breast, and lifted it lightly aside.

Wonderful, how quickly a surgeon's ears grew deaf to screaming. There was, of course, a great pottage of blood and sinew. Polidori, probing with a knife, drew these aside, as one might heavy curtains. Occasionally, the tip of his blade scraped across the boy's ribs, a rather delicious sensation, like the first touch of a freshly sharpened quill on parchment. At last, he uncovered the thickness of irregularity, a knuckle of fractured bone. He traced the rib's slight descent, its clamping pressure; and, with a dirty swab, wiped away the blood that drained into and obscured the wound, a valley that filled almost as quickly as he could clear it.

He felt, beneath his finger, the soft expansion and swift retraction of the heart. He was conscious, almost painfully so, of being a young man himself; and the prospect of his journeys with Lord B, then imminent, inspired in him an awful sense of the stretch of life before him, the extent of his expectations. In this frame of mind, the boy's vital organ, tenderly laid bare, struck him as an apt symbol for his own exposure to the fates. To have that power dependent in his hands! which he himself offered to the vicissitudes of the world! It was one of those rare thrills that justified him in adopting his father's preference for a career. And he remembered the opening lines of Byron's *Corsair*: 'Come when it will – we snatch the life of life'. Indeed, just *that* lay breathing under his blade. He attempted to soften the pressure on the boy's heart by lifting the bent rib slowly upwards in his iron grip – an easing-off rewarded at last, it almost seemed, by the gradual cessation of that organ which had protested so long and steadily against the forces acting upon it. The boy died beneath his hands; an unhappy omen. News leaked outside the surgery. Wilson was sentenced to hang, and the riots to free him began. But by that time Polidori had returned to London.

Other deaths followed.

He considered writing a story about a doctor mysteriously

in thrall to all the people he had inadvertently killed. His dead patients, hardly angry, ask him to perform a number of small jobs in their names; they want him simply to act as their living agent. This occasionally involves his dressing up – to satisfy the illusions of the loved ones left alive. Under various impostures, he makes love to widows, or tea for mothers, and so on. Mostly, these understand the nature of the trick being played, and play along. Their mourning is happy to make do with even the shabbiest make-believe. Worn out, the doctor eventually kills himself; though Polidori could not decide if he suffers most for his own pretence or for the wilful delusions of the survivors. In the end, Polly settled on a third alternative. His doctor, love-struck, attempts to woo one of the beautiful widows in his own shape; she coldly turns him from her door.

He thought he might just stop by Colburn's again – though not, he promised himself, to bring up the matter of the Byron memoirs. The silence of an editor, he supposed, was best left to take care of itself. Instead, he would try to interest him in this new story. As a sequel to *The Vampyre*, a comic inversion, to be called, *The Physician*: the tale of a living man who feeds off the dead. A much more common predicament . . . Perhaps they could leave the anonymity of it suggestively *intact*. Polidori felt the argument already warming on his tongue. Stepping out in his best suit, now respectably patched up, he discovered Eliza's note in his box in the hall. He had almost forgotten her name. He tore it open on his way through Covent Garden.

My dear Lord B –
You haven't been out of my thoughts three minutes together this past week, though I suppose you must be inured by now to the way you wander around people's heads when they hardly know you; and we tend, no doubt, to expect a reciprocal intimacy as soon as we see you

again. In that spirit, I am only writing to say, I shall be in Lady Walmsley's box this evening, at the Theatre Royal . . .

Tearing it up, he dropped the shreds in the gutter; and, afterwards, twice bounced the bones of his hands together on the underside of the knuckles – a habitual gesture, at something done with, left behind. He found Colburn, as usual, dressing to go out for the evening. His coat coal-black, his collar almost painfully white, his face, as usual, a rough living brown, composed of blood and sunshine and drink unequally mixed. Colburn said, 'Why don't you dine out with me and we can talk?'

Polidori feared he meant to decline his journals of Byron. It amazed him sometimes, when he was brought to feel the difference between utter and imperfect hopelessness. In a flurry of nervous spirits, he suddenly answered, 'I'm engaged to the theatre.' He hardly knew why he said it; he hadn't decided to go. But a little flirtation, perhaps, would cheer him up, even with a moon-eyed girl. And he worried Colburn was about to tell him *no*.

Instead, Colburn offered him his box; and before Polidori could think, acceptance of it had included the older man's company. He could hardly say no to that himself; but it struck him already, with a sweaty flush, that Colburn might give the game away, such as it was. Polly would have to be on his toes. He'd be hard put, under such circumstances, to get much satisfaction out of the evening – out of the girl, that is. It had already occurred to him that she might serve for the relief of certain inevitable frustrations; he had seen, first-hand, the lengths to which Byron's admirers, however innocent, would go. There was also a spice in the pretence. The necessary effort of his imagination, in playing the part, might add heat to his life. Like any exercise, lying warmed the blood. Well, if she had any sense, she couldn't help but see through him. The real Lord Byron could hardly go unde-tected at the theatre. Even so, a sense of recklessness inspired him to make the attempt, from the same instinct that led him at cards to risk his hand and his money at once. He wanted to know the worst.

Nor would it be the only time Polly had played the impostor. He remembered, suddenly, his first taste of woman's flesh: the night he spent in Dover with Lord Byron, on the eve of their setting forth for France. (Colburn, in his ear, was counting up sales. *The Vampyre* had almost sold out the first edition; a second was contemplated. The publisher took his young friend by the arm: 'How happy he was, to have settled that business of the authorship', etc.). Polidori, hardly listening, allowed himself to sink into one of his reveries. –

Hobhouse and he had kept each other awkward company on the road to Dover – Byron's old friend openly resented having to chaperone the young doctor. 'No doubt,' he said, 'that rascal Scrope is having a merrier journey.' Hobhouse, in consequence, couldn't resist the boastfulness of gossip, its flaunted intimacies. They dined, briefly, as the horses were being changed; to pass the time, Hobhouse launched into one of his anecdotes. 'B had taken a box at the theatre to carry on his flirtation with one of the actresses. She used, between acts, to come up to his seat, and on her hands and knees . . . Byron bragged that he could still see the glisten on her lips when she resumed her part on stage. His Lordship had the devil's own talent for seduction; and which was more remarkable still, no one's minding. Until now,' Hobhouse added, his plain handsome face falling dutifully solemn.

'Until now?' Polly echoed him. 'I suppose you mean his sister, Goose.' The carriage was ready again; but the ice, at least, had been broken. His own sister's marriage still weighed heavily on his mind. Frances and he had always maintained the curious intimacy of the first-born; their friendship mirrored their parents' own relations. They knew what the world was like before the rest of the family, that interrupted stream of brothers and sisters, arrived. Gaetano had taught them both Italian, too; he had wearied of the practice by the time a third was born. Besides, his professional duties occupied him more; and he retreated at length into the fatherly seclusion that follows the job of fertility done. Italian had become, for the oldest two, a private language. Frances had said to him when she first heard the news of Lord Byron's offer, '*Caro fratello*, you never doubted, honestly, that great things lay ahead for you? You never doubted for a minute, did you?' Yes, he had doubted; he told her as much. 'I never have,' she replied, kissing him on the chin. He put his thumb to the wet mark, distantly relieved. Then she added, more firmly, 'We rely on you. All of us. Rely on you.' She, too, had inherited the emigrant's sense of unacknowledged merits. She trusted to him the glory of the family name.

He was unspeakably jealous that her husband spoke Italian, a language to him almost as intimate as sex. The newly-weds hoped perhaps to see Polly on the Continent. Their honeymoon would deposit them at last in Milan. Mr Rossetti mentioned this, with a hand across his brother-in-law's shoulder, a fraternal gesture Polidori silently resented. Hobhouse bumped against him in the carriage and prattled on, meaning to shock. 'You know why he calls her *Goose*, don't you? From Gus, of course, short for Augusta. But Byron has other reasons.' He explained what they do to a goose, '*filling* it from behind, to make *foie gras*. Until it explodes, you see.' His manner, insistently knowing, came across as rather sour. He played the part better of upright Horatio. Sarcasm drew from him secret reserves of poison. In truth, Hobhouse was a little shocked himself. But he had begun to resent his reputation for sobriety and innocence and was hoping to push the burden onto someone else.

They arrived at Dover in the evening. Hobhouse insisted on bringing the carriage aboard in case the bailiffs followed them and seized it. But the wind the next day was contrary.

Byron, as usual, had risen late, but they still had an afternoon to waste. His lordship was in strange high spirits: both bright and squally, swiftly changeable. He never loved England so much, he declared, as in the leaving of it. A cemetery, he said, would suit his mood exactly. There is a kind of restlessness nothing but graves will satisfy. So they visited the church of St Martin and passed a pleasant hour in the churchyard, deciphering the gravestones.

Polidori was growing accustomed to Byron's suggestive pauses. 'One has,' Hobhouse whispered, 'always to keep a weather eye on his Lordship, to be certain, that in case he falls silent, it is sufficiently remarked upon.' It was the first kindly, conspiratorial word Hobhouse had addressed to the doctor. Byron had paused in front of a particularly neglected plot. 'Churchill's grave,' he said simply; 'only think . . .' Hobhouse and Polidori, catching, as always, quickly at the poet's mood, joined him beside the mossy gravestone. It resembled nothing so much as a tooth broken in a dirty mouth. The sexton then being nearby, his Lordship called him over, and asked if he knew whose grave he tended.

The man considered the stone carefully. 'I cannot tell; I had not the burying of him.' A yew tree cast its shadow and dripped; the day had been interrupted by sudden showers, out of a cloudless sky. The plot at the foot of it, uncut, had overgrown. It withered in its own shade, and the faint wet stink of yellow grass filled out the sea air. 'But I believe the man you mean was a famous poet in his day.' The three young men smiled at each other. It seemed impossible that Lord Byron could ever suffer from such neglect: it was a ghost tale, to frighten children, when of course there are no such things as ghosts. 'People often come out their way to pay him honour.' He had crooked, large-fingered hands, black as spiders, and a head of uneven growth, like a potato. Still, there was a canny look in the sexton's eye. 'And myself,' he added, 'whatever your honour pleases.'

Byron gave him a crown to fresh turf the grave; and the

51

old man hobbled away, three-legged, on his spade. Polidori, in his bright voice, just sharpened by his father's Italian, said, 'Only think' – elaborating, as he hoped, on Lord Byron's sentiment. 'Here stand two authors. One, the most distinguished of his age. Another,' nodding graciously at Hobhouse, 'whose name is rising rapidly. And a third scribbler, still ambitious for publication, for literary fame. What a lesson it is for us.' The wind off the Channel blew his collar up and his words away. The flatness of the sea, as always, seemed its most surprising aspect. Only human landscapes can't be taken in at a glance: the ocean exposed itself all at once. White rags appeared where the wind tore the water.

Hobhouse gave Byron a look. But the poet, more kindly, answered, 'Indeed. Indeed it is.' And then, after another pregnant pause, he dutifully added, 'I had not known you wrote.'

Later, Polly regretted showing them his tragedy. The party spent the night on shore and got drunk in the bow-window of The Grapes. Byron insisted on giving the play a reading. It was titled *Ximenes* and based on the sacrifice of Abraham. It did not serve to diminish their merriment. Byron himself took up the text and declaimed:

> 'Tis thus the goiter'd idiot of the Alps
> Follows the goat-tracks on the mountains'
>   scalps,
> And carols loudly to the peaks above,
> Of shepherdesses and their chilly love.

Byron singled out the word 'goiter'd' for praise. 'Goiter'd' was a fine word, a beauteous word. He had never before encountered it in verse. Then he added: 'Nor *scalps*, for that matter, very often.' The medical profession, it seemed, had a great deal, in the way of vocabulary at least, to offer the inky tribe. As for the shepherdesses, however, he hated to see the fair creatures maligned. Perhaps the doctor would speak more kindly of them, once he had kept himself warm at their indiscriminate hearts. Polidori, in the end, could no longer stand their laughter; he retired sullenly, in a hot stamping mood not far from passion.

The three young men were sharing a room. He encountered in it one of the chambermaids making up the beds. Not for the last time, Polly was mistaken for his master. She blushed to the roots of her yellow hair and could not look at him. A pretty girl, full-faced, with a long broad nose and a nimble mouth. Polidori found her thin lips peculiarly expressive, practically hidden, as they were, by the general rose of her complexion. One had to stare to keep track of them; they wriggled into sight. Her brightness suggested nothing so much as warm blood on a cold night. And as she moved to leave with her head bowed, he caught her by the shoulder and began to kiss it, shifting quickly from the rough, unsensual cloth of her kerchief, which made him feel foolish, to her neck. 'My lord,' she said, 'my lord,' patiently; then growing hotter, she lifted his head to kiss him back.

Polidori said, seeking a kind of revenge, 'Will you call me brother? As you touch me, will you say, sweet brother, sweet brother.' The scandals surrounding Byron's separation were fresh in his mind: the sight of Augusta in her négligé; the sound of Byron's low laughter; Frances's marriage. He was scarcely nineteen himself, and still a virgin. The maid, perhaps as little as a year younger, greedily complied. 'My sweet brother,' she whispered, between kisses, while he pressed her hands with growing force between his thighs. He felt the gradual blindness of ecstasy and closed his eyes. 'Will you miss me,' he murmured, 'when I'm gone?'

'My sweet brother,' she said. The room abruptly grew colder; he muttered, disconsolately, 'My dear, kind sister.' The maid, less embarrassed than disappointed, moved to clean her hands in the pail of water she'd left standing in the hallway. She glanced round quickly at him, but did not return. Only his head was hot now; he was terribly ashamed. Afterwards, when Byron and Hobhouse joined him at last in bed, he confessed his sins – omitting, however, his peculiar instructions. The urge to confess in him was strong as love.

Hobhouse said to him, 'It isn't only that you ruin your own reputation. There are others at stake, for which I care rather more.' He settled the cushions behind his head dramatically; nothing would serve; he wished it to be understood how much he had been personally put out.

Polidori had never before felt so far from home. The men whose company he kept seemed unutterably strange. He longed for his father's consoling reproofs. Gaetano was right; the poet's influence was pernicious. For the first time in his life, Polidori had sinned. There had been no consequences, and worse still, the pleasure was too brief; it was the after-silence that endured, that signified. The only respite, it seemed, was to repeat the sin. He felt again the girl's hand between his legs: to have *that* acknowledged, and cared for, which had previously been only a source of shame . . . which remained a source of shame.

Byron's reproach, in the end, was softer. 'You might at least have given me a cut off . . . your muslin.' He rested his palm on the young man's head, a kind of benediction; then turned to blow the lamp out against his hand. The three young men lay in the awkwardness of sleepless silence. Polidori was too frightened even to rustle in his bedclothes. Hobhouse, who slept by the window, turned pointedly away from the young doctor. His back bulked like a low wall against the moonlight. Byron himself broke the silence at last, remarking, that 'the world was never more terrifying – than when it *pleased* us. My first taste of passion,' he added, 'was rather thrust upon me. But the worst of it was that I longed to repeat – the trial.' Polidori cried like a child to receive this comfort; but silently, and Byron did not guess the effect of his words.

*

Polidori imagined, as Colburn led him by the elbow to the nearest chop-house, Eliza Esmond playing the part of the chambermaid. 'My brother,' she had said; 'my sweet brother.' He smiled somewhat shamefully to himself. Eliza's complexion, it is true, was worse on the whole, not quite so fresh; but she had the same long face and restless lips. Indeed, there was something about her eyes, a hesitation in them, which Polidori supposed might prove sweet in the drawing out. There was little, in the end, that Byron's mistresses tended to stop short at. Miss Esmond, it is true, had an air of innocence about her; but if he remembered her rightly, she wore it as other women wear their guilt, as a kind of complication. There were in her, undoubtedly, knots to be untied. Knots might just suit him; and he himself was rather more innocent than simple. Byron's remembered comfort had brought on other memories: 'And the worst of it was I longed to repeat – the trial.' At that, the smile on Polidori's face, and the shame of it, returned. Along with another worry: how completely he gave into these reveries. God knows what Colburn made of his stupid silence.

CHAPTER SEVEN

FTERWARDS, WHAT ELIZA REMEMBERED most was the constantly deferred sense of arrival. It was like a word on the tip of her tongue; the breakthrough depended on internal vagaries she couldn't quite bend to her will. First, Mrs Violet returned late from Hyde Park with Lady Walmsley's gig; she had wished, she said, to give the dogs an airing. One of them had entangled itself filthily with a gentleman's boxer. The untangling had involved them in very awkward explanations, which tested the young man's gallantry to the hilt. Mrs Violet's careful innocence was more a question of manner than matter; she touched every subject with a cold light, but there was nothing she wouldn't put her hand to. She raised it now to her cheek as she described her new 'beau'. A real blood, swagger-shouldered, in a bright red coat that just brought off his complexion . . . He meant to pay his compliments later at their box. Meanwhile, Eliza pressed her palms together till the bones rubbed. 'Oh,' Mrs Violet broke off at last, 'was you waiting for the gig?'

What a relief it was to be away; it was only in these interims she could breathe freely. The coachman, Mr Willis, a young man still, badly chapped by sunshine and rough leather, took them by the remains of St Mary's fish-market – the stench of the glistering trout, both fresh and foul at once, suggested to her more intimate decay. They shifted in the slick of their own loose scales. Risking her voice, she begged Willis to stop first at Lincoln's Inn, where she left a note for Mr P (the name he had asked her to use) with the gatekeeper. Her heart beat a sharp tattoo in her throat.

Handing over the ribboned card brought her a little closer, closer; something would happen soon; it must. If she pushed herself far enough, the natural gravity of events might take her the rest of the way. But she was waiting for the first slipping sense that she had lost her feet. Willis gave her an odd look as she climbed back in. He had a young man's curiosity still about his trade.

As soon as the maid let her into her sister's drawing room, Beatrice said, 'My dear, what's the matter?'

'Why, nothing,' Eliza answered in surprise. She was conscious only of the upright flame of her high spirits. It was Beatrice who seemed to demand pity: her small face swollen and thickened, the tip of her nose as tight-skinned as a flexed knuckle. She sat in the fat heat of a spring fire, on her hands and knees; they pressed carefully against a bearskin stretched across the hearth-tiles. She rose at last to greet her sister. Beatrice said, 'You look as if you've been out to sea; a real wind-blush.'

'Only I was so late,' Eliza offered.

'You mustn't overexcite yourself. It spoils your colouring; you haven't the pallor to carry it off. Too brown. Now let me look at you,' she said, holding her at arm's length. Eliza couldn't help sweating against the push of the coal-heat. The May day was rather bright than hot, but still she had caught a flush in the open air. She felt herself overflowing; the touch of her sister's hands against her shoulders was a tremulous containment, the lid on the pot that brings the water to boil. Suddenly, she confessed, 'I – I – have made an assignation, for the theatre.'

'My dear child.' Beatrice's voice ran thick and cluttered, unlike her. As if walking in borrowed clothes, a man's attire which didn't quite fit, she had to drag her heels. 'Wherever did you meet him?'

'At a bookshop. In a doorway.' It seemed utterly remarkable to her that the subject of her compressed excitement could be so easily let loose upon the air. A transformation, not from fiction into fact, but from feeling into action – as striking as if, dismissing a thought, she discovered the gesture had upset a candlestick. 'You have met him,' Eliza added coyly. 'You have danced with him – years ago.'

Beatrice's gossipy scream descended to a croak. There was just the hint of jealousy in it, too; the uneven pressure of a forced action. A flurry of questions followed: but who is he, where have we met, how far have you compromised yourself, and so on. Eliza only shook her head. It was a wonderful feeling, not budging. As if she possessed the greater weight. 'He sends his compliments,' she lied at last, 'but has particularly desired me to keep his presence a secret.' A secret from whom? His presence? Has he only just returned – from where? Was he a soldier, a sailor? Is he terribly battered, and ashamed to be seen? Eliza feared she had already given too much away. But a younger sister has large resources of silence, and she depended on these, shaking her head, pushing her chin out. Her drooping lip just revealed a line of wet mouth-flesh.

Time was pressing, however. They moved upstairs to the dressing room, where Beatrice began to fling clothes onto a low settee: morning and evening and afternoon dresses, opera cloaks, and mantuas, pelisses, gloves and scarves and hats. Eliza sat demurely to the side with her knees together and her hands pressed between them – as quiet as a corpse on a doctor's table. Her sister soon forgot her jealousy. She had that slight sweet generosity of pretty women; she delighted in draping, in petting and praising, her uglier sex. Eliza, unused to the shared fuss of being dressed, enlarged her eyes and drew in her lip and lifted her back in a drawn-out gesture of *hauteur*. Her vanity was doubled and redoubled by the various reflections, in the looking glass, in her own, in her sister's gaze. For a minute or two she felt like a broad palette of her own finer tastes and enjoyed that large freedom which extends even to the composition of the self. She had the making of a lady in her. They argued fiercely over the depth of her décolletage.

But the final gap had yet to be bridged. What she was straining against was her inability to act. Such make-believe was only a deeper assertion of her own carefully protected walls; it was the stepping over them that mattered. When the front bell rang, the sisters had not resolved the issue. Eliza pinched and tucked low the line of her dress. Small-breasted, she wished to suggest the pressure of her heart, outwards. The hoops of her ribs were visible; one could almost imagine dragging one's knuckles across them. A pink-brown fan of skin spread wide beneath her neck. Quickly, Bea tied a red band of velvet around Eliza's throat: a compromise, to draw the eyes away. Some of her hairs, curled after the fashion, had caught in it; but there was hardly time or attention to spare for her any more. She was being sent forth. Lady Walmsley waited in her carriage. Mrs Violet had carefully prepared a thin smile of praise to greet her. She was doubly annoyed at the delay; she didn't want it to spoil. Bea kissed Eliza quickly in the doorway, untucked her straggling hairs and glanced her over. 'You look lovely,' she said and thought: rather tightly bound. Her narrow face: long lip; sharp nose; ash skin. The fierce slight swell of her breasts; those tiny hips. My poor lonely sister, she thought. Not unsensual. God knows, of all that, what will first come undone. She softened suddenly, remembering forgotten fevers. 'Whatever you do,' she said, in a sisterly whisper, 'has been done before. Whatever happens, has happened to others. To everyone.' And she was gone.

Eliza thought, nothing that happens to anyone happens to me.

They dined at Wilmers first. Another place to wait, and defer arrival – the arrival of what, of whom, was growing to her increasingly unclear. If Lord B appeared, what should she say to him? Could any event answer the force of her expectation? At Wilmers the party gathered weight. Eliza was vaguely conscious of increase, the added difficulties in manoeuvre. There was Dab Hansen, the MP, a fat young buck with a twitch in his left eye and a charming stammer. He looked up painfully to Lady Walmsley. It was rumoured, after all, that she had once bedded Fox in his youth (in hers, too, of course). Lady Walmsley had, over the years, acquired a certain power of blessing, of bestowing favour, whatever was meant by the word. Her nod of recognition conjured significance out of thin air. Even Eliza was conscious of the warmth of her ladyship's shadow.

Then Admiral Withers 'had a sighting of them', as he said, and joined them at their table in the window: a heavy-headed, thin-necked old man, in a balding wig. Lady Walmsley, with her knotty hands, drew him to herself. She was particularly glad to see him; and they gossiped together at their end of the table, a flow of talk that did nothing to prevent his ordering several dishes of food. He tackled his turbot, Eliza quietly remarked, 'as if he continually hoped to surprise it'. Mrs Violet laughed; Eliza's sharp tongue sometimes startled the widow into undissembled amusement. At Lady Walmsley's age, to be making up to such an ostrich! Her ladyship wore a piled-up turban on her head; it was forever undoing, and required a constant and delicate 'putting in its place'. For once, Eliza indulged in unspoken condescension: poor old woman, petting herself.

Miss Esmond did not guess how little her own white gown suited her. Beatrice had tried to persuade her against it, but Eliza believed firmly that her chief distinction, the only thing her narrow features and form allowed her to aspire to, was *elegant simplicity*. Her nut-brown skin cast its dingy shadow across the lace; she looked rather unwashed. Yet her high spirits almost made up for it. A pink flush had begun to spread on either side of her nose; she seldom took wine at dinner. What could Bea have meant, that 'whatever you do, has been done before'? Eliza hadn't intended to *do* anything; she wouldn't know where to begin. She felt brave only in her thoughts. In these, Lady Walmsley and Mrs Violet, even the beautiful Beatrice, played unflattering supporting roles: the gorgon, the shrew, the wicked sister. Eliza, naturally enough, was the heroine of her own romance, the sweet, abused child making her way untainted through the world. And now the wine was making her talk.

Mrs Violet said, in the carriage afterwards, 'I wish, at least, we was going to a *modern* play. I can't bear anything old-fashioned.' The crowds had begun to fill the streets around Covent Garden; Willis, once or twice, cracked his whip to part them. Bridges Street itself was almost impassable; there was some kind of protest under way outside the theatre. Men filled the lane, shoulder to shoulder, their shadows doubled and redoubled under the swaying gas-lamps. Eliza caught the odour of them in the spring air, and covered her mouth. The press of people shocked her; the violence they threatened, their undeniable high spirits. Admiral Withers, at last, mounted the coach-box himself and roared a path clear. In spite of his age, he had a voice for all weathers. Hansen handed them out, and then Mrs Violet's new beau appeared, and 'cut a swath through them,' as he later said, 'with his stick. These pit-boys instinctively respect the force of a gentleman.' They squeezed together into the theatre-lobby, which was hardly less crowded or oppressive: a grand ante-chamber, square and high, overwrought with gold vines. Marble pillars guarded the doorways, topped by various busts: of Macklin, Cibber, Mrs Siddons. Eliza, in her strange way, never felt a clearer sense of *belonging* to her little party.

'The play is a great favourite of mine.' Lady Walmsley made a point of appearing undisturbed. They had reached the safety of their seats under the gratifying impression of a task accomplished. 'I remember seeing it first when Lord Frederic was courting me. He took a box, on purpose, across the gallery; and tried to cast the shine off his lorgnette in my eyes.' Lady Walmsley was plumply sinking into a reminiscence.

'Oh,' Mrs Violet responded, put out, 'but one knows what one means.'

'I do, indeed,' Eliza suddenly broke in. She had caught something of the crowd's high spirits; the wine, too, was beginning to take its toll. Her eyes as she spoke scanned restlessly across the way. A new fear was growing inside her, that she mightn't recognize him if he came. Besides, he was sure to disguise himself – for reasons she was dimly conscious of leaving unprobed. It pleased her too much, the sense of being in his secret, complicit. 'I have been saying to my father (you know my father writes romances), that he relies too much on histories and chronicles. Monks in abbeys, castles, harems. What is wanted, as you say, Mrs Violet, is the modern touch. Clubs, coffee-houses, and the like. A ride in the Park. The action of a play.'

The settling, unquiet air of the theatre reached a new pitch; then swiftly declined at the chastening hush of drawn curtains. Eliza noted that the pit was half-full. Mrs Violet's 'dog-friend' (as Lady Walmsley afterwards referred to him, in a tone impossible to convict of irony) informed the party that the theatre had raised its prices: these riots were the unhappy result. He was a square-jawed, handsome man; just the coal-black hint of the next morning's beard dusted his white complexion. His features suggested the rigidity of a mask, as if he suffered helplessly his own set expression of smiling self-regard. A Mr Tom Chancery. Not an unkind soul; he handed even Eliza to her seat and offered her the services of his fan. A mark of attention whose chief reward was the pointed and politic kindness Mrs Violet chose to show her for the rest of the evening.

As soon as the play began, all conversation resumed, a low rumble of talk as common and continuous as the sounds of carriage wheels on cobble stones. 'My father had this answer for me,' Eliza whispered, during a scene change.

It was all she could do to keep her head straight. Her glance darted here and there, leaving faint electric tracks in her mind's eye, the beginnings of a headache. 'He complained it was impossible; that the present day was too familiar. An author could not shape it as he pleased. His readers would for ever be comparing this or that against the real thing; his fictions could not but suffer by the contrast. There was another consideration, too. That what seems to us now terribly modern is only a matter of fashion. In ten years or so, one might not remember how we dressed or swore or passed the time. An author, my father says, who aims at posterity, had better set his feet firmly in the past.'

Admiral Withers intervened, clearing his throat with a swallow of something from a small hip-flask. 'But surely that is giving up the chase too easily; it shows a poor faint heart. The past is easily boarded, if you follow me; what we want is to tackle the present, in all its confusion.' Dab Hansen took the flask off him afterwards and passed it to Chancery. There was a general air of consumption and loose happiness – what Eliza thought of afterwards as 'manly snuggery'. Withers continued. 'Besides, I can never stomach all the monks and knights; call it the sailor in me. They talk painfully by the book. It's quite shocking, the way these historical writers steal from each other. I dined once, by the way, with Walter Scott. Perfectly amiable man; kept a decent table; and, as I learnt at dinner, his own *brigade* of infantry. Called them the Aldershots, or some such nonsense. Hadn't any notion how a war was fought. Didn't much care, either; admitted he only liked the dressing up. No, as Mrs Violet says, give me a modern play.'

Eliza found herself taking her father's side, somewhat against the grain. 'There seem to me a hundred different ways of dressing up, and not all of them require old clothes. It's an awful business, my father once confessed to me, and almost the worst of authorship: the eavesdropping, and peering over shoulders, just to see how other men live. More often than not, one only paints them like oneself regardless. It seemed, after all, more honest to him, beginning with make-believe; and from there, to work out his own ideas, without worrying too much over likenesses.'

'I only said,' Mrs Violet cut in at last, with a wincing smile, 'that I preferred a modern play, because it don't go on so long.'

There was a space of silence, of attention to the stage: the stage's own silence had produced it. It seemed that some-one had forgotten his lines; the quiet stretched out painfully. A man from the pit called out, 'Aren't you going to answer the gentleman?' General laughter. Even Lady Walmsley joined in; her handsome old head looked blind and common, screwed up in high spirits. Mrs Violet let out a shrill cackle; her tastes were really quite low. They deserved each other, after all, the old *grande dame* and her mismatched daughter-in-law: one pretty and foolish and young; the other, none of those things. Yet they were strangely complicit in their bickering. Eliza offered a half-smile. It seemed beneath their party to favour such outbreaks, but she didn't wish to appear sour-humoured. 'Might I ever,' the Admiral inquired, 'have picked up one of your father's books?' He had looked on disapprovingly. It didn't sit with his general ideas to laugh at strangers; he believed in keeping men in order.

'This is just it,' Eliza admitted, changing tack, 'this is just my point. He cannot afford a publisher; and none, as yet, has been willing to take on the expense. He should try something new, I tell him. Only, he lives a rather retired life. He spends more time among books than people. It seems only natural to him to set his romances among the scenes familiar from his daily life: his shelves.'

'But surely he lives in a house, on a street. He has neighbours. Eyes and ears. More particular memories.'

Eliza nodded. His life, since her mother died, had been uniformly drab. He spent his days at a desk in a wide hall of desks, tallying figures. His evenings at a table in his back room, composing. Weeks, years, passed without event. He seemed capable of acting only under the prick of his pen. She answered at last, 'My father once confessed to me that there were two great difficulties in *telling tales*. The first I've mentioned. Imagine yourself, he said, in a room full of people, of perfect strangers. So they seem, at least, until you discover that each of them, down to the merest child, bears your own face. Your own failures and habits; your own shabby knowledge of the world. Such terrible reproach they turn on you; as if to say, look, this is what you have made me – made us.' Eliza herself looked around, then, at the audience: at the pewter dimpling of a crowd of faces, their thumbprint impressions, the bright variations of pink. 'This unhappy family.'

'And the second?' Lady Walmsley inquired, somewhat recovered.

Eliza's social ease surprised herself, but the conversation was well-rehearsed. 'Forging the hand of Providence. My father admits to being a fractious and fickle god; his heroes tend to suffer under him – from the most unlikely coincidences. But he has no patience for the slow accumulation of events: it is too much like life.'

Lady Walmsley gave her a sharp look. Eliza's throat was sore from the wine and talking; she blushed at having forgotten her station, her dutiful silence. At having exposed her father to their indifference. Lady Walmsley said, 'I suppose, then, he is hardly surprised at remaining unpublished?'

Admiral Withers answered more simply, 'In the navy, you see, we have few such fears. We hope our men think as much alike, as much like *us*, as flogging will make them. And then, we are seldom short of circumstances to test their mettle.' Eliza gave him a grateful glance. Her father had always got on, she remembered, with intelligent, practical men. It once surprised her; he was so impractical himself. But now she had learned to expect it. Even the relation of his troubles brought out their sympathies. It was then she considered – hesitant as she was, of her voice, of her charms, of her place in society – how suitable her education had been. For wooing poets. Her father had taught her, if nothing else, the language of romance, of swooning and reproach, of love. If only she could put it to use.

Lady Walmsley broke in suddenly, 'I believe that's Sam Whitbread, giving himself presiding airs. And beside him, Henry Colburn. Do you see, Hansen? There, just across the way. With a third man, in a black coat, talking. I haven't seen him since he launched your little history of Ireland on the unsuspecting world. Flutter your fan at him, Mrs Violet. There. He has just caught my eye. I suspect we shall have his compliments at the interval.' Then, smiling with satisfaction: 'The actors must grow thirsty soon.' Eliza had seen him, too. Lord Byron's distant animation awoke in her a kind of pity – she saw what miniature his gestures were reduced to, at thirty yards. It wasn't quite the sense of arrival she had anticipated, but something near to it, nearer. At that range, he still seemed largely a creature of her own imagination; imbued, however, with the power of approach. Capable also of unguessed-at qualities; a life outside her mind.

CHAPTER EIGHT

A FEW HOURS EARLIER, OVER DINNER, Colburn had said to Polidori, 'Now I've had a look at your memoirs of Byron.' They sat in a back room at The Nose Bag, a tavern just off Grosvenor Square: low-roofed, stinking of men, spilt beer. Colburn cut bloodily into his chop. 'I'll tell you what the trouble with it is.' Polly's heart sank. It seemed to him suddenly he had spent his life listening to that preamble. 'Don't despair,' Colburn added, in his kindly, practical way. 'It's easily mended.' In Colburn's eyes, everything was merely a question of adjustment. He freely confessed he had no original talents, but prided himself on his gift for tinkering. What he professed to know – the way of the world, how to satisfy its tastes – was precisely in its way just what Polidori despaired of coming to grips with.

'The trouble,' he repeated, 'is plain enough. You've written a charming memoir of a young man's continental travels. Full of art and adventure and pretty girls.'

'This is just it! This is exactly what I set out to do. A charming travelogue, etc.'

'Only you've picked the wrong young man. You've written about yourself.'

'Naturally.'

'Nobody cares a damn about Dr Polidori. *I* don't. *She* doesn't.' He gestured at the waitress; then at a table of gentlemen, who were picking over a pot of mussels. '*They* don't. I suspect, really, neither do you.' Having caught the girl's eye, he ordered two more pints of porter. 'That's the trouble. Nobody does; though, as I say, it's easily mended. Shall I tell you a young man they might pay two shillings five pence to read about? Lord Byron. Shall I tell you a fitting subject for a continental journal? Lord B. Shall I tell you what John Murray would pay five hundred guineas, with a kiss on the lips, etc. etc.' Colburn, in the midst of this tirade, spotted an acquaintance at the bar; and touching Polidori on the shoulder, rose from the table and made his way over. One of his characteristic vagaries, that he could shift the full heat of his attention on a whim, leaving the young man to consider his position alone.

Of course, Polly knew it was true. Had always known it; had resisted just because he knew. He remembered landing at Ostend, shortly after that unhappy episode in Dover. Byron had proved a poor sailor, and Polly preened himself on being 'sea-worthy'; this at a time in his life when he could still fancy himself blessed or charmed, almost untouchable. When he trusted his sister's faith: 'We rely on you. All of us. We rely on you.' The months that followed helped him to revise that self-opinion. By the end of the summer, Byron had dismissed him; and Polly had put to the test his sister's preference, for her husband, among others, and come out second best. Being untouchable struck him in a different light, with a different meaning: he was unable to touch, make contact with the world. Reconsidered, his steady legs and iron stomach seemed only proof of how little life affected him, how out of tune he was. Byron's easy upset suggested his more sensitive gauge.

Still, it made Polly smile to remember the poet: how green and grateful he looked, to see the little town of Ostend, as the ship beat its way into the harbour. He shouted at Polidori, for standing to windward of him, for looking cheerful, for anything at all. By the time, however, they reached their hotel, his lordship had fully recovered his humour and his land-legs. He apologized to Polly for barking at him; only, he said, 'It helped him to keep down his dinner.' And then he fell like a thunderbolt upon the chambermaid.

She was a perfectly unremarkable girl of seventeen, who had reached just that age, that span of months, when her commonness seemed like the freshest, simplest language of youth and beauty. Round cheeks, that would soon hang slack; wide eyes, before they reddened; a full, plain mouth unlined by any fixed expression whatsoever. She hardly resisted him at all. Polly left his portmanteau on his bed and retreated to the hallway. He meant to descend to the dining rooms, but lingered a minute, listening to the sounds within. The maid, strangely enough, had most of the shouting to herself: a pigeon-like cooing deepening in her throat, till she lost her breath altogether and resorted to gasping. Lord B distinguished rather by his silence. Polly couldn't help but reflect on his own abrupt performance in that line; he had begun, as his father predicted, to feel the force of impossible comparisons.

They journeyed north and east through Belgium. At Brussels, they ran into a friend of B's mother, Pryse Gordon: a man of about forty, curly-haired, with a youthful, amiable expression, and a nose that looked somewhat bitten off. Lord Byron wanted to take in the fields of Waterloo; Pryse offered to serve as 'cicerone'. Polly guessed already that Byron was planning more *poeshies* (B's word), and secretly hoped to test his own muse against him. Indeed, Gordon's wife kept an album of occasional verses, in which Walter Scott himself had recorded his impressions of the field of battle. Polidori felt the exaltation of his company; he nursed secret hopes of 'announcing' himself by some grand poetical flourish. The mockery of *Ximenes* still rankled, though he had, on a calmer consideration, removed the offending words – stricken 'goiter'd' and 'scalps' from the MS. This was his second chance to prove himself.

The visit brought out all Byron's pomp and foolishness. His grand carriage had made a palpable impression overnight, not particularly favourable: it was only too faithfully Napoleonic. The farmers had suffered heavily in the war. B himself was on his worst behaviour. A certain, perhaps understandable, conflation in his mind made him sensitive to unintended slights. He had last travelled that way as a young man, with his life before him; an unknown. The journey, recorded in the first cantos of *Childe Harold*, had made him famous, and he expected some evidence of that fact to accompany his second pilgrimage like a glow of lights, an easing of the way. Of course, this was often the case. But even the best of travellers grow irritable at the inevitable delays and discomforts, at the obstructive indifference of the natives. And Byron's temper had never been steady. Their inn at Brussels had been especially foul; he violently fought off his ill-humour with forced wit and loudly repeated Pope's lines to Bathurst, 'In a bad inn's worst room', as their host left them a last inch of tallow candle to light their dirty bedside. All pretence of sanguinity left him when Polidori foolishly corrected him. 'I believe you'll find,' he said, 'that the line runs, In the worst inn's, etc.' Byron grinned horribly and then hissed, as Polly had known Italians hiss at women, with both hands raised. Later, more calmly, as they undressed, Byron insisted on making an early start, on rising at first light, in the morning's glory, etc.

For once he kept his word and refusing any breakfast himself, hurried Polly and Gordon hungrily out of bed for his sake. B not unkindly explained that he couldn't bear any longer the rude, titillated stares of his countrymen; and he hoped to escape their prying eyes by stealing a march on them during the feeding hour. 'The English tourist,' he quipped, 'also marches on his stomach.' Bad jokes were with him always a sign of high spirits. Only Polidori minded; afterwards he blamed the rumblings of his own stomach, and his sleepless head, for feeling so dull, for the long wide absence of inspiration, the waste of the day. Byron, of course, proceeded to make himself as conspicuous as possible, pulled a dark cloak about his ears, muttered audibly to himself; till even the farmers who hadn't a notion who he was, stopped their horses in harness, and stared.

They reached the Plain of Waterloo at morning twilight; cold narrow lanes of ascending sunshine stretched over the broken fields and broadened into daylight. Spring had returned; spring left no sign of anything but spring. Favourable rains promised a heavy harvest; their horses struggled in the deepening soil. Already the corn, morning-wet, reached to their stirrups. B dismounted, looking for bones, for rusted sabres. Gordon, in hushed tones, confided to Polly (he had instantly adopted the name), 'That he had never seen his Lordship so pensive and silent, in such a musing mood'. He explained that Byron's cousin had died at Waterloo, a soldier named Frederic Howard. It upset Byron particularly, as he had once insulted the young man's father, Lord Carlisle – 'out of sheer vanity, which made it worse' – with the quick, sharp tongue of youth. B never regretted anything as much as his own vanity; but his contrition, his sense of wrong-doing, was just as sensitive as his pride. 'An extraordinary man,' Gordon concluded; 'wonderful, how deeply he feels.' Gordon, as Polidori guessed, was a very good-natured fool: blessed by wealth and mediocrity, and an easy disposition, which saw no reason to alter either of his natural states. Polly dismounted, too; and kicked the ground. He began looking for bones himself, and feverishly beating his brain for rhymes, for feelings. It seemed only an ordinary plain, a spring day; there was nothing to be said, or felt.

By noon, the fields were dotted with curious visitors. Peasants appeared, ambling from party to party, offering, in a rolled up cloth, various broken blades, rusted and earthy; horseshoes, patches of tunic. Byron, high-spirited, had found his tongue; something had shifted within him, aligned his temper. His fresh colour suggested seaside nourishment, briny inhalations. In a benevolent vein, he bought a helmet for too much money; whispered to

Polidori, knowingly, that he had seen a farmer run his plough over it earlier in the morning, to lend it verisimilitude. This is what he loved above all, the false authentic – seeing through it, delighting in it, nonetheless. Polidori, revolving verses on his tongue, hardly said a word all day. B had discovered a fox skull stuck in a clump of mud. He carefully brushed away the earth with a handkerchief, till the fragile jaw appeared, parchment-thin, the colour of tobacco stains. He kept looking out for Englishmen. Whenever any approached, he lifted the skull to his eyes and began declaiming, in booming melancholy tones:

> Start not – nor deem my spirit fled;
> In me behold the only skull,
> From which, unlike a living head,
> Whatever flows is never dull.

So childish, and absurd; Polly couldn't help but warm to him. They mounted their horses again and galloped fiercely across the fields, chanting Turkish war-songs together. Polly consoled himself, there hadn't been the occasion for inspiration; it was rather a holiday from grandeur.

Byron went to bed early and rose late. A wide crust of tallow lay dried against his bedside table when Polidori retired at last. He had been drinking with Pryse Gordon. The next day, after dinner, Gordon took Polidori aside. The horses were being saddled; the coach had been repaired; Byron was eager to carry on. They could hear him from the dining room, instructing the servants, directing the boxes, till all fit snug. He liked playing the general; he suffered from what Polidori wryly characterized as 'intermittent gusts of practicality, the conviction that he alone could lead them forward'. Pryse ignored the doctor's attempt to draw him into a criticism of the poet. He carried his wife's album under his arm, and carefully opened it to the latest page. Byron had copied in a fair hand the following lines:

There have been tears and breaking hearts for
   thee,
And mine were nothing had I such to give;
But when I stood beneath the fresh green tree,
Which living waves where thou didst cease to live,
And saw around me the wide field revive
With fruits and fertile promise, and the Spring
Came forth her work of gladness to contrive,
With all her reckless birds upon the wing,
I turn'd from all she brought to those she could
   not bring.

Polidori had a sudden image of the fox skull; Byron, with his thumb on the joint, tenderly manipulating its jaw. It might have been an image of Polidori himself. Out of his own head only dullness flowed. It was as if he were hardly alive, as if he lacked the sense to perceive life, as if nothing that mattered, no feelings of significance, not even lamentation, could touch him. He was untouchable. What difference between them, in their clay, in their spiritual soil, produced on the one hand such a harvest, and in his own heart, only dust? The force of impossible comparisons. Gordon took him lightly by the elbow, and said, companionably moved, 'Sweet sentiments, are they not?' Polidori had been weeping. He replied bitterly, 'I believe his lordship hardly knew the young man; much less liked him.'

Small wonder he hadn't spent his observations on Lord B. He needed to breathe! after all; he needed to make a space for himself. His journals had been a steady source of consolation. In them, he insisted on precedence. Shortly after, Polidori began to feel a physical constriction: a tightness in his temples, spots of blindness, wretched nausea. He was hardly well enough to travel; the worst of it was, the patience and forbearance he inspired in Lord B. On top of everything else, to suffer his kindness! Later, on one of their interminable coach journeys, Byron confessed to Polidori that he wrote that little memorial 'as much out of guilt as any sweeter sympathy'. The young man, who, 'to do him justice, died gallantly', was a kind of cousin to him and every kind of fool. His lordship had once, by a tremendous effort of will, resisted making love to his wife. Or had almost resisted, it hardly mattered; in any case, all Byron could remember was the effort. 'False grief, then?' Polidori, stung by a curious jealousy, wanted Byron to acknowledge his hypocrisy. But the poet seemed hardly to have heard him. 'It is my curse,' he said, looking out at the tidy cheerfulness of Flemish fields, 'that whatever I love dies young.' No, no, no, no, Polidori wanted to shout; you did not love him, you did not suffer for his death. He almost shouted it now, in the gloom of the public house: no, no, no, no. You did not suffer; *I* suffered, I suffered more.

Colburn returned to find both glasses of porter untouched on the table. 'I'm looking forward to this evening,' the publisher said. 'I'm glad I ran into that fellow; Harding, by name. An actor. He gave me an appetite for the performance tonight. A bit of gossip. I'll tell you on the way.' Polly hadn't stirred; Colburn stared at him. 'Drink up,' he said.

They decided to walk from Audley Street. It was a fine spring night, just cold enough, as Colburn said, 'to make the stars look sharp'. Polidori attempted to interest him in his sequel to *The Vampyre*, 'a . . . a kind of comic inversion, to be called *The Physician*: the tale of a living man who feeds off the dead.' But he was tired of petitioning on his own behalf; he was tired of most kinds of dressing up. Playing the eager author seemed the worst disguise of all. Colburn nodded absently. 'Yes, yes,' he said, 'very interesting. It all depends, of course, on how you carry it off. A tricky business, I suspect.' In the middle of Piccadilly he took the young doctor by the arm. 'I'll strike a deal with you, John. Start from scratch. Put Byron this time where he belongs: at the heart of it. What he looked like, said; the girls he took to bed. Whatever you can't recall, don't be shy of inventing. Show me what you've got in a month; I'll cast my eye on it. If I like what I see, there's a hundred pounds on the spot, and four hundred to come. Don't beat your brains over it; we don't want anything clever. Simply remember who your hero is, and you won't go wrong.'

Polly said he would attempt it; he would do his best. 'Good man.'

Approaching the theatre, they began to fight the traffic in the streets: women of the lowest class, respectable tradesmen, a few drunk soldiers spoiling for a fight. Colburn, a bull of a man, led with his shoulder, and Polidori followed gratefully in his wake. A handful of gallants were beating a path for the ladies. Polly overheard one of them boasting, 'These pit-boys instinctively respect the force of a gentleman', but the voice, and the people behind him, were lost in the throng. Some men had climbed up to the first-floor balconies on either side of Bridges Street; they now passed a rope between them, and then slipped the hook of a lit lantern along the rope. 'There'll be trouble soon,' Colburn said. 'People want entertaining, and they can't afford it.' The men began to swing the rope back and forth over the heads of the crowds. A picturesque effect: the loop of light trailed shuddering black smoke and briefly illuminated, here or there, a dirty face fevered in the glow. Someone started a song, which was generally taken up, in great, if rather violent, good humour. Polidori felt the heat of the lantern hurrying by his ear and struggled to make out the words:

> We've burned it down before
> And we'll burn it down again
> The cheapest show at the Theatre Royal
> Is a fire in Drury Lane.
> Oh, we've burned it down before . . .

Settled at last in their box, Colburn said to Polidori, 'I wouldn't miss it for the world. Munden's acting against Kean for the first time. I hope we can see it out to the end.' He launched into a history of the two actors. Munden was the grand old man of English comedy; Kean, its *enfant terrible*. They despised each other: it was a perfect contest of age and youth. A new way to pay old debts indeed! Munden's gentle manner against Kean's ferocity. Colburn's friend at The Nose Bag had witnessed Munden rehearsing. The old pro was in a perfect terror; he hardly dared set foot on stage. He had prepared, as always, meticulously, down to the last nicety of dress, of manner, of speech. But Kean had such natural force, it couldn't be countered by style at all, it was the death of style.

Polidori looked around briefly for Eliza Esmond; recognized her at last by her long throat, bound by a line of red velvet. For an instant, he considered her in the fine sympathy of indifference. She sat a little aside from her party. A few feet away, some old dame (Lady Walmsley, he supposed) rested a flirtatious hand on the shoulder of a slender upright man in a large-buttoned coat. Polly admired the cold white beauty of Mrs Webster; her face, at that distance, had something of Byron's look, his trembling hauteur. He remembered the pains the poet took over his appearance, the bled pallor of his countenance, which suggested nothing so much as the exhaustion produced by vanity, by the perfect stillness it required. He imagined first the lady, then his lordship, undressing in the cool silver lake of a mirror: their spell-bound self-regard.

The cream of Eliza's frock did not suit her brown complexion. She had the touching appearance of a wild child prisoned in formal clothes, playing grown-up. Poor thing. Her shoulders so high and narrow, she seemed, like a fractious girl, to be held up from above by two hands under her arms. Why had he come? simply to tease her? Because he hoped to make love to her, and relieve, for a moment, the squalor of his life by her silly misapprehension? And for the first time, he guessed another reason – he wanted to see how far he could play Byron's hand, whether he could carry it off, whether he had it in him. She caught his eye and held it: he saw the electric shock of pleasure in her, her answered hope. And felt a jolt of it himself, transmitted along the wire of their gaze. He had never before known the pleasure of giving pleasure, and remembered one of Lord B's confessions: 'I am weak enough to love,' he used to say, 'anything on earth that appears to wish it.' Still, he could hardly approach her there, then, amidst such company. The gap between them, which equalled almost exactly the distance between who he was and who she took him to be, seemed impassable. For the first time, he considered the consequences of being found out. A woman such as Lady Walmsley, with an interest in the girl, could hardly be expected to take his imposture quietly.

Colburn said, 'I know that woman. Lady Walmsley. With young Hansen; I published his pamphlet on Ireland last year. They'll expect us to call on them, no doubt. Come, I'll introduce you. They may be able to do you a bit of good.' He tipped his hat at the old lady, and bowed. Polidori felt suddenly the moisture between his pressed palms and began to think up excuses. He couldn't be certain his lie wasn't criminal, the game he was playing, however inadvertently. But perhaps these nerves, these ridiculous sweats, were only the fever of another kind of anticipation, the sour foretaste in the mouth brought on by desire. He imagined his teeth in her brown neck and softly raised a single finger to his lips. Eliza nodded, and looked down. There was something sensual, he had often felt it, in the idea of the vampyre: it had, perhaps, to do with the submission of the girl, her quiet, selfless offering of life, of blood. 'Why don't you marry?' Colburn continued. 'You're not ill-looking. The daughter-in-law is pretty enough, I believe; and quite stupidly rich.'

Almost in spite of himself, Polidori was drawn into the action of the play. A young, dishonoured man, at the mercy of his debts, attempts to woo a rich and beautiful widow, if only to show the world that he's in favour again. Kean played the part of Giles Overreach, a 'cruel extortioner', the young man's creditor. Rubbing his hands, he asks one of his servants if the bankrupt has finally hanged himself? 'No, sir, he lives,' the vassal replies, 'Lives once more to be made a prey to you, a greater prey than ever.' Kean digs deep in his throat, crying, 'Art thou in thy wits? If thou art, reveal this miracle, and briefly.'

'A lady, sir,' the man says, 'is fallen in love with him.'

Was it so easy then? Perhaps what he needed was only the sanction of the world bestowed by marriage; a woman's touch. When the curtain fell at intermission, Colburn said, 'Come, I'll introduce you.' Polly was tempted for a minute to confess – his silly imposture, unintended. What had he come for, after all? Make an end of it, a source of laughter, momentary confusion and disappointment, soon made up. But he wasn't yet quite willing to give up the charade; so he hung back. Polidori said, 'If you please, I'd rather not.' And then, with false weight, 'I believe I've run into the girl in white before. Best not to mention my name.' He guessed, rightly, that this was just the kind of hint at confession Colburn instinctively trusted; confessions, after all, inspired belief by appearing to pay for it. Colburn answered, dismissively, 'As you like. But take my advice next time, and brazen it out. One can't always skulk.'

Afterwards, he saw Colburn sitting down beside the pow-der-haired woman. The girl with the narrow throat turned her sad face towards Polidori and gave him an understand-ing look. It seemed almost as if they had true grounds for separation, crossed stars, unlucky fates, etc. Her expression had the tenderness of parting in it, of unwilling retreat, across the sea of bare heads below them. For the first time it occurred to him how much they might properly have in common. Both of them were touched by fantasies. He saw, as bright almost as a halo, the spell these seemed to cast around her: the circle it made was the shape of loneliness.

She sat, in the midst of her party, silently staring out at him. Only when the long-necked old man touched her by the elbow did she turn away. But conversation put her in a different light. Her speaking face had an agreeable animation; her hands, too, seemed quick and lively. When she rested one briefly on her companion's lapels, Polidori felt, to his surprise, a pang of jealousy. What an awful fool she must be, he thought to console himself. Then: what a contemptible one he knew he was.

He remembered once, after Byron had gone out riding – this on Lake Leman, where his Lordship had taken a house for the summer – quietly stealing into the master's bedroom. Shortly after breakfast; Polidori was somewhat recovered from the journey, his terrible headaches and stretched nerves. He looked at himself in B's mirror; tried on his master's hat, his Albanian short-coat; postured at a graceful angle, leaning on his lordship's sword-stick; adjusted the muscles of his face, practising more poetical expressions. The balcony windows, overlooking the water, had been left open; and the air off them, still cool with early summer, reminded him how much of the bright season still lay ahead, its long days. A long life. Thus absorbed, he did not hear Byron returning on foot. The horse had come up limping on a loose cobble, and B could never bear any cruelty to his animals. He found his young doctor, costumed in his clothes, staring at his own reflection. Polidori was too embarrassed to move or speak. Byron approached him, and stood at his side, the pair of them doubled in each other, in the mirror. 'They become you,' he said. Polidori quietly undressed.

After the interval, circumstances conspired against Kean's Overreach. He lost his land to forgery, his daughter, in marriage, to a servant-boy. Confronted by his accusers and confounded on all sides, he gave way to a rage so pure it had the beauty of virtue. 'Why, is not the whole world included in myself?' he began, but his anger consumed his meaning;

79

the rest of his speech being scarcely articulated. A stunning display of natural power, Munden cowered before it, forgot his lines, was pulled gaping from the stage. The audience applauded in mid-scene; the contest was over, Kean had won, even as he lay breathless on the ground. Such fury seemed almost unacted. It wasn't susceptible to counterfeit, being so inhuman in its force; consequently, beyond the pale of comparison. Polidori was utterly involved in it. His eyes fixed on the prostrate figure, even as he felt himself falling in his seat. A rush of blood had swollen his head, and he gave way to its hot darkness, childishly: an almost conscious letting go, though it was consciousness itself that he let slip through his fingers. Still, it wasn't the first time in the past month he had fainted. Later, he found Colburn's large face bent over him, felt his hand against the bones of his neck. 'Why, feel how thin you've got, man; and you hardly touched your dinner.'

Colburn, with Polidori's arm bent at the elbow around his shoulder, carried him into the corridors and down the marbled stairs, out into the air. The crowds had dispersed; it was only a cold night under hot stars. Polidori had been watching his own heart tick in the line of his wrist, a little indentation of skin, pressed and released, again and again. How frail he was, his arm strained under his own half-weight. Colburn was right, Polly had let himself go. It was sheer weakness of vanity; without a mirror to remind him, he tended to starve himself. A headache had come to stay, one of that crowd of unpleasant, interior guests – blindness, tinnitus – which had visited him on his travels with Lord B. He knew how much depended on internal balances: our health, our vision. It required the constant adjustment of delicate sensory mechanisms to keep at bay a universal nausea, which threatened otherwise to overwhelm us. He both felt and enacted the clutch of his stomach, the upwards lurch. A stream of heat filled the sour path of his throat; he opened his mouth onto the cobbles, and retched.

God knows why Kean's rage had afflicted him so terribly. There was something both pure and purifying about his anger – without limits or modesty. Polly felt better for it afterwards, almost clear-headed. Colburn handed him into a hansom cab and left him there; he still wished to catch the curtain calls. Munden, he remarked in the pleasantness of admiration, had stood transfixed; the other actors had had to drag him off the stage, Kean's fury had undone him. He'd forgotten his lines. 'I wonder if the old man has the heart to come back on.' On the journey towards the river, Polidori permitted himself a weak tonic of self-congratulation. He had got out, after all, undiscovered. But more than that, the incident reminded him of how powerful his feelings still were, his appetite for life: Kean's rage had found its echo in him.

Colburn, it turned out, had not paid the fare.

It was only as he lay in bed that night, going over the events of the evening – the dirty pallor of Eliza's complexion was almost Italian and reminded Polidori of the peasant girls auctioned by their fathers under the balcony of Byron's palazzo in Venice; he used occasionally as he said to 'indulge their paternal pride', which didn't prevent him from haggling shamefully over the prices – that Polidori remembered Lord Byron had once attended a performance of Kean's; had been painfully struck by it; had collapsed in the theatre, and been driven home.

Byron himself had told him the story. He had met Kean in what he called the 'second blush of fame', shortly before his marriage. Hobhouse and he had gone to Drury Lane to see *Macbeth*, and afterwards dined at their friend Kinnaird's, where Kean himself appeared later, large-headed, quick with leftover nerves. He was ready to embark on, as Kinnaird put it, 'one of his happy *drunks*'. It was a night B never forgot. (For a famous man, Polidori often thought, Byron was peculiarly susceptible to fame in other people; the glow of it persuaded him of his own.) Even so, he always liked the company of men. And he'd just come back from the Noels' country place at Seaham, and a week enduring the 'inconstant ardours' of his bride-to-be, and the rather more 'unebbing' garrulity of Sir Ralph, his future father-in-law. That late dinner with a famous actor, a few friends, struck him as the best and last of his bachelorhood.

He mentioned all this to Polidori on a late ride home along the shores of Leman, to the villa he had rented overlooking the water. In the morning, Byron continued, somewhat chastened by a hangover, and tender on account of it, he felt the need to write to Annabella. He still remembered his letter, and recited some of it to Polidori. 'I have great hopes that we shall love each other all our lives as much as if we had never married at all.' Nothing was too private for Byron to delight in repeating it. Still, Polly couldn't help but acknowledge the charm of the line. It was just like the poet to squeeze a little sweetness out of the sourest moods. He looked at Polly now, reining in, and said, in his famously melancholy tone, 'I wonder, if we were still married, should I love her as much as I do?'

They had been up at Coppet, visiting de Staël. The conversation had turned to 'famous actors'; and the 'grand gargoyle' had been curious to hear Byron's report of Kean. 'I know no pleasure,' B had said, 'so sensual as *good acting*.' A lady novelist, just shy of her sixty-fifth birthday, had actually fainted away. Talk of Kean had awoken in Byron the whimsy of confession: his intimate manner was utterly irresistible, precisely because he seemed to need kindness so sharply. The warmth off the water put their horses in a soft sweat; the air had the taste of flat soda. Kean, he said, had played his part on either side of B's marriage, standing guard, perhaps, like the 'lions of paradise', or the 'dogs rather, watching the gates below'. The actor had presided over his 'last supper' as a bachelor. And then, in the course of his marriage, Kean had, on a number of occasions, thwarted Byron: innocently enough perhaps. Turned down the roles that

Byron, as a member of the committee at Drury Lane Theatre, had offered him; refused to read his address on the death of Sheridan, etc. Byron also took a dislike to Kean's acting. The poet had, in his 'old age', acquired a taste for modesty, for natural proportion.

Still, shortly before sailing for the continent, Byron had gone to see Kean at the theatre once more. B was carrying on a 'thoroughly pleasant affair' with one of the actresses. 'These,' he added, 'are rarer than one might think.' His marriage, hardly a year after that dinner at Kinnaird's, was in ruins: his daughter stolen from him, and taken to the country; his wife now cold to him 'as statues or virtues'; lawyers swarming 'like wasps at a picnic'; rumours of this and that flying. The bailiffs, 'as you saw, Polly' haunting his door. And that night, Kean went into one of his rages. Drunken spittle flew thick as grapeshot; he shouted his lines so loudly they drowned themselves in their own noise; the actors quailed before him. And it tallied so forcefully with Byron's own sense of futility and what the Austrians call *Wut* (to which the English owed their rather gentler expression of 'wroth') – at the world, at the way in which everything he loved had been taken from him, often by the objects of that love – that he absolutely fainted away, 'from sheer exhaustion at having his own thoughts so violently *voiced*'. Polidori silently inclined his head; he was afraid of disappointing such a confession by his own weak sympathies. Still, he remembered noting for the first time, after months spent wrangling with his jealousy and admiration, that Byron was unhappy. That he suffered, too; indeed, owing to the grander scale of his life and sentiments, that he probably suffered more than Polidori *could.*

Polly lay in bed, in the bloodless light of the moon, which poured through the open window of his bedroom and over his knees and ankles. The recollection had struck an almost physical blow; recovering from it involved a kind of returning to his senses, a feeling for wounds. Three years after

Byron's confession, Polidori had swooned at the theatre, watching one of Kean's 'rages'. It never for a minute occurred to him that he simply shared his master's sensitivities; it was clear to him that he had borrowed the poet's susceptibility, even to the point of unconsciousness. And, in fact, the fainting fit began to replay itself in his mind, from a sharper internal view. The wilful release of his balancing muscles, in his hips, his stomach; the unchecked rush of blood to his eyes as he forced them shut; his softly delayed collapse to the balcony floor. His waking gratitude, instant because anticipated, at Colburn's looming sympathies. For the thousandth time since leaving Byron's service, he sensed the hand of the poet on him. (A sound like Byron's voice, 'soft and low, an excellent thing in woman', sometimes surprised him at odd moments, under the noise of carriage-wheels on cobbles, in the cry of a woman scolding her child, calling after him. A scent like Byron's, like the violet of his toilette, once stopped him cold amid the general odours of spring.) Polidori felt haunted and began to be afraid. The space in which he lived and felt – in the solitude of himself, free of the taint of other lives and feelings – was shrinking. He felt a lightness in his heart like the weak beat after a loss of blood.

CHAPTER NINE

I N THE MORNING, Polidori had to pack up his books.
Wherever he went he bought books; he could hardly
read them as quickly as he acquired them. In Milan
alone, after Byron had dismissed him, for consolation he
purchased over three hundred volumes. Now they lay in
tumbled stacks about his rooms: Caesar, Pliny the Younger,
Sallust, Seneca, Tacitus . . . Byron had said to him once, not
unkindly, 'You are more an antique Roman than a Doctor.'
Their presence was a constant reproach: how little he had
read. Another world in which he had failed to make his way.
Better to sell them, to be rid of them, to begin again: with
empty shelves, an uncluttered life. Colburn had promised
to send a man around that afternoon to appraise them. As
usual, Polly had turned first for help to those who abused
his trust. The publisher would sell them on, whatever struck
him, for an 'honest' commission; and Polly could not
repress his filial relief at entering into relations with a powerful man.

It was a bright early summer day, dusty and glaring,
though not without its chills. Polidori sat on the floor in a
heap of books. He'd awoken, after a restless night on an
empty stomach, late in the morning, hollow-hearted and
red-eyed; but the sense of physical weakness had rather
sharpened than dulled the clarity of his thoughts. He was
cleaned out; he could fill up. The refrain of his intentions
ran through his head: I am going to set my life in order; I am
going to begin again, from scratch; I am going to begin. Yet
he could not lift a title without glancing in. His curiosity,

easily fatigued, nevertheless had its own kind of persistence. He liked to touch everything that came to hand. The
task sufficiently absorbed him that he did not notice the low
knock and shy step of Eliza Esmond, until she stood in his
room. Her cheeks were flushed, either with exercise, or a
consciousness of the risk taken. 'My lord,' she said, somewhat breathlessly. 'My lord.' It was just as she might have
pictured him: a poet surrounded by his inspirations;
dishevelled, dirty, indifferent to the sunshine beckoning
from the city window; a man of his words. 'I feared for you.
You left so suddenly. You would not speak to me.'

'I was taken ill, it could not be helped. The air in the theatre
was stifling. The press of other people.'

'I thought perhaps you were displeased with me. I
thought perhaps you suspected me of giving you away.' She
wrung her hands till the knuckles reddened unpleasantly;
her spareness betrayed a kind of greed, an appetite for life
that would not be satisfied by ordinary human foods. He
guessed that whatever she suffered as disappointment,
some internal heat transformed into guilt, into her own
wrongdoing. She could be easily played with.

'Not at all.' He decided to please her, to appeal to her
sense of himself. 'Only, I am very susceptible to the . . . the
force of others. Kean was magnificent. His anger was
tremendous; it undid me.'

'I know just what you mean; it took me just the same; it
was all I could do not to cry out when he shouted so.' There
followed an awkward silence. They could only speak when
their various postures touched upon each other, like glancing foils. In their natural shapes, they hung back, silently.

She, taking violent courage, began again abruptly and too
loudly. 'I only wished to say I had read your tale; I was never
more affected by anything' – she seemed to stagger slightly,
her agitation was painfully apparent – 'by anything in my
life. It is the finest thing you have done. I have not slept this
week.' She leaned in his doorway, and Polidori hastened to

support her. She wore a long peach-coloured pelisse, and a very small bonnet, shaped like a bee-hive. A charming dress; she was really not at all ill-looking. Her fidgets, her nerves, were only the checked expression of something rather fierce. She'd make, he thought, a beautiful consumptive, the way she fought for life. Besides, she had this fact tremendously in her favour: she had liked his book.

'You are very brave,' he whispered, taking her elbow in his hand and guiding her to his single chair. 'Very brave.' His open neck shamed him; he had rolled his shirt-sleeves to his elbows, and now carefully unrolled them again.

It seemed to her that a pane of glass, already cracked, had fallen away. The view was not only clearer for it, but the fresh wind in her face struck her with a kind of violence. She was almost free, outside herself, in the world. She had taken this step on her own – come what may, she had done her duty. This thought she repeated feverishly in her head. Duty to *whom*, to *what*, still undefined. He poured her a glass of water from his nightstand. She had prepared a little speech, and now, with his back turned, she summoned the courage to deliver it.

'I presume, I know, upon a very slight acquaintance: two dances at a ball three years ago. Or rather, only one; the other we sat out together. I suppose you've forgotten inviting me that night, to bid you farewell in the morning. You were leaving for Dover, I believe.' She paused to gather her thoughts; and then, as if entering at last upon her proper confession, continued. 'I came. You did not see me; but I watched you standing in the balcony window. I nearly called out to you – but the world was all before you, and I did not suppose it would wait for my interruption. I was hardly more than a girl. Your glance passed over me then, and as it did, I fell in love with you. It may seem a strange assertion, but it is none the less true that I place my happiness in your hands. If a *woman*, whose reputation has as yet remained unstained, if without either guardian or husband

87

to control her, she should throw herself on your mercy, if with a beating heart she should confess the love she has borne you many years . . .'

Polidori interrupted her with the glass of water; she had started to pant. He lifted her chin, and she drank. Her swallow, plainly audible, struck her as an almost shameful avowal of the physical self: she had really begun to believe she was all words and feelings until that cool lump of liquid passed down her throat into the stomach. He resigned the glass to her and retreated to the window. Bowing her head, she resumed: 'Could you betray me, or would you be as silent as the grave?'

It amazed him, afterwards, how easily he'd adopted his role. Childe Harold, of course, was the model for it. And Polidori, as he entered into the love-sick character, was surprised by the sympathy it taught him for Lord Byron. So this was it, the painful little contradiction from which the poet suffered: between the amusement one felt, at playing a part, and the really tender feelings it evoked. 'You hardly know what you ask of me, of *whom* you ask it. My touch,' and here Polidori paused and just turned his head till the sunshine caught the light sketch of his profile, 'my touch is contagion. There is scarcely a creature – who comes within my orbit – and does not suffer some terrible humiliation. Whatever is innocent and nourishing in this world, I corrupt and destroy. If, indeed, I could learn – if I could strive – to deserve the honour you have thus entrusted to me, my first thought, my first regret, would be – that I did not at once, for your own sake, turn you from my door.'

The pose seemed to carry his feelings with it, on the crest of which he forgot for a moment his various embarrassments. The dusty poverty of his rooms. Its odours: the mulching stench of well-travelled books, the damp oppression of a young man's solitary life. The port stains on his old silk shirt, the glare of his threadbare pantaloons, the loose-stitched squalor of his shoes. All the lies he'd told; all the patients he had killed. The lies he was telling still . . . For just that minute, his possession of the part was complete. It was only a whisper of self-congratulation that brought him down again. *Come*, he thought of saying to Lord Byron, *this is talking.*

She raised her eyes to him. 'My lord, I should die, I should perish. You could not be so cruel.'

It was almost too perfect, the way she played up to his role. And yet the tenderness she aroused in him could not be doubted. He imagined his palm taking the measure of her cheek, as Goose had taken his own face in her hand. The smell of her, as dry and sweet as powdered sugar, seemed to offer a return of the feminine into his life: its quiet promise of niceness. A world governed by taste and gentleness. This is what Byron had always enjoyed in the female presence: the way one appealed to it. They had both flourished in the world of their sisters' love; they had both suffered from being cast out of it. For the first time he looked at Miss Esmond and thought, *who are you*? And staring at her, he brought the question out. 'But what's your history?' he said.

'My history,' she answered, thrilling, for her part, with the sensation that for the first time she could speak openly, plainly, fatuously of her private passion, 'is books. The history of Zuleika, of Kaled, of Medora.' She passed over her life as a governess, as a servant; the bruises she suffered bumping against the human indifference around her; her cramped quarters, the loom of the eaves above her head as she slept, which cast its thick shadow even onto her dreams. She listed instead the heroines of Byron's eastern tales. 'I have been loved, abandoned, widowed, a hundred times over. The rest is blank.'

It wasn't the answer he'd hoped for. 'You seem very young,' he said, disappointed; then added, with an irony kindly meant, 'I mean, to have read so much.'

He could hear the porter on the stairs, singing and sweeping. The law-clerks bustled out at five; it was just gone half past four. Had she been observed? She had wantonly compromised herself – for nothing, for no one. The silence that followed was for him to break. 'What would you ask of me?' he said at last. He had a sense of waiting for an echo. The bell had been struck, but the answering tone hung uncertainly in the air. Perhaps by now Lord Byron would have brought her to bed, pulled up her dress by the hems, tasted her neck . . . A thought that carried with it an unpleasant image of his rain-soaked mattress and the unwashed sheets lying on the floor in the next room. Still, his imagination could not help playing the scene out. He inched towards her, unsure of his hands, which he buried sweating in his pockets.

'I do not expect you to love me.' She rose uncertainly. Then, with growing conviction, 'I am not worthy of your love. I feel you are – superior.' Her voice, wonderfully low, was like the shadow of a voice, that grows darker in a general brightness. It possessed an almost religious urgency. She held out her hand to him.

His palms were slick. He touched hers only with his fingers, to raise it to his lips. He kissed her knuckles. They smelled of books. 'Whatever I love is destroyed,' he said. 'Consequently, I have broken the habit of it.'

That last line had too much truth in it: he decided, for the moment, to spare her. Besides, Colburn's assistant was expected any minute, he'd be bound to give Polly away – a prospect that made the doctor flush with shame. It occurred to him that he was beginning to depend on what he thought of (in that vague language he used to prop up his self-love) as Miss Esmond's 'good opinion'. She had read and admired his story, after all, though under a false impression. And yet the image she'd fallen in love with had been his own: *he* had been standing in that balcony window; *his* glance had passed over her in the street. The world, as she put it, was all before him then; but he had more patience for an interruption now.

'May I call on you, at Lady Walmsley's?' he said, bowing.
'I'm afraid, I am expecting – a friend.'

He realized at once what this suggested, its instant charge, but could not retract it in time. Eliza, however, was rather relieved than otherwise; the effort to preserve her role had almost exhausted her. And she had her own secrets to maintain. If he visited her, he could not help discovering that Eliza's position at her Ladyship's house was far from unequivocal; that she was not even, quite, a governess to the two children; that her duties extended occasionally to the kitchen; that she slept with the other servants under the eaves. She said, 'I never expected you to sacrifice yourself; that is my part.' And added, 'On Sundays – that is, tomorrow – my father and I are accustomed to taking the air in the tea-garden at Bagnigge Wells, about two o'clock. He, he . . . is also a writer, a novelist. You may look out for us there, if you like. They make uncommonly refreshing syllabubs.' After a moment's embarrassment, she continued, 'He would be charmed – he would be quite overwhelmed, to meet you.' And then, lowering her voice, 'I need hardly say you may trust him absolutely.'

She now wished for nothing but solitude. She had fed almost too richly on the encounter; she wanted to pick more slowly over its crumbs. Her final words to him, as she stood in the doorway, had an almost business-like simplicity. They were a useful summing up. 'Well,' she said, turning away, 'you can do what you like with me.' He followed her steps along the corridor, down the echoing stairwell, and then walked to close his window – the season turned quickly – against the late afternoon chill.

He remained at the casement long enough to see her leaving. The sunlight had deepened in setting, a cold bronze glow. He watched her in it: she cast a slanting, implacable shadow along the pavement. It hardly shifted as it moved, a clear black shape slipping over the street. No wonder, he suddenly thought, Lord Byron used to fall in love so easily.

The pleasure of giving pleasure is a wonderful thing: the freedom of living, that is, in the confidence of being loved. It struck him that he was happier than he had been before her visit; a change in temper as forceful and obvious as an increase in light. She, for her part, had never been happier in her life.

CHAPTER TEN

T HAT NIGHT, POLIDORI BEGAN a second memoir of
his travels with Lord Byron. Or rather, he attempted
to begin it. He had taken over his rooms from a law
student, who had departed suddenly and without explanation, leaving behind not only several weighty legal tomes
(which Polidori had just sold as his own), but a writing table,
a mattress, and a bureau missing its hinges. Its doors were
held in place by loose paper tightly applied, and Polly, capable of almost any incuriosity, had not once looked within
after two months of residency. The writing table stood
beneath one of the parlour windows; he sat down uncom-
fortably to begin, crossing and uncrossing his legs with
difficulty under the low desk. His knees suffered several
sharp knocks. He was a nervous composer and the waste of
his energies overflowed in constant physical adjustments.
He needed something to write on and had almost
addressed his pen to the margins of his copy of *Childe
Harold*, when he remembered the scraps of paper wedged
into the bureau doors.

This was just the kind of practical diversion his muse
depended on; and he promptly rose from his seat and
began to prise open the cupboard. Inside he found, nailed
against the backing, a narrow shelf supporting three or four
low glass bottles, unstoppered. They were powdery to his
touch; the dust blended instantly with the perspiration in
his palms to produce a thick tacky surface to his skin, most
unpleasant. Polidori had a horror of unclean hands, and
was turning towards the wash basin when he noticed one of

the bottles had several inches of ruby liquid in it, and a leather string around its neck. He lifted it by this, put his nose to the opening and inhaled its pent-up acridity: laudanum. He hadn't taken laudanum since his days as a medical student. Well, if sleep wouldn't come that night, here was something to turn to. Composition, especially the blankness of failure, tended in him to produce the equal blankness of insomnia. He carefully smoothed the pages under the heel of his palm, and spread them over his desk. Only then did he soak and rub his hands clean; but since there was nothing to dry them on, except the dirty shirt he was wearing, the wet line of his small finger darkened the paper as he pressed the page to write.

'In the spring of 1816, I accompanied Lord Byron on his second tour of the continent. In the midst of a painful separation from his wife, he had decided to leave Albion's shores behind him; and had taken me on, in the capacity of medical attendant, owing to a series of physical indispositions, which, he feared, amidst the rigours of travel, might eventually transfigure themselves into an incurable mental malaise. His wife, he informed me in our initial interview, had alleged insanity among the grounds for separation – a particularly painful suspicion, he continued, given a family history not unblemished by incidents of psychological infirmity. Madness, he added, had always seemed to him the most likely consequence of that hot restlessness from which he suffered; madness or self-slaughter.' Polidori paused here, resting the quill against the lobe of his ear. He added after a minute, 'I mentioned to him my special knowledge of somnambulism – the subject of my medical dissertation – and other forms of psychic outbreak, which, I urged, peculiarly fitted me to the role of his attendant. After a brief examination, both physical and psychological, I could offer him the following consolation: he seemed, in my professional opinion, no more likely to end his days in the mad-house or the suicides' cemetery than I myself.' He dipped his pen into the inkwell and finished off the page, 'He engaged me at once. I was nineteen years old.'

But the thought of his youth put a stop to him: what a boy he had been, after all! He saw himself lift a hand to his sister's mouth; he felt her teeth against it. That morning he'd received a note from his father: Frances had returned, unexpectedly, from Milan. Papa Gaetano offered no further explanation. The curtness of the note demanded a visit, which Polly had, at least for the day, put off. For various reasons, not the least of them, the circumstances in which he'd seen her last: in Milan three years before.

Byron had girlish fingers, rather fat, even after one of his purges; there was something peculiarly trusting about their plump heat. In his mind's eye, he watched Frances open her mouth to receive them. Why do you not bite him? Why do you not bite? A three-quarter moon lay awkwardly on its back in the sky, but its brightness suggested the abrupt certainty of a struck gong. He seemed to be waiting for it to go out, as one waits for the ringing to cease. It continued undiminishing. He noticed only by the ache in his forearm that he was holding his pen-hand in mid-air. The trouble may have been those last few lines, their casual return to self: 'he seemed, in my professional opinion, no more likely to end his days in the mad-house . . . than I . . . I was nineteen years old.' In fact, he wasn't sure he'd said anything of the sort. The line had the freshness of a recent addition, an invention. It was the kind of thing that struck him now as true; he was writing himself back into the story, and worse still, imposing everything that was going to happen on the boy he once was, setting forth. He must begin again. He lowered his elbow to the table and did not move.

Naturally, his thoughts turned again to that summer on the shores of Lake Leman. Byron and he (how sweetly that *and* suggested an equality of companionship, a shared purpose – unmerited, of course) had been looking for a house to let for the summer. The Villa Diodati, which they eventually settled on, was rumoured to be taken. In any case, there had been a misunderstanding, and Polly and his lordship had rowed back and forth across the lake to no purpose, till the doctor, at least, was thoroughly out of temper. Getting out, they ran into a party of English travellers, which included the poet Percy Shelley, a slim boyish figure with the complexion of a fat child. Snippings of fair hair, Polly observed, lay on his neck, around his ears, on his fingertips – the marks of hasty cutting. He was accompanied by a pair of women whom Polidori took to be sisters: a pretty, flat-faced girl with short dark curls; the other was smaller, plainer, more composed. The hands and wrists of both of them were covered in short blond shavings, a fact that drew Polidori's instinctive envy. It made one itch to look at them. The women presumed upon a previous acquaintance with his lordship, and, in fact, Byron himself, who could be very charming when he was bored and anxious for company, pretended to a flattering knowledge of Shelley's *Queen Mab*.

Polly had learned to hate every introduction among strangers. Strangers were bound to ignore him. He was, after all, as he later expressed it to Mrs Shelley (by way of apology, after another embarrassing episode, in which he had challenged her husband to a duel) 'only a tassel on the purse of fame, a star lost in the halo of the moon'. Among familiars he might receive a little attention from just those persons whom Byron had, for whatever reason, chosen to neglect himself. But amid fresh company, he disappeared at once, like salt in solution. He took out the boat again in something of a sulk and lay on his back and let the water move him. The lap of waves sounded like the murmur of intimate conversation, distantly heard. His jealousy, an actual acridity furring his tongue, would, he thought, soon pass, if he indulged in the taste of it, just once. But as the summer lengthened, it concentrated, grew stronger, became almost unpalatable, indigestible.

Polly put his pen aside now, and rose suddenly from his

chair. Somewhere he had a copy of his old diary, unless it was mixed in with the books he had sold to Colburn. The thought brought on a sweat of anxiety; Polidori was beginning to be overwhelmed by a sense of how much that mattered in his life he was capable of simply mislaying. He found it at last, kept safe in the empty case for a pistol, a weapon he had hidden in one of his boots and carried with him wherever he went. (A habit he had picked up from Percy Shelley, who, in a schoolboyish way, liked to travel armed: the Pistol Club was one of B's affectionate terms for their circle of friends.) He returned to his narrow seat beneath the window, and began to leaf through the pages of his journal. He had, for almost a year now, denied himself this pleasure. His obsession with that brief period in his life was, he suspected, becoming unhealthy; nevertheless, a resolution was quickly and almost painlessly broken, for a second time within the week, he noted. He had, after all, just given in, under Colburn's prompting, to his love of gambling – though he still hoped to nip that passion in the bud.

What struck him most, as he glanced through the jottings of his diary, was how *casually* he had lived. These famous times had passed him by as lightly as any ordinary day. 'Tea'd and talked politics with B,' he read. And then, '. . . after dinner, jumping a wall my foot slipped and I strained my left ankle. Shelley etc. came in the evening; talked of my play etc., which all agreed was worth nothing.' The ankle, in fact, still afflicted him; it ached in wet weather. He remembered more of this incident than he had recorded at the time. Rain clouds had set in over Geneva. It was the first bad spell of their summer together, and just before supper, before the clouds opened, Mary Shelley had determined to 'get in' a walk along the shore, and had been caught out.

The flurry passed, and a black and purple twilight set in. Byron observed her from his balcony, as she mounted the hill towards Diodati with that peculiar air of drudgery of the recently doused. He turned towards Polidori and remarked,

'If you wish to be gallant, jump over the balcony here, and offer your arm.' Polidori felt a thrill of inclusion, but slipped as he landed on the wet ground, and his mood turned with equal swiftness the other way. Byron, to do him justice, hastened to carry his physician inside. Polly could feel, against his ribs, the triangle of youthful muscle formed by Byron's breast and the top of his arm. They were all young men still. Later, Byron descended the stairs on his hobbling foot to fetch his young doctor a pillow for his leg. 'Well,' Polly said, touched by his master's solicitude, and, from various motives, deliberately allowing that gratitude to curdle and sour, 'I did not believe you had so much feeling.' Byron did not answer.

The rain returned that night, and lasted, off and on, for much of the week. The company took on the close air of wet wool, a kind of smell. They were restless for some outbreak, of anger or amusement, and spent their energies on Polly's new play. He sat on the balcony with his hand hiding his mouth and stared out over the water. Such chastenings always rendered him childish. At supper he drank too much wine, and regained some of his spirits, a little ferociously. They were discussing John Abernethy's theories of the 'electric or spiritual fluid' animating the body – whether or not it was to be found in the blood. Mary, whose matronly manner grew with surprising ease out of her girlishness, suggested that any material conception of the life-principle would quickly run into palpable demonstrations of its absurdity. If 'life' was a substance that could be added or taken away, then death was merely a drought, easily replenished. Polidori, who saw in the dark girl the promise of warm sisterly comfort, cried, in overheated support, 'It was a theory for vampyres, not scientists.' Shelley remarked that in time even the subtlest fluids might be understood and mastered: 'It did not seem to him a question of materialism.' If the life-substance, in any form, was capable of addition and subtraction, then no subtlety could prevent the processes from being 'reversed'. As for the *comparative* nature of the animating principle, one had only to look around the present company to see proof of the fact that the 'vital quality' was unequally shared. A nod at Byron, who, for once, kept quiet over his wine. Polidori felt the heat rise to his face – another slight! And remembered his father's warning: the force of impossible comparisons.

They stayed up late into the chill of the early morning, reading from some volumes of ghost stories Shelley had discovered in one of the bedrooms. As the shadows of the candlelight began to dim in the false dawn, someone, nobody could remember *who*, suggested they each attempt a tale – a venture that became the single sustaining occupation of the week of wet weather that followed and more or less confined them to the house.

From the first, it was generally understood that Mary needed the greatest encouragement. 'Have you thought of a story?' was the question everyone asked, at breakfast, over dinner. And she was forced to confess every morning and evening, that she had not. It seemed to her that she was the last to begin, a delusion she afterwards cherished – that delicious suspension of spirit before the avalanche of inspiration. But the plain fact was that nobody had ever thought to inquire of Polly how he was getting on. Perhaps because he wasn't, quite, one of their party, being a mere travelling physician. Besides which, they had begun to treat him with the tenderness of condescension, not least because it had the effect of subtly hushing him.

Polidori remembered, as he sat under the low desk in Lincoln's Inn, the terrible blankness he had felt. He bit his quill, as he had bitten it three years before, and tasted the almost salty dullness of feathery bone. His thoughts began to follow familiar paths: what was the source of this absence, if absence could have a source? A man might be incapable, say, of mending a boat: this was a matter of skill or knowledge. If he couldn't lift a stone, it was a question of weight and strength. But if, in the quiet of the guest room at Diodati – with a clear run of white parchment and a view of water, its gentle unevenness, the low green hills surrounding, the peaceful traffic of the shoreline – he found nothing to say or think or write, to what absence of knowledge or skill or strength could this be ascribed? Perhaps his failure resembled barrenness most; the childlessness he suffered from was one of thoughts. He wrote in a fair slow script: 'The summer of 1816' and sat, pen in hand and nothing in his head, considering the phrase until a little variation in his breath recalled him to his conscious self. He turned the pages of his journal.

Towards the end of that wet week, without a word written, after five steady days of unremitting blankness, Polidori had attempted to take out his distemper on Byron. His ankle had more or less healed: at least he had learned that his licence to complain of it had run its course. He sat at the small side-table between the balcony windows. He wanted his composition to be remarked upon. But nothing came. His heart was as dusty as a summer road; he choked almost physically on the dryness of his thoughts. He had no talent for lies, and the truth struck him as both too plain and various to be worth the telling. He was surrounded by impressions: Byron's restlessness over a large Italian novel; the drip of rain on the patient water below them; his melancholy gratitude for the greyness of the light. With a headache brewing, he couldn't bear the sunshine. But how should he select among these details, when the only thing pressing its weight upon him was his own dull thoughtlessness?

'What are you writing?' Mary had asked, kindly calling over from her chair by the fire – she grew easily, girlishly chilled, and the wet weather had got into her bones. She lit a small blaze after breakfast every morning. Polly answered, with a malice equally deliberate and obscure, 'The story of a skull-headed lady, spied through a peephole.' Byron's ears pricked up at this; he was beginning to lose interest in their 'game' and could never grow bored without persuading others into boredom. He stretched from the settee and walked over to the doctor, resting his hand on the chair-back so that his knuckles pressed against Polly's spine. Polly tried to cover the blank page under his hand, but Byron had seen it, and remarked, 'I am relieved to see that your ghost, at the very least, dresses according to tradition in *white*.'

Polly knew that Byron was looking for a quarrel; still, he couldn't resist. In a dry spell the day before, just at twilight, the clouds too thick to let the rain through, some of their party had attempted to go out on the water. (Shelley had stayed behind; there were times even he couldn't bear what he called the 'weight' of B's company, and, in particular, the close evidence of Mary's crush. The fact was, he'd hardly written a word since they'd met.) The sunlight milky and moon-like over the lake; that peculiarly peaceful chill hour of evening after a day's rain. Deep breaths of pent-up spirits. Polly, who wanted to join them, volunteered to row and then resented his usefulness, the dependence it suggested. Besides, his ankle had begun to throb. In the cramped vessel, he let his arms pull wide; his oar struck Byron in the knee. The poet, especially in the company of women, liked to play the stoic. Mary sat in the bow, where Polly's carelessness just caught her, from time to time, with the odd dose of wet. It was his silent revenge on all of them.

Still, he could not suppress the feeling, that *he* suffered most, perhaps: from the labour of it; from the constriction his arms felt stroking through the rain-sodden waters; from the confinement of his own timidity. He daren't attack them in the open. These petty gestures suggested rather the constraint than the outbreak of his spite. At the third knock, Byron, wincing, hid his face against his arm; then, quietly, he asked the doctor to mind where he pulled. 'Take more care, for you hurt me very much.'

Polly seized his chance to bring their conflict into the open. In a rush of honesty not unlike physical courage, he said, 'I am glad of it. I am glad to see you can suffer pain.' Byron suddenly lifted his hand and retracted it again: the gesture of a gentleman refraining from striking another man's dog. After a minute, he said, 'Let me give you a word of advice, Polidori. People don't like to be told that those who give them pain are glad of it. They cannot always command their anger; they are liable to do something rash. But for Mrs Shelley's presence, I should probably have thrown you into the water.' Mary said nothing. It was the tacit sympathy in her silence, for Byron, their little communion, that upset Polidori most of all.

As he sat at the side-table, he felt the awkwardness of Byron's knuckles on his spine. Surely deliberate: Polidori was forced to shift in his seat to the side. And then, resenting his own accommodation, he suddenly asked, 'Pray, what is there excepting writing poetry that I cannot do better than you?' Mary, a smile already in preparation, looked up at Albé, as she called him, and waited for his reply. B hesitated a moment, without withdrawing his hand from the back of Polly's chair. In fact, he was just as out of sorts and fed up with the venture as Polidori; but he had the wit to turn his peevishness into a kind of gallantry. There were three things, he said at last. 'First, I can hit with a pistol the keyhole of that door. Second, I can swim across that lake. And third, I can give you a damned good thrashing.' Polly pushed his chair back against Byron's foot, stood up quietly and walked out. He did not come down for supper, and Byron, in the end, 'humbly' (this was his own word) came up to see him and beg his pardon.

The next day, having made up, Byron admitted that he had tired of 'prosing' and offered Polidori a piece of his own inspiration. Polly at last had the scrap of narrative on which he could feed his imagination: 'Two friends – shall we call them Lord Ruthven, and his protégé, Aubrey? – were to travel from England to Greece; while there, Ruthven should die, but, before his death, obtain from his young friend an oath of secrecy with regard to his decease. Some short time after, on Aubrey's returning to his native country, he should be startled to perceive his former companion moving about in society, and should be horrified at finding that he made love to his sister.' Out of this germ, *The Vampyre* had grown; but the thought of Lord Ruthven's seduction of Aubrey's sister put Polidori in mind of Frances, whom he had not laid eyes on since he walked out of her house in Milan three years before – another source of unhappy reflections. His sister breathed not fifteen minutes' walk from where he sat. It was a meeting he longed for and dreaded in equal measure, so he turned from the prospect of it, as if from a dark side road, into the bustle of the thoroughfare.

'In the spring of 1816,' he repeated, 'I accompanied Lord Byron on his second tour of the continent.' And then, keeping to the task at hand, Polly continued: 'From Dover, Byron said his farewells at last, to Scrope, to Hobhouse – the latter weeping freely as he ran to the end of the wooden pier. Hobhouse had been the poet's companion on his famous first pilgrimage: the young man's face, plain and strong as an elbow, hardly reddened or shifted as the tears streaked down it. He hoped to join us later; it was a part of Lord Byron's attraction that his departures seemed always more permanent than the journeys of other men. Byron pulled off his cap and waved it – afterwards confessing to me, that wherever there was grief at parting, he had a woman's appetite for seeing it increased. Only the servants remained in tow: Fletcher, Byron's valet, a Swiss named Berger, and your humble narrator, who counted himself (already) as a friend.' And who, in jealous greed, was hardly upset to see Hobhouse left behind. Once more, Polly's journal had shifted its attention inward; and again he stopped short, uncertainly.

To fill the empty minute, he stood up and retrieved the jar of laudanum from the bureau and poured a thumb's breadth of liquid into a glass. He had, in the past, been accustomed to a night-time dram, but had given up the habit after his student days. Before drinking, he sat down again and wrote, on a fresh sheet of paper: 'Among his many talents, Lord Byron was not least distinguished by his talent for *quarrelling*, and, which was perhaps still more remarkable in him, the grace of his reconciliations. He had tremendous powers of kindness, of forgiving, and of being forgiven.' He stopped again and recalled, with a force and precision that almost robbed him of his breath, the long solitary afternoon that followed their spat over the ghost story. A passage of time, which, for several reasons, he had allowed to gather dust in his memory. Polly, confined by stubbornness to his room at Diodati, had not stirred from the small chair at the foot of his bed for several hours. The light, grey as it was, had slowly darkened as the morning gave way to afternoon and evening. But for once his thoughts had ceased to race within him; they had rather the stillness of concentration. Clarity and certainty had replaced confusion and restlessness. They resembled a jigsaw after the last interlocking piece has been carefully smoothed into place: the perfection of the image came at the price of his freedom to adjust it. After sunset, he rose stiffly and fetched his medical bag from the foot of his bed; he stretched his legs, and particularly the tendons of his left foot, gratefully, as he stood at his dressing table and mixed a glass of soda with cyanide. He set it down and considered a minute whether it might be honourable to leave a note for B, when Byron himself came into the room with hand outstretched, a gesture, that, on seeing Polidori in tears, he quickly turned into an embrace.

CHAPTER ELEVEN

POLIDORI AWOKE DRY-THROATED and sweaty with leftover dreams. Still fully dressed, he sat up and noted, through the open doorway, the empty glass on his desk in the next room. In the white morning sunshine, it cast little webs and concentrations of light on the green baize. He had not slept well. The laudanum seemed at first only to expand his sleeplessness, to tug at it several ways at once. His consciousness stretched over many levels; these were connected by darkly imagined stairwells and abrupt shafts. He attempted to descend, further and further, into his thoughts but could not reach the waters of sleep, whose drip he heard everywhere multiplied around him. The dankness of the walls promised an imminent arrival; their slickness shone in a dim light whose source never became apparent until it grew and woke him through uncurtained windows.

There was nothing to eat, so he wiped the glass dry against his shirt and filled it with water from the pitcher on his nightstand. Some of its old acridity remained. The water was hardly even cool; it had been standing in the sunshine. He undressed and returned to his front room and sat down at his desk and for three hours did nothing – in a kind of suspension whose liquid base was the bright half-sleep of a morning after. Then, suddenly emerging from it, he dressed again and went out into the street: the bells of St Jude were ringing and had reminded him of his appointment.

*

It was a good brisk walk to Bagnigge Wells. The London traffic had the softness of Sunday, that little patience with delays and fine weather. Prints of spring leaves patterned the blue skies, which had a dusty spaciousness, a recently swept look. He sweated lightly into his collar as the terraces fell off from the roadside and gave way to the scratchy untidiness of farms. Ashamed of his own damp heats, he removed his jacket and carried it over one arm; the other held his walking stick. It seemed to him impossible, in the open air, in the blue light of day, that he could be taken for anything but what he was: a shabby young man looking for a turn in his luck.

Bagnigge Wells was, as Byron used to say, 'as dirty as Nature'. A warm unsettled wind had scattered the dust of the dry ground over the grass and the leaves of the trees. It was hardly empty. Strollers in twos and threes, examples of every class, occupied the weaving lanes, which touched and parted at irregular intervals like lovers' hands. There were trees between them, oaks and laurels; fences of box-hedge. And here or there a grove had been woven together from the top branches of an alley of holly-trees, so that between their netted fingers, the sunshine scraped through only in bright scattered edgings. Everywhere the sound of water, like coolness audible, from various fountains green with dust. A series of benches along the river, sectioned from the rest, served the ale-drinkers; and Polly heard, from time to time, mild cries of triumph and despair issuing from a bowling-green and a skittle alley. Polly had been, once, to Vauxhall Gardens, and though he expected nothing like its grandeur at King's Cross, still, he was surprised by the modest seclusion around him. It was the decent haunt of mostly respectable people who wished to taste, in suitable miniature, the pleasures of Nature. How ridiculous it was to imagine his lordship venturing into such a middle-class retreat, to pursue – in the company of her father! – a thin high-shouldered creature whose only charm perhaps lay in the girlish restlessness of her small breasts, long fingers and wriggling lips. Yet in spite, or perhaps on account of, the borrowed scorn he felt – in the role of the famous poet – he suffered from a familiar sense of his own internal silence, the contrast he made with the pleasant spirits around him.

One field over, a dozen cows stood at ragged attention, and their line of sight led Polly's eyes to a peaked brown hut in a corner of the gardens, under an ilex tree. It took him a minute to recognize Eliza, by the unwashed colouring of her throat, by her hitched-up shoulders; and then her father, by a slightly more muscular bulk around the armpits and his back, which still suggested the discomfort of a child being held up under his arms.

For a minute he stood back to observe them. They might, almost, have been mistaken for lovers. Her attendance on him was quick and fretful, and suggested that involved intimacy which scratches at and relieves an impatience with herself as much as with him. Like trees, they stood in the shade they cast themselves: everyone around them seemed to stand in a slightly different light. Privacy, even in public spaces, brings its own clouds. Their skins – a whimsy struck him – must grow very irritable with the constant chafing of their affections. The father had bought for Eliza, from the hut, a glass of syllabub; but in the exchange of money, had set down his own and tipped it over with his foot. The syllabub, Polly guessed by the way the father blew over it, was only dirty; at least, something in the way Mr Esmond protected it betokened a man stubbornly making himself contented with a treat he had spoiled himself. Eliza, pawing, was trying to take it from him; he resisted, and the motions of their mutual irritation drew them cloyingly and tenderly into each other's arms. Mr Esmond kissed the top of her hair, and they began to eat and walk at once, with some difficulty.

Polly almost decided to leave them on the spot. His interruption would seem like an intrusion, and he supposed,

with a blush of shame, that Eliza had never for a minute suspected so great a man as Lord B would ever take up her
humble invitation: she hardly had the appearance of a
woman expectantly glancing round. And yet something
about her fussing made him linger. The little game of her
concern reminded him of Frances. He knew, as well as anyone, the way a daughter's or a sister's love rubbed up against
a fuller expression, and grew pettish from frustration of tenderness. And he imagined her touching him with her thin,
long fingers, adjusting his collar, tucking his hair behind his
ear, and then his neck almost ached with the absence of her
hands upon it. In any case, she had seen him by now; and
the face of joy she made – her front teeth bared awkwardly
beneath her top lip as she tried to restrain herself from smiling too largely – awoke in him, to his own surprise, not so
much shame or distaste as something more nearly answering.

Her father limped slightly, lagging behind her; and then
made an awful, indescribable gesture, which Eliza didn't
see, and which Polly was too surprised to remark upon. Mr
Esmond seemed to bow, approaching; but then thought
better of it, and, having ducked his head, lifted it again like a
bird pulling its beak out of its feathers. Resenting his own
obeisance, he stiffly held out his hand. But Polly was too far
away to reach it, and Mr Esmond, stretching towards him,
stumbled and almost fell down; Polly, helplessly, had the
sense of letting him fall. Eliza's father caught himself in time
and staggered to a standstill – as if Byron's fame were an
impenetrable shield that a humble clerk such as Mr
Esmond dared not, could not broach. Eliza, who had
missed the performance, simply said, 'My lord, you cannot
guess how honoured we are, how happy you have made my
father.' And then the poor man attempted to fix an expression on his face to match her sentiments; it was rather
obscured by his beard. Polidori decided in the end simply to
nod at him. He remembered now what he had grown accus-

tomed to in Byron's company: the imbecility that his fame brought out, like a latent colour, in most ordinary people. Eliza took Polly's arm in hers (showing off, for her father's sake, an intimacy with the great poet she did not yet possess), and between the two of them, guided their steps through an arch of laced trees.

The beginnings were awkward enough. Polly, shyly, left it up to Eliza to take them both in hand; and she hardly had the character or confidence (as far as Lord B was concerned) to serve as cicerone. Even so, Polidori was surprised by how snugly engaged he felt. It occurred to him, how well such a family would have suited him: the company of loving and hapless people, their warm exchange of sympathies and failures. Mr Esmond offered Polly a taste of his syllabub. He was quite full and on the point of throwing it away. And Polly, having seen it kicked in the dirt, wondered whether there was any sly humour in the gesture – a quiet sort of revenge he was peculiarly placed to appreciate – and happily accepted it. He ate, with deliberate greed, pursing his lips around the heaped spoon and sucking. Perhaps he could shock them by a realistic display of the manners of a peer. And the childishness of it, and the rush of sugar (it was the first food he had eaten all day), loosened something in his temper, and he, kindly condescending, began to enjoy the part he had come to play. He said, to put Mr Esmond at his ease, a line borrowed from Lord B, 'Now confess, sir, you expected to find me a Timon of Athens or a Timur the Tartar: gloomy and misanthropical.'

No, no, Mr Esmond averred, shaking his long head. Nothing of the sort.

'Or perhaps you took me for a mere sing-song driveller, full of poetical enthusiasms?'

Not that either, no.

'Then what?'

'I didn't,' Mr Esmond said – he had stopped in his tracks and let go of Eliza's arm, and stood now face to face with the poet – 'I didn't expect yours was a character I had the wit to imagine. I didn't dream of imagining anything. I knew it would fall short.' He hesitated, he was visibly moved by his own humility, his humility indeed seemed to matter a great deal to him, and Polly had for the first time the occasion to look him up and down.

Eliza's father was, undeniably, a strange-looking creature: about the average height, but so narrow and straight, he appeared taller. His face was covered ineffectually by a beard, which, it seemed, no matter how long he let it grow, refused to thicken and fill in. His brow was high and noble in its way, with what seemed the print of an angry knuckle just above the strong line of his nose. His cheeks inclined sharply and, as it were, hungrily to his chin, but it was the quality of the skin that seemed most striking: smooth, beneath the hairs growing out of it, pale, utterly childish. Eliza's dark complexion clearly came from her mother, from whom she must also have inherited her animal restlessness and fine spirits. Mr Esmond never fidgeted at all; his long arms hung limply by his side. His lips alone, as pink as Eliza's, though a little encumbered with whiskers, allowed the expression of subtlety and humour. 'To tell you the truth, sir,' he added, conscious of venturing on something obscurely impertinent, 'I did not expect to find you at all, here. I expected to find that this was another one of Eliza's – I won't call them lies, because she's a good honest girl' – the good honest girl was writhing and blushing uncontrollably – 'but what we call in the family her Ideas. I expected to find you were merely another one of her Ideas. She can't help them; it's her imagination; I wish I had it. But Eliza's capable of believing anything she thinks, and she thinks a great deal, you'll have found that for yourself. All kinds of things.' Polly didn't know what to answer, was struck suddenly fearful he had been discovered, and for the first time guessed how little he wished to be found out, until Mr Esmond added, 'But there's one more thing about Eliza's Ideas, which is this, that they sometimes turn out to be true. You can't just reckon against them, not reliably. And I'm grateful, and honoured, I'm sure, to find that this is one of those occasions.' And he bowed at last, glad to have delivered himself, gracefully enough, of what he meant to say.

Polly felt mostly relief at the time, and bowed in return. It was only later he realized, and reflected upon the fact, that something important had been confided to him. A proper increase of intimacy. And that Eliza's misapprehension of him had in its way been blinding him to *her*. She was a girl who made things up, who lived, privately and powerfully, in the court of her own imagination. It wasn't entirely his fault; this kind of mistake was what she was always making, what she desired to make. He began to see her more clearly. If she was a fool, there was also a rareness to her, an indifference to present circumstances, not unlovable, especially for a man like Polly, given the 'present circumstances' in which he found himself, and, more generally, his own passion for dressing up. After all, he couldn't pretend that her mistake was groundless, that he hadn't played into it himself, that it didn't, also, reveal something about *him*. They suited each other, in fact.

And he began to like her father. He wasn't at all what Polly had expected, the gloomy misanthrope Mr Esmond had at first appeared to be. Failure seemed to agree with him; it had made him humorous; it had taught him to enjoy himself. Once his tongue had been loosened, there was no holding him back. Polly, with a charming modesty he could only carry off in the role of Lord Byron, had begun to flatter Mr Esmond with questions about the old man's historical romances. Wonderful, how much it lifted his heart, to tell his tales. His inert limbs would spring into violent, and worrying, life. Time and again, he let go his daughter's arm to make a point more forcibly, to act out the gesture of one of the desperate heroes of his unpublished imagination. In his first novel, *The Garden of*

Interrupted Spring, his heroine fights off the attentions of an ungentlemanly suitor, while walking with him in the family orchard. She heaves at him the body of a crow, who seems to have died from surfeiting on rotten apples, and who, mysteriously, revives to beat his wings against her assailant's neck. Mr Esmond played the part of the crow; Eliza's neck played the part of the ungentlemanly suitor's. Polly wept with laughter; conscious that he was being deliberately amused, and that there was also something cruel in the fact of his amusement. Also, he dimly envied her father's freedom with Eliza; she bent her head girlishly against her breast to ward off his tickling.

'Luckily,' Mr Esmond said, subsiding and winking, and consciously giving himself airs, 'I never wrote to be read.' No, exactly, Polly answered, missing the wink, hoping to make up for his laughter by playing one of Byron's familiar tunes: poetry for him was merely the lava of the imagination whose eruption prevented an earthquake . . . 'Or,' Mr Esmond cut in, 'in his own case, prose was the drizzle which prevented a shower.' No, no, said his daughter, taking his arm again, and squeezing her side against his.

Yet what joy it gave Eliza to see him happy, how sweetly it suited her. And there was something about their company that suited Polly, too: the easy assumption of their insignificance. His own father was hardly as genial. Gaetano's fatness belied him; he was cold to the touch with disappointment in his son. Polly imagined passing his Sundays with the Esmonds, the comforts to be found in their small corner, their quiet warmth. The Bagnigge Wells appeared; and for a minute they stood observing the dirty stagnant waters surrounded by cracked urns, the loose sketching of the midges flying over them. Trickles of overflow gathered dust and thickened. The ground was scored with the tracks of wet shoes. Should he confess now? Did he dare? He slapped a mosquito against his cheek; Eliza turned to look at him fearfully. Mr Esmond said, soberly, in a moment's quiet, 'Joking aside, I wish to make clear how much we feel the honour of your . . . how much, in particular, I myself, as a humble practitioner of a craft . . .'

Polly couldn't wait to interrupt him. He was terribly embarrassed, and also, just a touch, gratified and humbled by the mere expression of the sentiment, as if the words carried a weight independent of their truth. 'I assure you,' he said, 'nothing would give me greater pleasure than the chance to look over some of your works. Eliza, perhaps, could offer me a sampling.' Mr Esmond nodded his large ungainly head; and Polly thought, what a world Byron lived in, the powers he had of giving joy. He also remembered the way his own dramas had been received by the circle at Diodati.

They parted at last at the door of Mr Esmond's cottage, a short walk from the Gardens. A very humble home. The pointwork was going, the yard was a tangle of weeds and rose – this early in the spring, mostly thorns. A coop of chickens made scratching, irritable noises, somewhere out of sight. Polly, lingering, said he was grateful for the air off the canal; it was always cooler, as if it lay in shadow. He had removed his shortcoat and held it again over one arm. A clump of his fine chestnut hair stuck to his brow. Mr Esmond remarked: that may be so, but the damp did terrible things to his bones. When he came home from the naval registry and sat at his desk in the evenings, which he made sure to do, the one virtue his muse could boast was her patience!, besides which, the desk was very prettily placed, and he overlooked the slow drift of water, a row of poplars, a field just now beginning to show its corn . . . Besides which, he repeated, conscious of losing his way, but unwilling to see his lordship go, the life of a widower was rather quiet, now that Bea was married, and Liza out of the house. But what he meant to say was, that, as he sat at his desk, often the only thing that came into his head was the ache in his knees; and he had to rise every few minutes to shake it off, before he sat down again.

Eliza had never looked fresher. Suppressed pride had

brought colour to her cheeks, and vividly expressed her sense of having carried off a difficult enterprise. Now she impatiently ushered her papa inside, and said, she would only just point the way for his lordship and be back in a minute to put on his dinner. Polly himself took her arm this time as they walked into the road. She thanked him with downcast eyes; and confided, what her father had managed to whisper to her in the course of the afternoon, what a wonderful thing it was, the acquaintance of poets; how much impressed he had been by his lordship's grace and humility. What a fine young man he seemed. Polly could only repeat a phrase he had often heard Byron use when he wished to be kind, when he wished to please: that he was always better entertained by the company of honest scribblers than famous authors, who tended only to puff their latest book. Then he urged with heavier sincerity, that Mr Esmond seemed to possess the true passion for his craft . . . Eliza at this stood on tip-toe, just balancing her slender weight on the point of contact between her long-fingered hand and the soft upper half of Polly's arm, and then she kissed him quickly on the lips, tasting of lemon and cream gone slightly sour from the syllabub she'd eaten earlier in the afternoon. Before Polly could take her head in his hand and answer more fully, she was gone, skittering back with her skirts held in her fists above the dusty footway, and not even glancing back. Polly almost had to sit down on a rock, he felt so faint-headed; he rested instead both hands on his walking-stick. He had hardly eaten. He had hardly known, in months, in a year, the kindness of her sex – that sense of being blindly forgiven anything that a face pressed against one's own seemed to grant. After a minute, he set off the way she had pointed, in the direction of town, where he was engaged to dine at his father's house, to welcome Frances home.

CHAPTER TWELVE

F RANCES WAS ASLEEP WHEN Polidori arrived in a hot-weather stink that seemed to him to announce against his wishes something unhappy about his temper and circumstances. His mother said to him, first thing, hardly rising from her chair in the stony garden: 'Lower your voice; we've given her your old room.' Its window overlooked them, not five feet above Polly's head. Glancing up, he saw that she had left it open on the shady air. Polly heard a kind of reproach in his mother's news: as if he, of all people, should sympathize with Frances's weariness; as if he had a special understanding of its cause. But perhaps he was only going mad. 'How is she?' he asked, but his mother only repeated, 'Hush, keep your voice down.' He said he would just go inside to wash.

His sister Esmé ran helter-skelter down the steps to give him a warmer greeting. She had heard him come in. She was being terribly punished for some unnamed offence; they had compelled her to play with William, her nephew, just arrived. 'Is William here as well?' Polly said. 'I thought she had left him with his father.' She held onto Polly's legs as he bent his face to the basin. 'Compelled' was the word Esmé used herself. The girl was now almost seven; it seemed to Polly that she had aged as unhappily as he. 'Oh, it's cold,' she complained, as a few drops from the splash on his face struck her skin. She let go. Gaetano had once remarked to his son, that he wondered if perhaps Esmé was the 'cleverest, most prodigal of them all'. Polly thought she probably was, but the child could not bear changes of any kind and had what seemed to him an unhealthy firm grip on things past. Even at six, she wore the same little bonnet she'd been given three years before, ragged as it was – loose threads of it grew tangled in her hair, fell around her ears; the same frock, which bit into her shoulders and pinched her armpits and exposed an inch of freckled skin above her knees. She always clung to Polly as soon as he arrived, and would not let go without being prised free in a manner that seemed to her brother too brutal to be frequently attempted. Gaetano had always indulged her; but, having been his darling, she now seemed the object of a less happy, more frightened dispensation. She wept bitterly, extravagantly, whenever Polly left.

'How is Frances?' Polly said to her, holding the girl up to his face. 'Have you seen her?'

'Frances is unutterably old,' Esmé answered.

Polly, in fact, did not lay eyes on her till she came down late to dinner. A cloud hung over the meal. Polly could not put off the growing conviction that something was wrong – that the more normally everyone strove to behave, the worse it was. Gaetano intoned grace, over a fine roast lamb. The sour sweetness of an apricot gravy filled Polly's nose; but he was too upset to eat, being all nerves and fine feelings. His father, he noticed, had got so fat, he could hardly get his arms to the table; Ellie, the maid, had to help him to his potatoes. There was something wilful and selfish about his weight; he had built, it seemed, these comfortable walls around himself, and now no one could reach him. God knows *when* the family began to go wrong, but that something was off was as easy to taste as sourness in wine. It probably began, Polly reflected, in the usual way of things, with the eldest son.

Frances appeared at last, in that way she had when late: just opening the door sufficient to let her narrow hips slip through, and shutting it behind her with the flat of her

116

hand. She had, she said, only just got William to sleep. He'd got used to having her in bed with him; she had spoiled him. She hadn't the heart, these days, to let him cry. And then, quickly, seeing her brother, she said, 'Polly, my love, how cold of me, how are you?' And came round the table to take his face in her hands from behind. He hadn't been able to make her out clearly, so quick she was. He felt only her hands and her warm breath on his neck and closed his eyes.

He said, as she sat down now to her plate of food, 'The last time I saw you, you were . . .'

But she interrupted him, laughing, 'Many years younger, I know.'

He looked at her now, and couldn't keep out of his glance the chill of assessment. Her face was older, true. She seemed to have aged without any clear outward marks, but the essential difference was still strongly conveyed. She hadn't got fat or thin or grey; her dark complexion hid well the rough use of the Italian sun. But where before she had the unwashed look of a lively child who wanted scrubbing, her face now had a more durable weathering, as if no amount of bother could ever rub her pink again. Still, the cleft chin and the sharp hook in her nose suggested an unblunted spirit; and her brown eyes, large and clear as Polly's own, were quick and liquid still. But her hands had begun to show the purposes to which they were put. He saw the fine green leaf-print of veins along the back of them, a faint arthritic swelling in her knuckles; and his cheeks remembered from her recent touch a dry aggressive sureness.

He had not seen her since that autumn in Milan, three years before. That long summer, Polly had felt Byron's patience with him slipping, and the more he tried to please, the worse he succeeded. He was conscious of what an irritant he had become. He suffered from it, too: it was his own irritation with himself, like a poison-rash, that wore off on others, infectiously. The polish had come off his eagerness, his vanity – one was liable to cut oneself on the surface underneath. Byron, after a month of Polly's purging him, had got lean and hungry again. As his master grew healthy, Polly began to give in to little complaints, a bad stomach, headaches. He wanted, of course, Byron to take care of him in turn. He wanted to feel, on one side or another, the tenderness of the nurse, of the patient. It was the only intimate role Byron had reserved for him. His lordship had always possessed, among his charms, a winning weakness; but as his strength returned, he began to deny Polly the doctor's power to be kind, to be loving towards him; and it stunned Polly how bereft he felt, at this rejection. He tried to flatter Byron into taking care of him. He missed terribly the sick-bed warmth of their relations; but Byron, recovering from a difficult year and disastrous spring, felt that he had the world before him now. He always tired, in the end, of his young men.

And when everything else failed, Polly began to get into fights. He wanted to show Byron what the passion of loyalty was. He wanted to show Byron what a young man of spirit he was. Polly knocked the spectacles off an apothecary's nose, for trying, as Polly insisted, to sell them 'bad magnesia'. Polidori was arrested; Byron had to plead for him in court. And the doctor got off, with a fine of twelve florins, and a thin, wild sense of elation, that B had gone to such trouble for him. He considered the result 'a triumph', and couldn't help boasting to Byron, to tease from him an expression of concern. 'I think,' the poet said, 'you might cause me less bother in gaol.'

Later, he got into a silly scrap with Percy Shelley, who beat him in a boating contest, by 'stealing his wind' at the start. This gave way, afterwards, to several punning put-downs; Shelley could never resist his own flights of fancy, especially, that is, after winning anything. (He was beginning to suffer, too, in Byron's company; and took out his ill-humour on the doctor. Shelley, guiltily, secretly, loved winning: at pistols, at cards, at boats, at love.) Polidori said, in a pale and

118

pompous heat, 'I have become sensible that in this party I have begun to be treated with contempt', and challenged Shelley to a duel. Shelley only laughed. The fair young man grew rosy in high humour, and nothing amused him more than the lightness of his own indifference to propriety. 'I never duel,' he said, 'especially with doctors. It seems ungenerous, when mostly we pay handsomely for you to kill us.'

Polly answered, 'Well, as for that, for no charge at all, I'll shoot you where you stand.'

Byron in the end stepped in. 'Remember: though Shelley has some scruples about duelling, I shall be perfectly prepared to take his place.' Polly, in tears, backed down; he stood at the edge of the water, while the boats knocked against the pier. Shelley was balancing on the cross-bench, an occupation that seemed to require his full attention, and made him look boyish and happy. It was nearly lunchtime; in spite of everything, Polidori felt the simpler claims of hunger. Byron, in a curious gesture the doctor never forgot, touched the side of his forefinger to Polly's chin, and flicked it up. Polly hadn't shaved, and the rough stubble against Byron's nail made a noise like a struck match. Polidori couldn't tell, if Byron had meant to cheer him up, or suggest the cocking of a gun against his face.

Not long after, the poet and the doctor parted company. What Polly could bear least of all was the thought of disappointing his father; but he consoled himself with the reflection, that Gaetano had said from the first it would end badly and might take pleasure from the fact of being proved right. He wrote to his father at once, in terms carefully chosen to flatter the old man's sense of his son. 'We have parted, finding that our tempers did not agree. He proposed it and it was settled. There was no immediate cause, but a continued series of slight quarrels. I believe the fault, if any, has been on my part, I am not accustomed to have a master, and therefore my conduct was not free and easy.' But Polly wasn't yet ready to return home and burden his father: 'I hope I am still off your hands for some while.' He planned to 'walk over Italy and look over the medical establishments – see if there proves a good opportunity to settle. Besides,' he added, 'I might look up Frances and her *amante* in Milan.'

Byron, the morning Polly set off, seemed listless and peevishly affected. He lay sulking in his rooms 'like a dog', as he put it. And Polly had to seek him out in his bedroom: he smelled the thick air of Byron's sleep as he took the poet's hand. Byron would not rise from his low couch. 'Well, it's your own fault,' he said pettishly, raising a few limp fingers to be touched. And then, 'I am sorry to see you go. I soon get attached to people.' Polly asked for permission to look him up, should their paths cross in Italy. 'You may do as you like,' Byron said, 'it's all the same to me. Everyone leaves me in the end.' Polly, as he turned in the doorway, told himself to fix in his memory what might be his last view of the great poet: his angel's face, in which the beauty of man and woman were so remarkably mixed; his full curved ears, half-hidden in dark curls; his startling blue gaze. He looked pale, with a little colour just under his eyes, to show he had slept poorly; his lame foot hidden in the fold of an oriental rug, for he was never too idle or sad to attend to the necessary adjustments of his vanity. Polly had learned to recognize B's famous melancholy for what it was: the grace of his peevishness. But he now learnt to see beneath his self-pity another warmer melancholy. Byron was becoming lonely. He had learnt for the first time in the past year that he hadn't the charm or the patience to keep his friendships, even the least of them, intact – in touch.

In fact, Polly saw Byron again before the year was out. His lordship decided to pass the autumn in Milan, where Polidori was staying at his sister's establishment: her new husband, Rossetti, had been appointed consul. It occurred to the doctor, as soon as the news of Byron's visit reached them, that he had now at his disposal another means, another attraction, by which to bind the poet to him once again.

Frances and he hardly had a minute to themselves all evening. Which was just as well: what had passed between them, all those years ago, was present to both of them, and too difficult a subject for them either to broach it or leave it unmentioned. Besides, Frances was being, as Esmé complained, 'treated with cushions'. Even Gaetano insisted that she drink a little wine, not too much; that she eat well; that no one plague her with questions and news. Frances hardly seemed to need such indulgence. She was quite well, she insisted, and hungry and thirsty enough to let her own appetites guide her. But she gave way, after a few protests, to their 'cushioning', if only because she guessed, in the end, that it softened the shock of her presence for *them*.

After dinner, Gaetano and Polly withdrew and drank cognac and smoked each half a cigar. Polidori asked, if Senior Rossetti was shortly expected? Gaetano, who rested his glass on the button of his waistcoat, said only that 'Senior Rossetti was a very important and busy man. Also, very attached to Italy; he could not bear to leave it in the spring.' Polly said, 'I have not yet seen William.'

'No,' Gaetano agreed. 'A charming child. Exactly like his mother.'

Polidori, who had hoped to refrain from boasting of any of these things, said 'that he had begun to write again. Henry Colburn, a very reputable and successful publisher, had promised him a large advance for his memoir of Lord Byron; it wanted, he said, only a little adjustment.' When Gaetano did not answer, Polly continued: 'I have not asked you if you have heard any mention of a new gothic tale, *The Vampyre*, which has sold already in the thousands, and received a great deal of attention. As it happens . . .'

'I have never, as you know,' Gaetano interrupted, 'bothered myself over such trifles.'

Polidori drank and looked into his glass.

'Your godfather,' Gaetano continued, 'has written me to say, that you planned to enter the law. He did not think it a good idea. I must say I agree with him. At a certain age, for a man to change profession – I don't think you would find it easy. Even if you managed to establish a career in the law, about which I am by no means sanguine, even in the best case, that is, it would look unsteady, a sign of weak charac-ter. Your own profession seems to me perfectly satisfactory.'

'Why,' Polly asked, with more spirit, 'which profession is that?'

'Doctor, of course,' his father said.

Polly thought, I kill whatever I touch, I have always killed whatever I touch; but said nothing.

Gaetano announced at last 'that he wasn't so young any more, he could suffer himself to drink a second glass of cognac, or finish a cigar.' He rose and brushed the ash from his stomach. 'I wish you good night, son,' he added, turning in the doorway uncertainly round. He had aged, too. The girth of himself, self-made, seemed now an unhappy encumbrance; he couldn't, even had he wanted to, have reached his arms around himself to embrace his son. 'Your mother,' he muttered, 'asked me to tell you, that neither of us consider, that what has . . . brought Frances home . . . has any relation to you – to what happened between you in Milan, that is. I mean with Lord Byron. Your mother asked me particularly to reassure you.'

Polly ducked his head, blushing so hot that he couldn't say a word. His father, taking this gesture for a bow, bowed himself, and quietly shut the door behind.

Frances managed to catch him alone just as he was going. He had stepped outside and taken a breath of the dense spring evening, cold with cloudlessness. As he turned to close the door behind him, he felt a soft resisting weight. At first, he couldn't understand it, and pushed harder, until a little cry from his sister made him stop, and he saw her face in the crack. 'I wanted to say goodnight,' she said, and followed him out, leaving the door on the latch. This was the second time that day, he noted wryly, a girl had seen him out and on his way.

'I feel we've hardly exchanged a word all evening,' Frances said. She sat on the cold front steps and pulled him down to her. He had the sense of being taken in hand – as if he were the last of her goodnight duties to fulfil. There was little traffic in the road. The waning moon had the sky to itself and appeared both plain and large, its skin marred by blemishes, like any human face. Frances asked permission to warm herself on him, and when Polly said nothing, she slipped her hand around his back and under his arm, and pushed herself against his near side. The comfort of this almost made him tremble, but he with difficulty restrained himself.

'We mustn't tire you with questions,' he said, mockingly.

'That only counts for the rest of them. We have always answered to each other, haven't we?'

'Not in years. Not in many years.'

She nodded at this, taking it in; and then, consciously adopting a different line, asked, 'Well, how are you then? Papa I can tell is . . . hopeful for you again.' And then with kindly irony, she went on, 'He feels you have had enough of . . . your own way. He thinks you are ready to listen to him, again.'

'On the contrary,' Polly said, 'I am almost free.'

Frances had nothing to say to this, and for a minute they sat, companionably enough, in each other's arms, and watched the lights in the houses opposite come off and on. A thick-set man on a slow horse looked at them, trotting past, letting his head turn with them; and they met his stare, without offence or curiosity. Frances broke the silence again. 'I had forgotten how vast London is. It is almost a relief after Milan.'

'What's happened to you?' Polly said, giving in at last, ungraciously, to the gentle insistence of her intimate tone.

But she drew back now, and recited, as if repeating a difficult declension she was always getting wrong: 'Nothing, only . . . something slowly became clear, which I had hoped to conceal. It has brought about, when it could no longer be denied – when it could no longer *usefully* be denied – the expected consequences. But concealment was never for the best, and I am glad of it now, I am glad. Only too sleepy to go over it all again. I'll go over it all again tomorrow.'

'Perhaps I shan't see you tomorrow.' And then he added, rather grandly, 'I've got out of the habit of coming home.' It was the voice of the child who had stayed on, boasting of his new life, to reproach the child who had gone away – for knowing nothing any more about the family she had left behind.

'I see.' She looked him over. 'Well, another day then; it isn't a bedtime story.' The words seemed to summon the scrabbling on the stairs they heard behind them, like the sound of a dog struggling on hard ground. And just as the door pushed open against their backs, Frances said, 'The short of it is' – she looked up at him, smiling a little, 'I've been given my congé, too.' And then, 'Oh, William, my love, why aren't you in bed?'

Polly had never met his nephew, who was born within the year after he left Milan. He made space for him now, easing away from Frances, who quickly replaced her brother with the child in her arms. She kissed his sleepy face. The kisses seemed to bring out her son's tears and quench them at once. The boy was not yet three years old, girlish in figure and complexion, and extraordinarily pretty, with features Polly recognized at once: his rich locks, fine, harp-shaped ears, and astonishingly blue eyes. He almost wept himself to see them again, so carefully reproduced in miniature; but they inspired in him also a sense of the full horror of his shame. Frances had risen, the child was shy and buried his face in her neck. Polly stood up and took a step towards the road. She looked helplessly at him. 'He doesn't sleep any more without me,' his sister said. 'We've grown used to each other, lately, on our travels. I've been very weak, but I can't refuse what's so comfortable to us both. Not yet. But I wanted to say, brother, how sorry I was, for everything that happened. I never got the chance before. I hardly dared write and ask you to forgive me; but I very much hoped that you had.'

Polly put his hand around the boy's bare foot, which hung at his sister's waist, and rubbed it. 'There was never anything to forgive,' he said. 'And what there was, I believe, was mostly on your side. But perhaps we can agree to call it quits.'

'Thank you,' she said, and as he turned to leave, she added, 'William, bid your uncle good night.' But the boy was too shy, and Polly heard nothing else as he walked away.

CHAPTER THIRTEEN

C OLBURN'S PARLOUR LIGHT WAS LIT. The house was only a little out of his way home, and Polly, not knowing why, had taken the road that ran past it and for a minute wondered whether to knock on his publisher's door. He wasn't in any case ready for sleep again. He also had, in the first shock of his recent knowledge, an idea of coldly putting it to use. Colburn, he believed, would be very much interested in the story he had to tell. Even if it touched, rather intimately, on the personal; he now had his claim to the private closets of Byron's life. But then the parlour light went out, and the street darkened with it, and Polidori had the sense of a quiet turning to rest that a doused light always suggests. The sight of it put him in mind of his own bed, and having stopped in the street, he now continued on his way: sobbing dryly, with a forced grief akin to anger, which it quickly turned into.

An unhappy hesitation had begun to infect his least decision. There seemed to be no one on St Giles, aside from drunks of various degrees. Then a woman in a doorway called to him, in a plaintive voice not unlike a cry for help, and exposed, in the light of the moon under a ragged skirt, a scarred red knee. He didn't at once understand what was offered – for an instant he stopped in sympathy for the stricken and shelterless – and when he did, it amazed him, how the simple fact of the offering could colour her abused form: the dirty line of the bone in her ankle, the free play of her toes in their torn slippers. These now hinted to him the pleasure that might be had from something willing to be roughly handled. He tested himself for such desires. He was unhappy enough to act on anything that might put off, for an hour or so, the consciousness of it. And he had brought a prostitute to bed before: the daughter of an Italian peasant who stank of garlic and who had cheerfully bartered his child, hoping perhaps to advance her fortunes, to the famous English *milord*. Byron had a reputation for charity towards his cast-offs. And in fact having haggled and paid for the creature, who also reeked sharply and sexually of the kitchen, he took a kind of pity on her and declined to touch her after she undressed. His sympathies were like sudden fancies: she had stood before him in the blue pallor of girl-hood, her knees and elbows pressed shyly together. They did not, however, prevent him from passing the use of her onto his young doctor. Cast-offs, both of them. She had long, high-arched feet, and was by no means as innocent as she at first appeared. But the thought of her reminded him of another girl Byron had shown less restraint in enjoying, and, tearless and angry now, Polidori said to the woman in the doorway, 'Cover your shame. In this condition you inspire only disgust.' The outburst gave him no relief.

Turning away, he thought he saw Colburn himself passing ahead of him in the road, a broad-backed man with a brisk deliberate stride walking in the direction of Gronow's, his club on Drury Lane. Conscious of clutching at straws, Polly ran after him, across Shaftesbury Avenue, and onto Endell Street. All the while, one of Lord Byron's quips repeated itself in his thoughts. 'The doctor,' B once said (it was Shelley who cruelly passed on the joke) 'is just the kind of man, who, if he were drowning, one would reach him a straw, to see if the old adage be true: that drowning men clutch at straws.' But the image seemed to him now more unhappy than humorous – almost as if Byron from the first had seen the pathos in it, sympathetically. He caught up with the broad-backed man at the door of the club, a simple blue house-door with a hat-shaped knocker. By this time, in spite of the coolness of the cloudless night, Polidori was unpleasantly damp with sweat. It *was* Colburn. He seemed scarcely surprised to see the doctor, and said smiling, 'Finished already? I thought I'd leave you to it.' Polly was too hot to hear him, and, asking Colburn for a word, was duly invited inside.

Gronow's was fashionable among the theatre set and those gentlemen who wished to entertain their sporting but professional acquaintances in a mixed crowd. It sprawled over several floors of a narrow house. Candles lit the dark small rooms, which were heaped with furniture, and the smell and heat of tallow thickened the air of confined humanity. The atmosphere suggested guests making free with the hospitality of a host who has been unexpectedly detained from home. Colburn, in high humour, said he liked the place because the poets who came were always too drunk to plague him with their manuscripts. They descended, gingerly, the fretted iron stairs leading to the basement. Polly put his hand on Colburn's shoulder to steady himself, and then hardly liked to let go of his comforting mass. In the uncertain light, the publisher's broad, pock-marked face had the look of a friendly devil's.

Colburn ordered brandy for both of them from a waiter wearing tan doe gloves. When it came he set his glass against the ledge running the width of the room, and glanced over the tables occupying the middle of the floor. 'It is best to survey the field,' he said in his heavy ironies, 'before one ventures into it.' The rattle of the dice sounded like the quickening of a pulse; and Polidori, in spite of everything, found himself thrilling to the rapid and plain unfolding of fates the games represented. It amazed him always, the *fact* of chance: the notion, how hopeful! that his life might depend on the action of inhuman forces; that it could be redeemed by luck. It was clear to him by now that whatever depended on his own will, on his human qualities, on *himself alone*, was doomed to failure.

Gronow's was slow to take up new fads, and the game of

the hour was still hazard. Cries of 'nicked it' and 'crabs' rang out, variously, from the several tables in operation, among the haggling over bets laid. Colburn was looking for a lucky hand before joining in, and Polly, repeating something B had once said to him, told the publisher, 'I have a notion that gamblers are as happy as most people – being always excited. One tires of everything else before long: women, ambition, fame. But every cast of the dice keeps the gambler alive. Besides one can game ten times longer than one can do anything else. As soon as I hear the dice I feel – entirely *awake*. And by the contrast afterwards see how much of my life I pass in a kind of half-sleep.'

Colburn nodded, and then, in a quieter gap, said, 'It's the gamblers themselves I never tire of observing. How hopeless they are: whatever they win will be lost in a minute. I play only to keep my hand in. As I said, it's the spectacle of them that moves me.'

'You have, however, the reputation of a sharp.'

Polly had wondered whether he was being insulting, but Colburn turned and smiled suddenly at him. This was the kind of praise he enjoyed, with a spice of resentment in it. His large face reddened benignly; he liked being kind to those he was capable of hurting. 'I'll tell you, Polly, the secret of it: indifference. You'll never win anything if you care a hang for it either way.'

'I suspect then,' Polidori said in a high whisper to push his voice above the noise, 'that I shall never win anything.'

Colburn, coming to a decision, clapped his hands together, and called for *rouleaux*, a cup of coffee. He sat down at one of the tables and pulled out a chair for the doctor. Polidori asked for another glass of brandy; he was beginning to lose his head and beginning to enjoy it. There were four other men gaming with them. A young captain named Sheetcroft with thin pale hair and a white face and very pale blue eyes. He had been losing steadily and plucked nervously, in rapid alternation, his thumb against his forefinger: Polly imagined he could hear the rub of the skin. 'The thing is,' he kept saying, 'I'm about to be married, you see.' Polidori recognized another one of the players, a friend of B's, known as Scrope – to rhyme with 'dupe'. A small, compacted man, he wore a severe collar, very stiff and high, that brought out the green in his narrow face. His pupils twitched restlessly, and he half-blinked, in a kind of eye-pinch – an expression in which Polly recognized the suppressed frown of calculation. 'I believe we've met before,' Polidori said, feeling the brandy in his chest and reaching his hand out, 'in happier company. Doctor Polidori.' Scrope looked him over quickly, then touched his fingers to Polly's palms. He clearly had no recollection of the doctor. He had aged since the four of them set out, that long-ago summer morning, for Dover: Scrope and Byron in that ridiculous carriage, Hobhouse, resentfully, confined to the calèche with Polidori. 'I expect you mean I owe you money,' he said, with a thin smile. Polly was almost glad to see that he wasn't alone in falling on hard times since parting with B.

'No, we got drunk together at The Grapes in Dover, the night before Lord Byron left for France.'

Scrope, still unremembering, said, 'I expect we did. Getting drunk with Lord Byron was one of my better habits.'

'Are you playing?' Colburn cut in.

Polidori put his wrists together and opened out his hands. 'I haven't got any money.'

'I always thought that was why one gambled in the first place,' Scrope said, who had the cast and threw down the dice with a practised gesture. Three 'mains' running brought a pretty heap of rouleaux between his elbows. Colburn began to follow his lead, putting his bets on the 'dapper little fellow', as he called him; though secretly, between rounds, he complained to Polly of Scrope's 'miserable dandified manner'. Colburn had lately affected a prejudice against the whole tribe. It was a 'terrible waste of niceties', the attention they gave to their collars, their cuffs; their odds-tables. There were two other players, a small rounded gentleman named Tulk, who owned quantities of Surrey. He said little and bet heavily and marked all his winnings and losings in a notebook he kept inside his bright yellow waistcoat. And a banker whom Scrope referred to chummily as K. He had large hands and a slow manner, and whenever Scrope won, he carefully extracted a portion from his friend's pile, and arranged the chips in a neat row beside his own.

It was almost two in the morning before Polly joined in the game. Colburn had grown 'tired of the sport', having won a little for himself, about a hundred pounds. 'The trick,' he said, 'was knowing when he was bored. He always quit as soon as he was bored; there was a very fine line between indifference and boredom, but everything depended on knowing when it was crossed.' He was also sober, unlike the rest of the company, and wanted to enjoy the contrast with greater detachment. Polly, by this stage, had a brandy-fire in his head; the easy exchange of money, of fortunes, thrilled him as it always did. The thought of what he might do with a hundred pounds! There were tradesman's debts to be settled, of course; but even so, he'd have enough to take up that apprenticeship in the law. 'He had a fancy for the law. It struck him as an honourable profession' – he was beginning to explain himself, carefully and loudly, to Colburn; it seemed to him very important that Colburn should understand his position. What he wanted to say, what he wanted Colburn to see, was that his own particular difficulty, the blankness or barrenness from which he suffered, might count for less in the law than it did in the literary game. But even in his inflamed state, Polidori guessed this was the wrong line to take with his publisher, and he said instead, that experience had taught him that nothing ever turns out as you think it will, and it's a nonsense to say that it turns out better or worse, it simply turns out *otherwise*, and by otherwise he means of course worse. And that when he was young it struck him as the most natural thing in the world that the most famous poet in the world should seek him out and beg him for his professional services. *Beg him*; and that in fact Polly, at a very green nineteen, had, at the time, for some time hesitated whether or not to *oblige*. He wanted Colburn particularly to understand the way he used to think, of the world, of his place in it, when he was young. But his father from the beginning had warned him that he would suffer, and he had suffered!, from the force of impossible comparisons. There were some things it was impossible to compare. It was impossible to compare Lord Byron and Doctor John William Polidori. Yet they were in some ways very much alike and had on more than one occasion been mistaken for each other. A fact he considered highly suggestive . . .

This train of thought put him in mind of Eliza; and he wondered sentimentally how far a hundred pounds would go towards setting them up in life together, in a little cottage, like her father's perhaps, in Somers Town by the canal. Though, of course, he would also have to explain himself and his conduct to her very convincingly. He, paradoxically, began envying Lord Byron afresh, believing that the poet's powers of persuasion would make short work of any apology he had to offer for pretending to be the poet. It was a motto of Mrs Shelley's that 'everything came easier if you were Albé.' Seeing Frances had loosened something in his affections; he no longer clung to the memory of her, to the memory of the affection he felt for her. It occurred to him that the time had come at last for him to find her replacement, for him to replace the comfort she offered with new comforts and pleasures. And he tasted again Eliza's warm breath, the leftover sourness of the syllabub on her tongue. Colburn asked him, bending his mouth to Polly's ear, how he was getting on with the memoir of Lord B. There was always something conspiratorial about Henry Colburn; he tended to demand a full and hushed attention, especially from his authors. Polly almost said to him, you always seem to be conspiring over the most natural arrangements in the world. But instead, he said, that he had recently begun a sequel to *The Vampyre*, which had lately occurred to him, owing to a piece of gossip that had come his way from Byron's life abroad, of a very intimate and scandalous nature. That it concerned a brother and a sister, and the issue of an illicit connection, but he didn't wish to go any further into a description of the story, as he often found it spoiled his appetite for telling it later, in the quieter company of a goose-quill and a sheet of paper.

It was at this point that Colburn offered to stake Polidori what he called a bit of play-money, for playing with, as he said. Colburn liked to experiment with people and situations. He also liked his acquaintance to be beholden: it left him such scope for generosity and manipulation. His large friendly devilish face seemed to have swelled in the course of the evening, in the glow of the candles, until it loomed over Polidori as bright with blemishes as the moon that had illuminated Polly's chat with Frances on the doorstep of their father's house what seemed now several night-times ago. As an advance, of course, Colburn continued, on the fulfilment of various arrangements understood between them.

Polly again was tempted to complain of Colburn's conspiratorial manner, which seemed to suggest that a simple transaction between men of the world had sinister undertones. But thinking better of it – and this struck him at the time as a lucky omen, that, drunk as he was, he had managed to forestall his own stubborn penchant for what Byron used to call his 'getting into scrapes' – he simply accepted the sum of a hundred pounds, the full ration of Colburn's earlier winnings, by raking the heap of them with his forearms onto the green baize between his elbows on the table. A rough gesture that signalled his willingness to take his chances, roughly, and live by the results. 'Come when it will,' he thought, 'we snatch the life of life': one of Byron's lines, which served as a kind of refrain to his inward commentary on the rest of the night. He felt like a young man striding free again, for the first time, after a long bout of illness; or – and this was perhaps the apter image – after leaving behind the constraining company of an ageing father, whose arm he had taken, and to whose gait he had adapted his own.

Sheetcroft had by now two spots of hectic colour on his cheeks, round and pretty, as if painted on. He had continued to lose heavily and played on in the not unreasonable belief that since he was ruined already, the only swing in his fortune that signified was an upward turn. He rolled up his silken shirt-sleeves, and set his forearms on the table. Tulk, the landowner, had done very well by hedging against the captain. He was the kind of man who could not repress the satisfaction in his pity. Pity, in fact, was the only sentiment that inspired in him fellow-feeling. 'I'm beginning to warm to you, Sheetcroft,' he repeated, a little smirk playing on his lips, as if it took the full strength of his character to prevent the outbreak of a smile. He put his plump-fingered hand on the young man's naked wrist. 'I'm sorry to say it, but I've done rather well off your bad luck.'

Sheetcroft turned briefly towards him, with the timidity of a man about to depend on the kindness of the rich. 'I thought I'd just have a quiet game or two, to see if I was *warm*. I'm about to be married, you see; I thought it might bring me luck.' He had the cast, and as he said it, touched the box against Tulk's wager and let the dice fly. Tulk recorded the result in his little book, a two and a three. Sheetcroft took up the dice again, and rolled a two and a five. 'A good "chance",' Scrope kindly remarked; but he didn't trust Sheetcroft's run of fortune, and hedged with a bet of five pounds, at three to two odds, on the 'main'. The captain shook the box and threw again: he was hardly breathing. A six, a nine, another six. Polidori said, 'I love the glorious uncertainty not only of good luck or bad luck, but *of any luck at all*. These little postponements, when nothing, after all, has been decided.'

'No, no,' Sheetcroft replied. 'It's much worse, waiting. I'd rather lose at once if I'm going to lose.'

Polly took this as an ill omen for the captain, and laid down five pounds on the 'main'. Colburn, being out of the game, had decided to get drunk again. He ordered a pint of arrack punch from the waiter, and then called after him once more, and, on his return, asked for a beefsteak and an apple tart. 'Anything for the doctor?' he added, but Polidori did not hear him. The waiter, a handsome thin-faced man with honey-coloured skin, stood hesitant, until Colburn kicked him in the foot, and sent 'Narcissus' on his way. Sheetcroft rolled, and exhaled again, painfully, when another seven came up. His smile was sweetness itself, the soft brightness of winter sunshine. Even Tulk had the graciousness to congratulate him; Polly watched his five pounds being raked away. Well, it was only the beginning. He had the sense of entering at last, after a long absence, the arena in which he could do justice to his passion for life. He felt invincible, and was savvy enough to recognize the feeling as the result of brandy and sleeplessness; at the same time, he couldn't entirely discount it as evidence of the luck he was in.

Sheetcroft's fortunes were turning. On his next cast, he threw a three and a one, and, with the betting heavily against him, two twos: another four. 'Nicked it, by God,' Colburn cried; and the captain gathered the stakes to himself. He became expansive. Once, off the coast of Cherbourg, he let a French frigate, a 34-gun beauty, high in the water and quick on the turn, get the gauge off him. He fired, for what it was worth, at range; broke a stay, and awaited the returning volley. But the wind backed suddenly and caught the Frenchman across his bows. A rough day with long rollers, the gale had been steady all week – what a lucky gust it was. It showed, if you were looking, as a faint flat row of silvering over the tops of the waves. Sheetcroft let it fill him from the quarter, and followed it through the Frenchman's wake. Giving up the gauge for good, he crossed the stern of the 34 and raked her up and down; broke her mizzen, which tore from its stay and fell flat across the deck, till the wind caught the loose sail and pressed her like a dog from behind. She struck at once. But what he'll never forget is that *quiet* in the blow just before the wind backed; not so much calm as noiseless with the tension. You felt the pressure in your ears like ten feet of cold water. He thought he was dead, by God; he thought he was dead for sure.

The blood had filled the rest of his face; he was getting his colour back. 'I should be in bed by now,' he said. 'I promised Margaret I would be in bed by three.' He looked round the table, anxious to confide, to exchange intimacies, and declared, as if for the first time, 'I'm getting married in the morning. But I'm just beginning to enjoy myself.'

'Congratulations, old man,' Tulk repeated, largely out of habit.

Polidori, by the end of the first hour, had lost sixty pounds. 'He was getting his hand in,' he joked. Scrope was losing, too, very quietly, under great control. K said to him, 'Easy, easy,' when the dapper little man reached over, stretching the starch in his collar, to retrieve the chips from his friend's pile. 'You didn't expect to keep them,' Scrope said, lifting his brows. 'Well, we'll settle accounts, afterwards,' K replied, giving way. 'I thought you'd take the sporting view,' Scrope answered. And added, with only a touch of what B used to call Scrope's Special Horseradish, 'after all, you're only a banker by *trade*.'

'Easy, easy,' Colburn echoed, taking Polidori by the arm. He wasn't yet drunk, and had begun to fear for what he called his 'investment'. 'Sit out a round and eat something. It's bad luck gaming hungry.'

'I eat the air,' Polly said, strangely high-spirited. No sense of loss had yet afflicted him; he was proof against his usual quick response to misfortune. He tended, sensitively, to fall in line with it; but now he felt impervious. Another good omen; he drank half a glass of brandy to fix the feeling of it within him. His spirits were just on the boil; he didn't want them to go off yet, he dreaded the inevitable flatness to follow. He said to Colburn, 'I believe that gamblers, even those confirmed in their depravity, feel freer than most men. Their profession demands a cool head and a calculating mind; but in the end, they give themselves over, night after night, to a quite inhuman force. The fall of the dice or the turn of the cards has more to do with their happiness than any qualities they possess themselves: they step, as it were, out of their own skins. They are unbound.'

And, in fact, his luck turned, and he began to win. First he shared the spoils with Sheetcroft and then, as Sheetcroft began to lose again, with Tulk. He took a particular pleasure in seeing his own successes carefully recorded, in a cramped bad hand, in Tulk's book. 'Yes, write it down, write it down,' he cried. His drunkenness was becoming obtrusive; he kept looking over the landowner's low round shoulder, to see exactly what his little notes recounted. 'Write it down,' he repeated: he had the sense his good humour was lacking an echo, something to resound against. 'I am going to be married myself,' he said, taking Sheetcroft intimately by the elbow. He too wanted something to confide, and picked Eliza as the nearest secret to hand. 'To a very pretty girl,' he went on, 'who is under a . . . certain misapprehension regarding my character. She believes I am what I am not. She believes I am not what I am.'

Colburn at this point asked for Polly to return his stake; he was retiring to bed. 'You have plenty there to be getting on with.' Polidori looked happily at his winnings. 'Would you like to count them?' And then, suddenly sad, touched by presentiments of the ease of loss, in the broadest sense, he urged his 'old friend' to 'stay, stay. It was only for the happiness of the thing that he continued. It was only to keep the company in spirits. They were all bound together now, were they not, by ties of pleasure?' The light of false dawn was beginning to drift through the bars of the window that gave onto the street above them. Most of the tables had emptied. There was an ugly streak of red wine on one of the waiter's gloves. His face looked haggard now; his prettiness was only for show, beneath it lay a mean, tired spirit. Polidori yawned wide and slow. 'It was only a release of nerves,' he insisted and ordered coffee with a dash of brandy in it. In fact, he felt himself standing on the edge of a tremendous coming-down. The least slackening would leave him boneless, childish with misery. His sister, his poor sister. He was, perhaps, some two hundred pounds to the good. Tulk was ready to call it quits; Sheetcroft had fallen asleep at the table, and K was standing to go, when Scrope, who had lost five hundred pounds in the course of the evening, said evenly, 'I believe the cast is mine' and took up the dice. Polidori's coffee arrived. K sat down again. Sheetcroft woke up, with a raspberry of warm blood lingering on the tip of his nose and the creased skin of his forearm where they had pressed together. Colburn called for another beefsteak, beaten thin, a glass of Tokay.

When true dawn came at last, white with the promise of a hot day, Polly had lost everything. The first two hundred pounds had 'dried up' (Sheetcroft's phrase) within the hour. Then, fighting hard again, and grimly, soberly awake, Polly gambled away the rest of Colburn's stake by sunrise. A disaster which, in its own way, seemed strangely to suit his mood. He had a strong, almost comfortable sense of the snug fit of things: the way people lived up to their habits and fates in the end. Scrope had cleared his debts and come out again on the other side; he and Tulk rose victorious from the table, and followed each other up the corkscrew steps, delicate and careful with somnolence. Then out into the street again, into the air, light-hearted and blinking against the light. Polidori followed Colburn; his knees ached with sleeplessness. He stumbled at one point and steadied himself on Colburn's ankle. The publisher waited for him to let go, then resumed his climb. Standing outside again, in the air already pregnant with the heat of the day, Polly could just make out the flow of people on St Giles: the business of ordinary life continuing. He said to Colburn, 'I wonder if most men suffer from a sense that their life has not amounted to what they thought it would. I wonder if that is a general lament.'

Colburn answered, that as he got older, he put more and more of his faith in 'mere pleasure', which he had found to be a simple but effective physic against any, and even the most spiritual, malaise. He was often astonished at how happy he could make himself simply by satisfying his appetites. He had ceased to worry over his place in the world. When he was low, he ate a beefsteak; when he was hipped, he drank a bottle of champagne; when he was bored, he counted over his money.

Polly, taking the hint, said that it was 'very decent, very white' of Colburn to lend him the hundred pounds; he was only sorry it had gone to waste.

Colburn said, not at all, he intended always to get what he paid for, and Polidori knew very well what he had paid *him* for. Then, taking his watch from the fob, he added, 'I expect we both have business to attend to.' Bidding the doctor good morning, he set off towards St Giles; his gait slower than it had been arriving, the night before, but strong and steady still. Polly watched him go, he didn't dare keep pace beside him; and only after Colburn's broad back had disappeared into the traffic of the high street, did he make his own way towards home. Sheetcroft, patiently shy, stood waiting for him at the corner of Macklin Street. He had, just about, got off honours-evens by the end. Large-hearted and sleepless with relief, he was fastidious about his farewells. He wanted to feel that no one had been hard done by, he wanted to touch all hands. 'I thought at first that I had missed you, that you had gone ahead. Is it very bad?'

'Nothing is very bad any more,' Polly answered.

'That's just it,' Sheetcroft said, 'that's just what I remember thinking,' and bowing, he took his leave.

The sun had already risen above the terraces by the time Polidori reached Lincoln's Inn; he could see it glancing off the windows of his rooms. It cast shifting squares of light on the houses opposite. He nodded, in spite of everything, with the satisfaction of the late-returning, at the porter, and climbed the stairwell not so much heavy-hearted as confident that in some way his present manner of living would be brought to an end. He could not go on as he was. For the first time in many days he fell asleep as soon as his head touched the pillow.

table. A level sunset, coming through the window to the back, blinded him to his daughter; he spoke more freely at the glow of her. 'I had expected arrogance, and he was not without a fine sense of his own high spirit. But there was a softness to him, a willingness to please. One felt almost that he depended on it, and this was very charming in itself.'

And then he continued, with a pleasurable heat and interest in his own words; he did not see Eliza slowly giving way to tears. 'I have been very poor in the company of men. Your mother was my great love but also my first love, and I was by some years the younger. She had seen more of the world than I, and I was happy to take what she believed on faith: you know how much I relied on her. After we married, I found the roughness of men uncongenial. They presume too much upon . . . shared humours; they have no respect for what is womanish in us and delights only in the company of women. Our best nature. I felt this strongly at the time. I found it impossible to put up the show of indifference to all things that I felt was demanded of me. But perhaps I was too squeamish; and in fact, I saw so little of life, first-hand, so little of the world outside your mother's view, that I think even she began to despair of me, and she sometimes complained, that there was nothing *hard* in me to push against, I was always giving way. I'm afraid none of this is very clear. What she wished for is that I could give her what she had given me, a firm shape, if only by resisting now and then, by standing fast. When Captain Simons (he was a mere lieutenant at the time) courted Beatrice, your mother wanted to know what manner of man he was, if he could be trusted. He was so sure and easy that she couldn't confidently judge him, she had not the comparisons inside herself to hand. And I was forced to confess that I knew as little of such men as she, that I stood in just the same awe of them. She grew very angry at this. It was proper for a man, she thought, to have a fighting sense of life; and this is just what I saw in Lord Byron. Here is a man, I thought, who has seen the world, and who has not been afraid to put himself in the wrong. I have been too willingly constrained by a woman's understanding of harm done. I have hardly touched the world at all, I was so frightened of spoiling something. The friendship, even the company, of a man like Lord Byron, might have done much to . . . might have given me an appetite for . . . success.'

After the meal, they sat together picking from a bowl of plums, which Polidori had bought for them at a stall outside the Wells – each eating and sucking and laying the stones with wet fingers in the dirty pot. Eliza's father repeated his remark about the 'acquaintance of poets'. 'It is wonderful,' he said, 'to feel properly *observed*.' Eliza was too happy to interrupt his flow. She also enjoyed playing her mother's part, feeding him, listening, clearing up afterwards – he had always depended greatly on the women in his life to hear him out. It was one of her mother's sayings: 'Let him talk.' It kept him happy, a steady blood-letting. She was also conscious, just a touch, of falling away from him – she saw him through Lord Byron's eyes. What was his phrase, an honourable scribbler? Yes, she had confined herself too long to her father's narrow expectations of life. She understood now, at last, the game Bea had played in catching Captain Simons; her strong desire to leave home. How strange, how false, her sister had first appeared to her, as a lover, a seductress. But this, she thought, is what being in love is like. You can recognize it most clearly by the little cold ticking of calculation in your thoughts: perhaps I can change my life.

Her father insisted on accompanying Eliza home. He was restless; in any case, too restless to write. He wanted to think and talk; he wanted to go over everything. Besides, the sun had gone down a half-hour before. There was only the glow of it, cupped in the hands of the horizon, and tossed upwards. Even that was streaking and disappearing. By the time they reached Oxford Street, the lamps had been lit. Her father took her more closely by the arm. They walked like lovers almost, close-hipped; their shadow, under their feet, had only three legs, a bulging middle. It was one of his beliefs, that intimacy, its display, forms an inviolable shell, that lovers were less likely to be robbed. She understood him, how starved he was of human warmth; she after all had the two children in and out of her arms. She had Lord Byron's kiss.

Even so, when they reached the door of Lady Walmsley's house, she was grateful for her powers of detachment. They stood in the milky shadow of the broad stucco façade. All was softness. Even the air smelt costlier than the wind that blew across her father's yard, and she felt the slight retraction in his posture. He had put on, already, that humility of manner which embarrassed her in the company of Lady Walmsley's set. He said, to keep her a minute longer, 'I have always been proud of you, Eliza. Your mother and I were always proudest of you – perhaps because Bea never worried us, she had everything so well in hand. But your mother feared you would never be rated as you deserve.' She unwound his arm, and then her fingers from his hand, and kissed him, retreating already, with one foot on the steps. He addressed her now, looking up, and continuing, 'She worried that you were too much your father's daughter! and I am only sorry she has not seen such proof, of the esteem in which you are held; that the first poet of the age has taken such an interest in you . . .' And she stooped and kissed him again, scratching her face against his soft beard. He blinked at her; his pale childish skin reflected flatly the light where his cheeks were wet. At the top of the steps she waved him off, in truth glad to return to the glittering world, to leave her father, the homely air of his honourable humility, behind her. And only when he had disappeared, with a backward glance, around the corner, did she skip down the steps and hurry along the alley towards the servants' entrance at the back.

Sundays were her day off, and she just stopped in to tell

the cook that she had dined already before she retired to her room – to read, as she believed. But the books, which had once been her only solace, seemed poor comfort to her now. Eliza wondered what this signified, about her, about Lord Byron. Her room had a squat window, just at the height of her knees, overlooking the gardens behind. Often, in the mornings, she refreshed her eyes on the beeches rising high as houses, on their patient, superior company, their growing indifference to the little lives below. But in the shine of her candle, the window reflected blackly at her; and if she got down on her knees, she could see herself in it, peering back. Her feet and calves were tired from walking, but she pushed the books away, and, candle in hand, crouched to her own crouching image and considered her face. Her ashen complexion and stubborn lower lip; her thin, delicate, pernickety nose; her almond-green eyes, that gave her narrow face just the look of true elfin wildness which saved her from appearing merely stingy and hungry.

Was there anything to fall in love with in her face? How greedy she seemed to herself, with a fierce little selfish appetite: greedy and . . . and finicky at once. The look of a child who wants more and more, and disapproves of whatever she is given. She had never liked her face; but now as she stared at it, imagining in herself a man gazing at the woman she was, Eliza saw the promise of something else. There was innocence, there, but also a touch of cruelty, not unsensual. She looked like a girl who could give as good as she got. She looked like a woman willing to go certain lengths to please herself. (After all, hadn't she risen on tiptoes suddenly to kiss him, unbidden?) And Eliza supposed that there might be something irresistible, to a man, in the fat scorn of her bottom lip.

But her knees had begun to hurt her, and she looked again and saw only a sleepy and stubborn child, wide-eyed, who needed to be told to go to bed. She blew out the candle and breathed in thickly the masculine rough sulphurous odour of its snuffing; then squeezed into bed, with the weight of her books at her feet. The moonlight cast a ladder of light across the boards of her room, climbed over her knees. She was happy, she was happy at last. Lord Byron had kissed her. It seemed to her then that the passage into adulthood resembled nothing so much as an entrance into the world of her books – a world she had pored over and dreamed of, and which she now touched and tasted for the first time without the medium of the printed page. Small wonder the books themselves had begun to pall. And she kept herself warm with the thought that whatever had been done could not be changed or superseded; not till the morning at least.

Her father decided on his walk home to stop at Bea's house, which was more or less in his path. At his age, he had need of certain practical remissions and could use in any case a small glass of something to speed him on his way. Eliza had told him that Lord Byron wished to keep his presence in London a secret, and that he wasn't to breathe a word, etc. but he needn't give his name away. And besides, he didn't see how any harm could come of confiding in his elder daughter just the *news* of Eliza's little triumph. Bea and Eliza offered him such distinct comforts. Eliza, whom he loved more, was cut from his own cloth. And just because of this, she never quite satisfied his desire for a sensible margin to his dreaming life, which his dead wife had given him.

At the same time, he always relished those occasions when he could prove to Beatrice that his own view of the world had its basis in plain ordinary facts. When he could show her that Eliza (and, by extension, *her father*) wasn't entirely the fool of books. It was an old argument, almost comfortable from rehearsal. He would say, you see how well Liza gets on, and she would angrily retort, it was only her own practical interventions that had preserved that girl from the squalor of the schoolhouse, or the chill of the convent. And together they worked over and rubbed down the sharp edge of their fears for themselves and each other: that he was hopelessly impractical and she, worldly and loveless.

The captain was away from home, dining late at his club, when Mr Esmond arrived. This pleased him; it seemed a good omen. He felt awkward, large-footed, in the presence of his son-in-law: he guessed that he was the introduction of a wrong note, that he brought in, when their door opened for him, the cold weather of the family's humble past. Well, Simons himself was no better; at least, he had only *made* himself so. Bea received him in her dressing room; it was late and she had let down her hair. A handful of fire burned in the grate, just enough to cast shadows. Bea was very partial to fires in all seasons, fond of the twin luxuries of heat and waste – she liked, in any case, to draw out her convalescence, the sympathies it inspired. As she'd said to her husband, complaining, she had only just risen from her death-bed, and he couldn't deny her the comfort of a fire . . . In its light, with her long hair fallen to her shoulders, she looked almost like a creature of his own gothic imagination: astonishingly grand and beautiful. She had got all her colour back.

Mr Esmond had confessed to Eliza once that he was rather in awe of her sister, her high looks; and Eliza had said to him, nonsense, whenever she saw a pretty woman, all she could think of was the self-control and sheer *graft* that went into her appearance. Mrs Violet, for example, Lady Walmsley's daughter-in-law, spent more time at her toilette than Eliza herself wasted on books, which was saying a great deal . . . And her father remembered this now, and smiled: grateful, as always for the sly nourishment of his daughters' gossip, which fed his starved sense of the world, of women. He said, 'I wonder if you'll guess where, and with whom, I've spent this pleasant Sunday afternoon?' He found himself, in Bea's company, often adopting the teasing banter of a suitor. She, in turn, always answered him with what Eliza called her kindly *out-of-patience* tone. 'I expect,' she said, 'since it is so late, that you've been walking Liza home; I expect you've spent the afternoon with her.'

'Just so. With her, and her *admirer*.'

'Oh?' She turned swiftly in her chair now – she had been facing her own reflection in the mirror of her dressing table – and leaned forward, her small hands holding her small knees. 'Tell me everything. I can't bear Liza's little mysteries.' Her manner had changed towards him, grown more girlish and eager, more daughterly. And her father sat back and enjoyed the picture of her curiosity. Her wide blue eyes, like jewels too big for their rings, seemed to fill her face. 'She begged me not to say,' he said. 'She positively made it a condition.'

'Now you're teasing me. That's unkind, Papa. A condition of what? Confess: he's horrible and small and she's ashamed of him.'

Mr Esmond shook his wispy, childish head. Bea petulantly crossed her legs. 'Well, if you won't talk, you won't and there's nothing I can do about it. I don't see why I should care. But you might as well grant me, at least, that he's four feet tall and looks like a potato.' And when her father only smiled, she crossly continued, 'Admit it, he's an oyster-monger and smells like a bucket of fish.' But her gossiping joy broke though, and she began to enumerate, upon her fingers, the list of his possible occupations: a grave-digger, a ship's cook, a shoe-blacker, until he broke in, to put her superior airs to shame, with, 'He's a gentleman, as it happens; a poet, rather; a lord.' But she, blind with bottled laughter, whispered (it was all the wind she had left for her voice), 'I don't know why it amuses me so, the thought of a man taking an interest in Liza, in dear little Liza. I don't see why they shouldn't. I don't see why they shouldn't fall about her feet, in any numbers.'

Her father couldn't help the infection of her humour, and tried, unsuccessfully, to sit up in the softness of her low settee. He rested his weight on his hands and said, 'She tells me you danced with him, once. Years ago.'

'Yes, she told me that,' Bea said, recovering. 'Now confess, it isn't fair, to keep a secret of somebody one danced with oneself, now is it?' And her father, perhaps acknowledging the justice of this, admitted, that the gentleman in question was a man in whom he had his own reasons for taking an interest – as a poet, as a man of letters. And then, with cruel self-irony, 'as a brother of the pen'. He continued, more earnestly, 'What a wonderful thing it was, the acquaintance of poets' – a sentiment whose repetition seemed obscurely to comfort him. Bea, seeing the chance of a joke, a good thing (she was her father's daughter, after all) interrupted, 'I never dance with poets; they keep counting their *feet*' – but before he could answer, and in an utterly changed tone, she sighed, 'Oh, Liza, poor Liza.' Her father recognized this tone, had lived in fear of it much of his married life. It was the tone her mother used to adopt whenever she stumbled across what she called another 'one of his fancies' – anything that revealed his hopeless ignorance of the world's workings. And Beatrice had learned to treat Eliza in the same manner.

Mr Esmond and Eliza both despaired of this tone, acknowledged the power of the common-sense behind it, hated it, resisted it whenever they could, and gave in to it in the end. 'What do you mean, poor Liza?' he said, and continued, trying to sit up on the settee and give his posture more dignity: 'He was perfectly charming, and not the monster of misanthropy they make him out to be. He brought us a bag of fresh plums, from Brazil. We walked around the gardens together. He admired them exceedingly.'

'You mean Lord Byron?'

'I do. I mean Lord Byron.'

'You mean, that he spent the afternoon with you, in Bagnigge Wells. That he took tea in your cottage. That he has an honourable interest in Liza. In you.'

'I do. That's just what I mean. But as for tea in my cottage, he was called away, and left us at the door. Liza herself saw him out. I believe they have formed what they call in novels an attachment.'

She turned back to her reflection in the mirror and looked at her face – just as prettily sober now as before it had been prettily amused – as if to read in it how serious the situation had become. 'Poor Liza,' she said again.

'What do you mean, poor Liza?'

'She has taken you in again. *He,* whoever he is, has taken you both in. This is just like her: to fall for a hopeless impostor. In fact, they are perfectly suited. I've no doubt she's mostly to blame herself. Is it any wonder, the way she wastes herself on books, that she imagines one day Lord Byron himself has come to woo her?'

'I don't see why you should take this line. You are worse than your mother, giving yourself airs. Just because you *get about* in society. I tell you frankly, I dislike this manner; you should correct it. Why shouldn't she catch his eye?' And then he added, to show he was a realist himself, that he saw things squarely, 'which, as for that, is hardly rumoured to be the most discriminating. She says, you danced with him yourself.'

'I did, three years ago. Before he left for France, for Italy, God knows where. Never to return.'

'Just so. He particularly wishes her, she tells me, to keep his presence a secret. A trust I have now broken.' But the false hurt honour of his tone effected its own persuasion. The whole thing looked so shabby and plain through his daughter's eyes. So obvious: he couldn't quite shake off her view of it. What a pair they were, Liza and he; their shameful *willingness* to be flattered, to be taken in, struck him for the first time. And he said, in a very different voice, with his chin in one hand, 'What shall we do now?'

'How far has it gone?' Her father said nothing, helplessly; he didn't know. 'If he's touched her,' she said, 'I'll see he's hanged for it.'

CHAPTER FIFTEEN

ELIZA HAD SO OFTEN DREAMED of being in love, dreamed practically, as it were, in great detail, about particular men – how they looked at her and the promises they made – that when she awoke happy with a pale sunrise on her lap, for an instant she felt the little coming-down that always followed these dreams. The gradual return of her illusionless life. How much sweeter, then, the second surge of reflection, which reminded her that Lord Byron had met her father and been approved of, had charmingly accompanied them on their Sunday promenade. That she had kissed him at last, to his pleased surprise – had risen on tiptoe and taken his face in her hands, outside her father's cottage. She lay in bed warming those hands in the sunshine and delaying, minute after minute, the start of her ordinary day.

In a moment, she would rise and dress the children and bring them downstairs to be fed. She would present them to their grandmother at breakfast. It was then she could snatch an instant's solitude, to eat whatever the cook had saved for her meal. After that, the lessons would begin, leaving no respite in sight but tea till the end of her day. Still, as she pushed off the covers at last and sat up in bed, with all the common pains of waking, she was conscious that her life had been altered, irretrievably; conscious too that it might end in heartbreak, and that, at least as she saw the affair in her present uplifted mood, she wouldn't regret it if it did. She couldn't, in any case, go on as she had been going.

By noon a shadow had fallen over the happiness in which she'd awoken. Not so much as a morning's pleasant recollection of the previous day had been granted to her. Lady Walmsley, when Eliza presented the children, said that Mrs Simons had sent a note to say that she would be calling at eleven, and wished to see her sister in private. Lady Walmsley sat up comfortably in her own bed. Eliza, at her nod, stooped to the side-table to present her with the dish of tea, which her querulous hand uncertainly accepted. At another nod, Eliza retrieved it and returned it. A heap of papers lay on that half of the bed which had in the past been intermittently occupied by her husband. Lady Walmsley, who was fond of repeating amiable sentiments, expressed how delightful it must be for Miss Esmond to have so attentive a sister; what a blessing it was. And Eliza, who understood the purpose of these repetitions, their gentle insistence on her continuous state of gratitude, bowed her head. Lady Walmsley said that she didn't mind if they 'had the library to themselves', and that Miss Esmond mustn't forget to tell Cook to prepare something 'suitably refreshing' for Mrs Simons – who, poor dear, was only just recovered from her cold.

For the rest of the morning Eliza worried over what Bea was going to say. She suspected at once that Bea was coming to 'spoil everything', though why it lay in her sister's interest or power to do so, Eliza couldn't guess. Hopewell and Caroline sensed their governess's distraction. And it was among the things that frightened Eliza, about her own state of mind, that they had picked up something of her tremulous susceptibility, to the surges and retreats of happiness, and behaved themselves with a respectful decorum that was always on the verge of lapsing into tears. By the time Beatrice arrived, 'with the wind behind her', as their mother used to say, in the rush of her own importance, Eliza had already got her hackles up; and not the least of her sources of irritation was the freedom Beatrice assumed in her use of Lady Walmsley's house. She sent the cook down twice, first to steam her cup of hot milk again, and then to add another spoon of honey to it. Beatrice had decided to adopt, for the purpose of persuasion, the role of the put-upon sister dragged out of her sick-bed to set things right.

The interview got off on the wrong foot. The library was really more of a storehouse for whatever Lady Walmsley disliked among the objects her husband had left behind on his death. Their marriage was not an intimate one, and, as the weaker party in it, Lord Walmsley had taken to travel to relieve the monotony of home-life. His collection of weapons, ornamental and practical, which he had picked up in the Levant, was part of his sly revenge on a wife who greeted his homecomings with the chill of immaculate propriety. Most of them were considerably rusted now; but they served to prop up the heavy-bound volumes of parliamentary and Roman history that Walmsley had bought, as a single lot, from the remnants of the sale of the Alfred Club, of which he had been a founding member – another guerrilla sally in their matrimonial warfare. It was a gloomy, dusty, odorous room, that smelt of unwashed men and damp leather. Two tall windows looked over the gardens at the back, but these were partly obscured by the drapery of curtains (which were drawn neither at night nor in the morning, and had begun to sag) and the trunk of a tall beech tree, which rose with dark magnificence between them. A walnut card table, ruined by water-marks, had been pushed against the pane of one of them, with a chair on each side; and there the sisters sat. Eliza, after a while, took some comfort from the velvet thickness of the curtains, against which she pressed her cheek and ear, hoping to drown out half of what Beatrice was saying.

But she began more sharply. Eliza complained that Bea mustn't boss the servants around, as she often depended on their kindness and was in no position to give herself airs. Bea waited for her cup of hot milk to arrive, thanked the girl who brought it with cruel exaggeration, and then, after a sip, shot out, 'Now tell me at once, I must know, how far it has gone.'

Eliza pretended not to understand her.

Bea continued regardless, 'I meant to come earlier, but I wanted to speak with a lawyer. I supposed even *you* couldn't make any trouble before eleven o'clock in the morning. And I wanted to know if we had a criminal case – if it comes to that. Mr Wilmot assures me that we *may*, but this depends a good deal on just what was said and done. On what he called the *nice particulars*. Or rather, the *not so nice*.'

Eliza felt already the awful closing in of everybody else and their opinions – a sensation not unlike the pressure on the brain in high weather, before a storm. She yawned, out of nerves; but had the cheek to stretch it out luxuriously. 'I suppose,' she said, 'it's simply a matter of jealousy. He's very handsome, of course; but there's something irresistibly charming in the idea of playing one's part, you know, in his inspirations. You can't bear to see me preferred, especially when you missed your chance at him yourself.'

Her sister leaned forward and took Eliza's hand. 'I haven't come to be silly.' She paused a moment – Eliza could feel that she didn't mean to let go of her. And then began again, 'But I want to hear you say whom you mean, out loud. So that *you* hear what it sounds like; so that we both do.'

Eliza stubbornly bit her bottom lip. 'I won't give in to you this time,' she said.

'Will you say it?'

'No.' But even she felt the weakness of her position; either course involved a kind of concession, but she had chosen the worse. Not to admit his name seemed childish – a child clutching a lie to her heart by keeping silent. Better to brazen it out; and yet Eliza knew that once she said *his* name whatever had happened, whoever he was, would be exposed to the full force of her sister's *common-sense*. Bea looked at herself in the window. She confessed to herself that she performed these sisterly duties not without pleasure; but she took consolation in the thought, that it was only the pleasure of doing good which moved her. Her fine colouring had returned, and in the grey light – it was a messy, windy morning outside, not entirely sunless – her pink cheeks had a particular vividness, which pleased her.

Eliza, looking at her, could not help but admire her sister. She knew that men mistook Bea's loveliness – the small-headed tilt to her long neck, her large eyes and childish features, still soft, it seemed, with being formed – for sympathy, for invitation. But her beauty was only the efficient instrument of her hard will. Only her brown teeth, which she hid as well as she could beneath reddened lips, gave away her age and something humble in her birth.

Bea, warming her hands on the cup, had turned to look out the window. In a different tone, she said, 'I remember how much kindness, a sort of clever, *careful* kindness, was required, simply to dance with him. He was terribly embarrassed of his foot. As we waltzed, I had to press my hip against his; we swung our legs around together. But you couldn't on any account reveal that you knew what you were doing. He would have walked off, or rather limped off, at once. One felt – mothering towards him, I remember that well. It surprised me. I had expected to feel something much more thrilling. I was practically a girl at the time, just barely a mother myself; but the first thing I wanted *from* him, was to look *after* him. Not that we didn't tease each other. His manner was quite perfect, gentlemanly and engaging. But what made it still sweeter was, that one guessed the pains it cost him, to please. He had his mind on other things. He inquired, very attentively, of little Louisa. He had a daughter, too, he said. There was nothing he liked better, he said, than the *weight* of a daughter, in one's arms.'

Eliza, softening, said, 'There is something like a woman in him, but without that air of *show*, that women put on.'

155

Bea gave her a look, and continued, 'He told me that he was having his tailor make up a cushion to the exact heft of his little girl, filled with eiderdown, rosemary buds and grain, and that he planned to take it with him on his travels, and lift it in his arms whenever he missed her. The tailor, he said, had offered to make up a dummy of his *wife* as well, stuffed with virtues and potatoes and thistles, he supposed. An offer, which, on reflection, he had decided to decline. I remember flirting with him shamefully. *If only you had married me, my lord,* I told him, *I shouldn't have minded who you brought to our bed.* He replied, I might have married almost anyone but *her* I did. Not that it mattered any more, he added. England had had enough of him. He had had enough of England.' And then, leaning forward, she took Eliza's hand in both of hers. Eliza felt how warm and moist they were still from her cup of hot milk; how cold her own had become. She was almost bloodless. 'How long have you known this . . . impostor?' Bea asked, and repeated, 'How far has it gone?'

Eliza wriggled free of her sister. 'He said, he did not remember you.' Eliza was lying now, and this fact upset her as much as anything else. 'I described you in great detail. I said, a very cold-hearted woman, with a mean face and a common-looking husband.' Eliza had always had terrible tempers, a foul tongue. She turned horribly spiteful when denied; her face seemed made for spite, too, narrow and sharp, with that stubborn sulking and fat bottom lip. It was a part of the tenderness with which she was treated, by her father and sister, that these tantrums were dismissed as more of her childishness, quite harmless. 'She was once a lovely girl, but lost her looks with motherhood. Still, she can't bear to be outshone, and clutches, in every ball, at the nearest single gentleman, begging him to flirt with her. Lord Byron,' it was the first time she had confessed his name, and the sound of it gave her a blushing courage, 'admitted, that he was used to the attention of unhappy mothers. It seemed to him only charitable, to make a little love to them.'

Beatrice was accustomed to her sister's tirades, which in fact left Eliza more miserable afterwards than anyone else. Bea stood up, and briefly checked her appearance in the window. Behind her face, she saw a boy hold down a rose-bush in the wind; the gardener clipped it. The wind repeatedly tugged at the thorny branches and let go. A cherry-tree had blossomed and shed a few petals on the paving. She was thankful, after all, with age, to spare more attention for the world, to spend less on herself. It is true, she was happier than Eliza, she must show pity. 'I can't help you,' she said, 'if you won't confide in me. I shall have a word with Lady Walmsley, tell her to keep a sharp watch – on you.' And then, taking Eliza's head in her hands and holding fast, 'I know what ideas you get. I know how you suffer, living as you do. I feel it – here,' and she let go, and pressed her hand against her breast. 'How nothing compares to the life you lead in your books. You're as bad as Father. You want everything to turn out as you imagine it. You must learn to make do.' And then she gave in to the need to explain herself, to defend her principles, for her mother's remembered sake, for their part in the old family argument. Eliza had touched her nearer the quick than she let on. 'What you don't see is that practical-minded people find as much to love in each other as any hot-headed dreamers. The captain and I . . .' but she thought that Eliza was weeping, and added more gently, 'I promise to take you in hand. I'll find you a suitable young man.'

But Eliza had only bent her head in rage; she was angry at her own silence, as much as anything else. 'I should like a soldier, perhaps; I've never cared for the navy.'

Bea lost patience at last. 'Even if Lord Byron himself fell head over heels in love with you, what good could come of it? You haven't any position in society; you daren't risk the scandal. You don't, for God's sake, think he'd marry you?'

'What does it matter, what good comes of anything, really?' Eliza asked, looking up. Bea's assurance had a way of hushing her, but she was glad, for once, of having said just what she meant. How much she disliked her sister's efficiency: the intimate collusion of her ends and means.

'Oh, it matters, it matters.' She rang the bell and waited for someone to come. They stood awkwardly for a minute in silence, until the door opened, and the maid put her head round it. 'Ask Lady Walmsley if I might have a word with her,' Bea said. And then added, 'thank you, my dear.' Remembering to be kind, for her sister's sake, to the servants.

That night, Eliza turned again to her books. She picked up the third volume of *Childe Harold's Pilgrimage* and ran her finger over the publisher's mark: John Murray, Albemarle-Street, 1816. The leather of the binding had the smell of a man's hand; the pages, faintly discoloured, shifted under her breath.

> Is thy face like thy mother's, my fair child!
> Ada! Sole daughter of my house and heart?
> When last I saw thy young blue eyes they smiled,
> And then we parted, – not as now we part,
> But with a hope.

Strange, that he hadn't mentioned his daughter. It worried her a little, what Lord Byron had confessed to Bea about the 'weighted cushion': it had the ring of truth, of his voice, a tenderness whose overtone was irony. It suggested an intimacy she had not yet surprised him into. And she realized that what had upset her most about her sister's insistent question (how far had things gone?) is that they hadn't yet gone far enough. Nothing had been done that could not be undone again. If only she had some great irreparable sin to lay claim to, to silence their fussing, to put herself beyond the pale. To bind him to her.

Her father had stopped by in the evening. Lady Walmsley had never met him. She was pointedly charming; she said, 'I've told Eliza a hundred times, I'd like to meet you. We've become rather dependent on each other. I think of her quite as a daughter.' None of it was true – Mr Esmond was being coddled into taking *their* side. Yet even Eliza was flattered by her insincerity; perhaps she wasn't as forlorn a creature as she believed herself to be. Father and daughter took a turn in the garden. A high moon rode between the trees. It was cold when the wind gathered weight, but they had the warmth of each other, until Eliza abruptly inquired, 'So, has she persuaded you?'

'Your sister,' he began, but she let go of his arm and broke in, 'You can't have forgotten his charms, so soon. *The acquaintance of poets.*'

'Your sister has made me sensible of my duties, as a father. You and I, my dear, have let our enthusiasms run away with us, again.' And then, more bitterly: 'I do as I'm told. Perhaps it's for the best, this once, you do the same.'

'Has it made you happy?' she asked.

As she lay in bed, she hardened her heart once more against the unkindness of that last remark. 'You have a cruel tongue,' he'd told her, taking firm hold of her hand, which she had tried to wrench from him again. 'Everyone is *grabbing* at me,' she'd shouted. 'I don't want to be *touched* any more.' She needed to break free at last from her cramped innocence; she couldn't *breathe* in it. What had her father said earlier? . . . that he was too afraid of putting himself in the wrong?

She sat up, with quick decision, and kicked the covers away; sleeplessness had made her palms and feet sweat. Under her bed, she kept a writing-box with pen and paper in it. She searched for it on her knees, then brought it out and set it on her bed. Still on her knees, she began to write, feeling entirely practical and clear-headed – not so much passionate as conscious of taking a *decisive step*. This was

CHAPTER SIXTEEN

I T WAS DAYLIGHT WHEN POLIDORI AWOKE. He'd dreamed in his sleep of the wind's kicking up. The rattle of a sash window in its block had obtruded itself upon these dreams. Someone was trying to get in. In his dreams, he woke fitfully, and disturbed by the noise, rose to look out the window. Streets and houses had disappeared, and in their place, the prospect below him of a wide unsettled sea hardly surprised him. He tried to make out the horizon, but thunder clouds had cast their entrails into the water, and all he could see was the light shot through them. No land in sight. Lord Byron, he knew, in spite of his adventurous pride, was a poor sailor; he would suffer heavily if it came on to blow. And Polly considered what physic to make up for his relief, and then, a little spitefully, turned over in bed to sleep more. Well, let him suffer, too; there was time enough in the morning to play doctor. When the banging continued, he had the guilty but not unpleasant sense of being demanded, of putting somebody important off.

The knocking at the door brought him at last to his senses. God, he had needed that rest. He tried to guess the time and felt the luxury of being able to go back to sleep, if he liked, straight through the day again and into another morning. Was there anything to get him out of bed? He knew how late he'd got *into* it; and the memory of that ushered in others, less comfortable to him. 'I'm ruined,' he thought; and when the banging persisted, called out, irritably, 'For God's sake, what time is it?'

'Almost three, sir.' A young man's voice, respectful, common enough, but unembarrassed.

'Who are you?'

'Jeb Willis, sir. I've been sent –'

'What do you want?'

'I've been sent by Miss Eliza Esmond. She was very particular I deliver it straight to your hands.'

'Deliver what?' Polly called out, as he got up to answer the door. Was the feeling that rose in him, at the mention of her name, more shameful or loving? What an odd mixture the two made – how strangely they enhanced each other. A memory, suddenly, returned to him, a fragment from the wreck of the day before: Eliza standing on childish tiptoe to kiss him, the sidelong nudge of her nose against his. Another gift of credit he couldn't make good on. His power of disappointing her inspired in Polidori great tenderness; he knew what it was to be disappointed.

Mr Willis was a burly young man with freckles that had begun to thicken into blotches. He gave Polidori a small envelope, sealed with the initials E. E. Polidori, thanked him and moved to shut the door. 'Expecting an answer,' Willis said. So Polly sat down on his bed and began to read.

My dear Lord,

I did not, as you know, expect you to love me; yet much to my surprise, more to my happiness, you betrayed passions I had believed no longer alive in your bosom. Have you then any objection to the following plan? On Tuesday evening we may go out of town together by some stage or mail about the distance of ten or twelve miles. There we shall be free and unknown; we can return early the following morning.

  They are trying to keep me from you; but I shan't be kept any longer. I am being constantly watched; and shall appear before you, if you accept my offer, disguised. Your honour is safe; rely on me to approach you at the appointed

hour. I shall ever remember the gentleness of your manners and the wild originality of your countenance. My
happiness is in your hands. I will be waiting at seven
o'clock, tomorrow evening, at the Bull & Mouth, 40,
Regent Circus, Piccadilly.

Ever thine,
ELIZA ESMOND

Poor, foolish girl, he thought; what a pair we are. And he
smiled: how perfectly suited. Then he remembered that
Willis was waiting for him. 'She is,' the boy began, more hesitantly, 'she is a most kind-hearted lady, and much put-
upon. Have you anything to reply, sir?'

'Tell her, yes,' Polidori said.

He had a night and a day to wonder at himself. After Willis
left, Polidori finished the ruby dregs of laudanum in the
glass vial, and tried to sleep again. He took it as a sign of
good luck, of constitutional revival, that he managed to
recompose himself. He awoke this time in a stream of
morning sunshine, feeling light-headed and refreshed. He'd
hardly eaten in three days; starvation, he reflected, suited
him, and he remembered his spirited boast to Henry
Colburn: 'I eat the air'. It was one of Lord Byron's favourite
lines.

He washed and dressed, with greater than usual attention, and decided to go out. A fine, brisk day, sunshiny,
where even the shadows of the clouds had a black brightness to them and cast illumination. The air, spring-cold,
was very clear and rich to breathe. He wandered along
Regent's Street and took pleasure in the sight of the shops
and the gentlemen shopping. It was only a question of how
to tell her, that he couldn't go. It was only a question of
breaking the news, gently and confidentially. This was the
trouble; he didn't want to compromise her position. He
stopped off at The Nose Bag for a pint of porter, and lis-

tened, with real pleasure, to a pair of bucks betting over a game of vingt-un. For a minute he was tempted to join in, but he had no money in his pocket. He was also surprised by how perfectly the role of mere observer had satisfied him. It was time he got his affairs in order. He knew now, with final certainty, that he would never write another word. He'd known such conviction before, of course, and understood himself well enough to suspect above all his sense of *certainty*. But the relief he felt, at the thought of giving up – his ambitions, everything – made him want to justify this intuition with a decisive act. Colburn had once pointed out to him a money-lender named Nathan, who lived off Oxford Street, in the basement flat of a vivid green town-house. A very reasonable Jew. Expensive, true, but what mattered more was, he understood an Englishman's sense of *honour*. He didn't kick up too much fuss about the forms.

Polly, feeling pleasantly busy, decided to search him out. Finding the house gave him a little surge of satisfaction, on the strength of which he managed to convince Mr Nathan (a surprisingly florid young man, straight-backed, with large familiar hands) to lend him two hundred pounds, at one hundred per cent interest annually, on the security of his father's name. Barred sunshine made its way into Nathan's front parlour; Polly sat with his back to it, trying to read the terms spread out on a round table. He had to push his chair over – his shoulder was blocking the light – and then he forged his father's signature, without a second thought, on the deed of loan. Nathan, licking his thumb, counted out the money. 'On a day like this,' he said, 'I like to keep the door open to let the air in.' Polly set a loose volume on the signed paper, which was threatening to blow away. A copy of *The Vampyre*, he noted: another good omen, another shot of pleasure. 'I can see by the way you look at the book you're an admirer,' Nathan said. 'Though to my taste, not one of his finest. My uncle is a good friend of the author. He set some of his poems to music.'

'Indeed?' Polly said.

He asked to borrow an envelope and a sheet of note-paper. 'My dear Colburn,' he wrote, 'I hereby discharge my debts to you. Your servant, P.' After he'd dropped off the sum – he didn't wait to see if Colburn was in – it was almost time to meet Eliza at the coach-station. He didn't have anything else to do; and there was still a hundred pounds left in the envelope he carried inside his light coat.

He arrived at The Bull & Mouth ten minutes late. A very mixed crowd loitered outside the Western Coach Office. A thirst for travel, he reflected, brought together a stranger assortment of men than the other, simpler thirst being satisfied at the public house. There was a mother, well-dressed, taking leave of a small boy. She held the hem of her skirts in one hand and gave him a faint embrace: clearly, anxious to be gone; the press of people upset her nerves. On her way out, she unfolded from her sleeve a scented hand-kerchief and began to breathe through it. The boy, happily enough, sat on his school-satchel and peeled an apple. There were two young men setting forth together in sleep-less high spirits. They pitched their banter above the general noise, making a great display of affection. It was only a sense of their tenderness, the embarrassment of it, which occasionally hushed them. The family of a vicar, a short, slope-shouldered gentleman with a moley complexion, sat in little heaps on the makeshift furniture of their portable belongings. Their father was warming a glass of ale in his hands.

The loose wind in the course of the day had blown away the clouds; the heavens were high and clear. A hundred stars burned growing through the dusk. It was cold, too. A pair of drivers gathered at the bar to fill their flasks. Polly couldn't see Eliza. It struck him for the first time, how unhappy he would be if she didn't come. What he needed, he decided, was a nip of something, to keep up his spirits;

and as he waited for the attention of the bar-man, he felt a boy jostle him, and was about to push back when he saw who it was. 'I've only just managed to escape them,' Eliza said breathlessly. 'I've only just got away.' She wore a page's costume. Her faded hair was bunched and hidden under a peaked cap; a high ruffed collar flowered around the narrow branch of her neck. The cut of her trousers and the little fawn tunic dressed her in straight lines, like a boy: from her shoulders to her hips to her shoes. Her breasts were hidden in the loose hang of it, and Polly found nothing so tantalizing as the small secret of them. He wanted, comically, to reach out his hand and make sure of them. She had never looked prettier, in fact, more feminine. Fine dresses, by contrast, emphasized only her boyishness; the uniform exposed, to a knowing eye, what was womanish in her, softer and unshaped. Lord Byron, Polidori remembered, had once expressed to him his delight in late girlhood, which combined, he said, the beauty of the boy and the woman. The doctor suspected him at the time of merely dressing up less palatable desires, and Polly himself still burned with shame at the recollection of an afternoon, when, in the wake of their master's ill-temper, he had covered the page-boy Rushton with a series of caresses, which encroached upon, and finally overstepped, the bounds of comforting. Yet now he saw the simpler truth of Byron's claim: how delightful it was, innocently, to play with desires one could not explore so fully and clear-headed in their guiltier enjoyment.

Eliza, looking up, said to him, 'My lord, where will you take me?' Her pupils, he saw, had shrunk in the blue of her eyes. She was in high, feverish spirits. That stubbornness or disdainfulness which resided in her bottom lip, in the narrowing line of her jaw, and usually embittered her looks had been transformed into something appetitive and capable of delight. He guessed there was nothing she would stop short at, now; it was only his pity, or forbearance, or the failure of his desire, which could save her from ruin. But for the first time he suspected himself of a real attraction. She had gone quite mad with what she was willing to risk.

He said, 'Shall we make our escape?' At the coach-office, he bought two seats, inside, on the Brighton mail. They were harnessing the horses even then, and Polidori and Eliza had to push their way anxiously through the crowds in order to take their places. A comfortable-looking professional man with a bag of dried figs on his lap sat opposite Eliza. His face was very healthy and red, but mostly hidden in braids of white beard. He said, 'A kind master, who pays for his boy to ride below.' She smiled at him painfully, not yet trusting her voice. Polidori said, 'It's such a clear night, I guessed it would be cold.' There were four of them in the plush interior; already, the air was softening with their combined warmth. A plain square-jawed woman in a black bonnet – her plainness bespoke neither kindness nor cruelty, was in fact the absence of either quality – took out a ball of grey wool and began to knit. What a relief it was when they were off at last; Eliza, he could see, had half expected to be caught. Only after they were finally, snugly, settled (the unsteadiness of the coach pressed them helplessly into each other) and the road had dipped into the fields and woods south of the river, did they begin to feel the awkwardness of their situation. Even the friction of their silence, however, tended towards an increase of heat. Polly began to consider what they might do to each other when alone.

A gentle exchange of intimacies proved impossible given the confines of the carriage. They were both, in their ways, grateful for this fact: they hardly knew each other. Eliza was mindful of the woman's eyes upon her. They seemed to narrow with suspicion, and Eliza felt positively inflamed by the alternation within her of bravado and embarrassment. Of course, a woman would see through her at once. But then Eliza noticed her hands resting loosely on her lap in a tangle of wool, and realized she was only asleep. The gentleman with the figs followed soon after. His head fell back, leaving his mouth wide open; strands of his beard shifted in his noiseless breath. Polly bent to Eliza's ear and whispered, 'I suspected him for a snorer.' The tension in her was almost singing; she couldn't repress the snort of a giggle. But then, she looked for something suitable to answer in reply, lightly conspiratorial, and nothing came into her head. She could only think of his hand on his thigh which touched her own, from time to time, in the shift of the carriage. They both began to drift into and out of the shallow waters of a travelling sleep.

At midnight they stopped to change horses and stretch their legs. The skies were high and utterly cloudless; a moon on its back burned the colour of lit parchment. Polly, by nature of the roles assigned them in their masquerade, was forced to take the lead. 'Would you like a sip of something, Rushton?' he said. The name only then came into his head. He bought a bottle of scotch, and in the light of the carriage lamp, they passed it from hand to hand. In spite of the cold, the scent of fresh horse dung, not unpleasant, reached their breath. They were both particularly conscious of the slickness of the bottle-mouth, wet from each other's lips, as they raised it to their own. Polly opened the carriage-door and gave Eliza his hand, helping her onto the running board. He followed her inside. Their fellow travellers had not yet returned, and while Polly stooped to take his seat, they began to kiss, with an instant fierceness, that made it nearly impossible for them to recompose their breathing as Polly sat down and the red-faced gentleman clambered in behind him.

Eliza felt she could not bear the tension between them a minute longer; but the minute passed, and the driver returned, somewhat unsteadily, and whipped the fresh horses on their way. The bearded man offered around his bag of dried figs, which only the lady accepted. She chewed with a hard, practical thoroughness. Eliza watched the dimpling of muscle at the hinge of her jaw. But the pair of them were soon asleep again, and Polly passed the bottle of scotch, releasing it slowly, into her hands. Eliza, feeling the fire in her head and throat (she had never tasted whisky before), summoned the courage to ask Polidori a question. 'My lord,' she said, pitching her voice just above the rattle of the wheels, 'there has been something upsetting me.' Polly bent his ear to her mouth. As soon as she spoke she was conscious of the change in tone she was ushering in. Their conversation had not yet learned the intimacy of their hands and lips, but she continued nonetheless, and felt perhaps more easy and natural in this form of discourse than in the other. 'Last night, I re-read *The Vampyre*; the beauty of it moved me again to tears. You have, I am sure, never done anything finer. But I was struck again by how terribly sad it was and wondered why it seemed sadder to me than all of your other sad tales. Until it occurred to me that for once you take no pity on yourself – on your hero, I mean. For Conrad, for Lara, even for Harold, you show some forgiveness; but for Lord Ruthven, there is none. No pity at all; no sympathy. And I thought, the man who wrote this cannot be happy. The man who wrote this is living without hope.' Polly at once saw his chance, to explain himself fully – to a woman he'd lied to and was beginning to care for. Fully, that is, in his own roundabout fashion, and conscious of the risk he was taking.

They were both now perfectly awake, in that tender sleeplessness which survives the first drowsiness of the evening, and grows stronger and more expansive after midnight. The rattle of the wheels, the night-sounds, the canter of the horses' hoofs and their thick animal breaths, the intimate mutter of the coachman, cast a kind of veil over their conversation; and they had small fear now of rousing their companions. 'I have a confession to make,' Polly began, and then paused to summon his thoughts. 'Three years ago, as you know, I left this country – for good, I believed at the time. You came yourself, you said, that early summer morning, to see us off. You stood in the shadows of Piccadilly Terrace and watched our balcony. There, you saw a young man emerge, wearing a black coat and a white cravat, under a high collar. You supposed him to be Lord Byron; it was then, you said, you fell in love with me. In fact, that young man was' – he paused a moment, if only to take his leave, in passing, of a chance he acknowledged but would not grasp – 'my physician. I was inside, enjoying the consolations of . . . my sister. But the resemblance has often been remarked upon; we might have been brothers.'

They had reached the end of a long incline, and just at the beginning of descent the woods fell away on either side, and Eliza and Polidori could see the darkened farmland below them, with the flat shine of a river laid across it like the off-cut of a ribbon. He looked at her closely, to catch a trace of suspicion; but in her wide eyes was only the pity of adoration. 'I have been the ruin of that young man,' Polly said. '*The Vampyre* is an account of what he has suffered for my sake. I have come back now to make amends; but he refuses to see me, and his family have turned me from their door.'

As the hours and miles unrolled, lightening, and the cold of midnight gave way to the chill of dawn, Polidori began to tell what he called 'the true story of the vampyre'. After the heartbreak of his separation from his wife, and more particularly, from his daughter, 'whom I have not seen to this day' (Eliza nodded at this, with an expression of sympathy only just shaded by relief), he decided to leave England behind. His friends persuaded him to pay for the accompaniment of a physician, to watch over him in a general way, for neither his physical nor mental rectitude could be relied on. His legal adviser recommended a young man named Polidori – the son of an Italian émigré – who had lately come down from Edinburgh. His knowledge of the language 'and the warm endorsement of my sister' proved decisive, and together they set forth for the continent.

Their relations from the first suffered from an inevitable strain. Polidori was a young man of great spirit, but little common-sense; he balked continually at his dependent role. 'Perhaps,' Polly confessed to Eliza, 'it was my duty to relieve the worst of the injuries sustained by his self-love. I tried to tease him, affectionately, into a more sensible view of himself; I called him Dori, or Polly-dolly, to make him feel easy in my company, perfectly at home. What he wanted, however, was not my affection. It was my esteem. He had ambitions as a poet, a playwright, and after our good-nights, was always slipping a sheaf of MS under my bed-room door. The worst of it is, he was a man of good parts, honourable and loving, who might, in other circumstances, have made a name for himself. Yet something laughable about him could not be denied. *So oft it chances in particular men*, as Hamlet has it, *that for some vicious mole or fault in nature*, etc. *His* was peculiar; I could never, quite, put my finger on it. He had a kind of foolishness that turned everything it touched into nonsense. How he made me laugh! His chief talent, I once told him, was in making himself ridiculous. Putting himself in the wrong. *Their virtues else, be they as pure as grace* . . . You know the rest. In my own defence, I was less cruel than my companions, who used to cut him up rather fiercely. His damned poesies in particular. Perhaps they were jealous of him, too. But it could not be denied, he was always getting himself into scrapes. And after several months of this, I grew weary – of getting him *out* again. I gave him his congé.'

'There is nothing in that, my lord, for which you need reproach yourself.'

'No.' The first ghost of dawn had crept across the horizon; and in its light their faces appeared to each other pale and distinct, lined with sleeplessness. How familiar they were after all! or so it seemed to them. Their tired looks offered a

171

confession of the ordinary and material self that each found comforting in the other. The tension of the night before had eased away as quietly as soda in water and left behind it this flat loving-kindness. The horses were flagging, too. The beat of their hoofs had slowed with just a tease of irregularity in it to occupy the ear as they struggled up the last sharp hill before the descent into Brighton. 'The worst is to come,' Polidori said. The doctor, he continued, had a sister named Frances. She had recently married an Italian gentleman, a Mr Rossetti, who had accepted a position as the English consul in Milan. 'Polidori spoke of Frances with a fondness verging on regret, and used to describe her to me in loving detail.' Her looks, in which the liveliness of the 'warm south' had been combined with the gentler elegance of the north, to great effect; her sharp tongue and wit; her warm heart always overflowing. 'It was, he often said to me, strange proof of our own fraternal resemblance: our unembarrassed attachment to our sisters. Among his reasons for accepting the post of physician was the opportunity it afforded him to see her again. Polidori frankly confessed, he had been dead against her marriage. After we . . . parted company, he said to me, that he was almost glad of the chance to set off at once towards Milan.'

Polidori, as he spoke, remembered again the misery of those days. Lord Byron had settled their accounts honourably. He was always generous with money, and had included in the final sum a private gift towards the purchase of a watch. The Genevans, after all, were famous for their time-keeping. Even so, Byron refused to come down to see him off; Polly found him skulking in bed. His lordship always hated being left behind. He much preferred, as he put it, 'taking the *leave* himself'. Polidori planned to cross the Alps on foot and set off in a late-morning haze. His ankle had never properly healed, and by dinner-time it had swelled around the bone into a violent red, fleshy and indistinct lump. Not that he'd prepared any sustenance for his journey, consoling himself with the familiar refrain: 'I eat the air.' Every mile or two, when the pain in his foot grew too great, he sat down in the grass to weep. The influx of childishness, at least, afforded him some relief. Whenever the mountain road took him past some precipitate edge, he had to crawl along the ground with his hands on the inward slope. He had no particular fear of heights, but was terrified, rather, of giving in to temptation.

'That autumn,' he continued, 'I did in fact take up residence in Milan; it was only natural that our paths should cross again. Polidori was staying at his sister's house and seemed determined to flatter me into engaging him, on the old terms. I could see how unhappy he was. Whenever the doctor was unhappy, he forgot to eat. And the lines of his skull stood out till he looked like some repentant devil, staring through the bars at Paradise. Rather handsome in his way.' Polidori, searching for the response in Eliza's eyes, continued: 'I was perfectly pleasant to him, but explained that I didn't want a doctor I had to nurse myself. But the young man was growing desperate, and, by way of binding us together again, began to *put me in the way* of his sister, more and more – who, to be fair, was a very charming and agreeable girl, with rough patrician features of the kind I always admire. We shared a box at the Teatro alla Scala; sat beside each other at a farewell dinner given in honour of di Breme. She offered to translate for me some letters, original and amatory, between Lucrezia Borgia and Cardinal Bembo; I was absolutely enchanted by the Ambrosian Library. And she – delighted by her powers of enchanting. It wasn't my fault she fell in love. Polidori, in the event, proved right about her husband: a handsome, gracious man, but there was a chill about him, the deep chill in which you can hardly feel yourself shiver. That's how Frances put it to me; she saw how cold she'd grown only when a little warmth returned. But Polly could not forgive himself for the way Frances was channelling all her youthful unhappiness into this . . . infatuation. Her passion knew no bounds, lacked all discretion. And I, I – always alight on the nearest perch. (I mean to show you as I really am. I mean to warn you against me.)' Eliza, at this point, turned away and began to stare out the window. She watched a grove of birches approach, and then, by degrees, come to a standstill beside them. The driver had stopped the horses. Her first mad thought was, they had been caught at last, thank God.

But the horses had only tired on the slow ascent; the coachman, too weary either to bully or beg, simply requested his passengers to walk the rest of the hill. The square-jawed lady took exception, and was chivvied along, genially, by the man with flowing moustaches. Polidori began to involve himself in their conversation. It was always a sign of happiness in him, when he trusted his powers of persuasion. The woman – 'a widow,' she complained, 'twice over!' – was beginning slowly to fold the knitting, which had draggled over her lap, when Polly noticed that Eliza was gone. He left the gentleman to hand her down, and stepped out. Dawn, he could tell, was breaking somewhere below them on the far side of the hill. The sunlight made the trees crowning it burn blackly. Then he saw a narrow figure hurrying along the side of the road, and ran to catch up with her. The air was very sweet and thick with coldness. He filled his lungs; the chase, the nervous tenderness with which he approached her from behind, contributed to his sense of that awakening strength whose name is joy. And yet he tasted even then, like a trace of blood, the bitterness of revenge in his high spirits. Against whom? for what?

Eliza, he could see, had been weeping; she shook off his arm when he tried to seize it. 'You asked me,' he said, 'why I took no pity on myself.' And then he repeated, 'I mean to show you as I really am.'

On one side of the road, a triangle of woodland fell away into the crease of a river, which ran into a cluster of farm-buildings and out again through the fields. On their right, a shelf of flat land had been sewn with grain, waist high already and chattering like insects in the dawn wind. The emptied carriage trotted past them, and Eliza could see behind her the loose string of passengers making their way on foot to the summit. She said, with a thin vein of pride at her own courage pulsing in her, through her more general heart-break, 'I will hear everything out.' She stepped into the grain-field. The dew dripped visibly along the stalks and wet her shoes. He had to run to keep up.

Polidori said, 'Polidori began to regret the affair; he saw it could only make Frances unhappy. Rossetti was not the man to overlook his – rights. Worse still, Polly was jealous of Frances; of her attachment to me. Of my attachment to her. They were very fond of each other as children; and the fond-ness had survived their growing up, without quite finding a new language for its expression. He used to surprise us at all times. The Rossettis had a wonderful terraced garden, with an alcove built into the hill away from the house: perfectly cool on a hot day. I used to sit and write there, translating, and Frances would join me. If you opened the door, you could see their vineyard falling away, and the river behind it. There was only a table in it, a low couch. We had become . . . indiscreet. Though to be fair, by October, the weather had turned, and the room was too cold to sit in for long, without a little shared heat, a little exertion. Polidori discovered us there one day, in the midst of this; his sister saw him first, and stopped. I – I confess, made a gesture with my free hand, which he perhaps took as a sign of invitation. And he, to his everlasting shame, I believe, stepped towards us, hopefully, until Frances, wrapping her dress around her waist, moved to shut the door against him. But I had grown tired of Milan already. Frances had lost all sense of restraint; and in the first week of November, I shifted ground to Venice. Afterwards, I heard, through various channels, that she had given birth to a boy. Perfectly charming and healthy; only, perhaps, too much his *father's son*, for them to sustain for very long the conjugal illusion. Rossetti has now cast her out, both mother and child. I came back to London to take on myself . . . the burden of his education.' They walked on in silence; and when he tried to take her hand, she permitted it, so limply, however, that he let go of her again.

He remembered every detail of the scene. How he saw his sister's arm, and the soft outline of her breast, before he saw her face. The little involuntary stirring that preceded recognition. Lord Byron, wearing only his shirt unbuttoned to the navel, seemed very casually to possess her; she, on the other hand, looked helpless with unhappiness. Byron had no sense of shame, of his own exposure. He slowly turned over his palm, as if to show, he had nothing to hide, come in. And it struck Polidori now for the first time how neatly their positions described the difference between them: Lord Byron's free enjoyment of the world, of his sister; Polly's more intimate constraint. The one, inside; the other, looking in. Polidori dared not taste what he desired; and he remembered, that long-ago summer morning, Augusta answering the door in her swelling négligé. Then the low, sweet laughter coming from the poet's bedroom, while Polly stood in the balcony doorway, listening. There was nothing in life Lord Byron would not try, whereas he was everywhere hemmed in by . . . what? by pieties – a word that conjured up again his father's warning: the force of impossible comparisons. 'Now you know the worst of me,' he said.

'What did they say to you?' Eliza had shrunk within herself. She walked with her head inclined, almost paralysed by fear: the thought of what she had put herself at the mercy of.

'Who?'

'Her family.'

Polidori wondered what their response would be – to Lord Byron, if by any chance he came to beg forgiveness at their door. What Gaetano would say to him . . . Polly could hardly repress a rueful smile. No doubt his father would invite the poet to stay for dinner, but the son at least took his chance of describing a sharper, more appropriate response. 'They would not admit me; they would not open the door.' The saying of it released a flood of high feeling in him. 'They refused even to address me by name.' She nodded with returning sympathy at his emotion, misunderstanding the source of it. 'And what became of the doctor?' she asked at length.

'Dead, by his own hand.' And he repeated, sardonically, 'That is the true story of the vampyre.'

They had reached the crown of the hill, where the coach was waiting. Below them they saw in the glory of sunrise a town glittering at the edge of a vaster shimmer: the spread of the sea. The other passengers lagged some way behind them, and the driver was busy feeding his horses from a sack he had tucked into his belt. Both Eliza and Polidori were conscious of the murmur of his professional affection, the modest and ordinary undertone of their grand romance. She rubbed the stickiness from her eyes with the palms of her hands, and turned around to look at Polidori. Her misery was the misery of a child: resolvable, he saw at once. She said, in a haughty voice quite unlike her own fretful and companionable manner, 'Man marks the earth with ruin – his control stops at the shore.' He recognized the line, one of Byron's, and continued more simply: 'Upon the watery plain, the wrecks are all thy deed, nor doth remain a shadow of man's ravage save his own.' She sighed, heavily, with false deliberation, and fashioned for him a look of painful sweetness. 'Last night,' she said, 'as I rested against your shoulder, I thought: I have never been happier in my life. And now I know: I will never be happy again.'

'Liza,' he murmured, 'my dear child.'

The wind was salty and fresh, coming over the sea; they both had a touch of high colour over the pallor of sleeplessness. Cold, too, in a careless way; with the promise of more cold behind it. 'I want you to know,' she said, 'that I forgive you.' She was blushing now, conscious of her presumption, of assuming her rights over a man. Her statement had the force of a wedding vow. And she continued, 'There is something that matters more than happiness, more than virtue. And I have found it out, God help me.' By this time, the last of the stragglers had arrived; the horses were harnessed and ready. Polidori could not help reflecting, how young she was, still. The false note of her forgiveness awakened only his sense of her innocence. He was overwhelmed by the desire to protect what had been corrupted in him; a desire, which, paradoxically, teased him with sensual rewards. And she slept against him, trustful from sheer exhaustion, as their coach made its way into the city.

CHAPTER SEVENTEEN

T HEY ARRIVED OUTSIDE THE WHITE HART as the bells
of St Nicholas were tolling eight o'clock. The sea air,
heavy and sweet as fresh towels, gave a softer
rebound to the clangour. One felt everywhere the presence
of that flat expansion, the Atlantic. Gulls cried their scissor-
ing cry. Salt scarred the foundation stones of houses. Eliza
found, carefully descending on the strength of Polidori's
hand, that her two hours' nap had left her on the pleasant
side of sleepiness. And, as they turned a corner of the lane,
the angle of another alley gave a narrow glimpse of sea: a
pale white line, with the bluish grey of the water below, and
the greyish blue of the morning sky above. She clasped her
hands together and kissed her fingers and thought, smiling
a little at herself, I have forgotten already to be unhappy.

Years later, she remembered always the pleasantness of
the day they spent together. The town was small enough
they could take it in in a morning's perambulation. The sea
was still too cold for swimming; but they could look at it and
drink its waters, from a stall set up on the pebbles advertis-
ing 'Russell's Restoratives'. Polidori, hoping to show spirit,
bought a concoction of crab's eyes, snails, and tar, com-
pounded into a pill. He swallowed it with a pint of sea-
water, making a face. It made him feel, he said, as thirsty as
a fish; but he confessed that it bucked him up after their
sleepless journey. Eliza, retreating almost physically,
declined. From time to time when she fell quiet (they had
many hours to fill before the inevitable night), he whispered
to her that he could feel the snail still crawling inside him: a

flight of whimsy always rewarded by the shiver of her disgust.

A windless day. Even at eight in the morning, they sensed the gathering heat of it, and by noon, with the sun doubling off the water, Eliza became conscious of her own slick odours. She would have liked to remove her cap, but feared the tumble of girlish curls it would let loose. Only in the gardens of the Pavilion, behind a row of cherry trees, did she dare, for a minute, to shake her head free of its constraints, while Polidori took her neck in his hand and stooped to kiss her. She waited for him to finish and then carefully clipped the bunching of her hair on top and restored the cap. Not that she suffered his ardour in silence, but she felt, after his confession, and for the first time, sure of him; and this security had instantly suggested to her the more conventional role. She had the patience to tarry till the evening; though the thought of what awaited her then surprised in her, from time to time, a fit of trembling Polidori himself was too preoccupied, by his own growing expectations, to note.

He felt he had left everything behind him. His father, Frances, the debts of every kind he owed in London: filial and brotherly, financial, literary. Polidori wondered now why he had been so slow to fall in love. Eliza, it seemed to him, had the courage to confine herself to a life lived narrowly in her imagination. She wasn't restless for proof; it was enough for her to colour what she saw herself. And Polidori had often thought that if he had never known Lord Byron, if he had never travelled to Italy with him, if he had never been cast off, he might have been content to do the same. Ended up, perhaps, like Eliza's father: a man for whom introspection was the secret of an indifference to everything else. But Lord Byron had taught him what it was to live in the world, to put one's sense of self to the test. It occurred to him, now, that he had been so slow to appreciate her charms only because, in Lord Byron's shoes, he enjoyed a privilege of selection he didn't dare aspire to in his own. The story he had spun for Eliza, about the true nature of the vampyre, had allowed him to see his own life in the clear warm light of self-pity. He was another sufferer. Another helpless victim of Lord Byron's appetite for life. Another innocent, etc. The recognition allowed its own measure of freedom: to love a poor girl who hadn't understood yet what a fool she was making of herself; what a fool her lover was. He wanted to let Eliza know he had suffered, too.

Again and again, in the course of the afternoon, he endured in silence the temptation to confess everything to her. He couldn't get out of his thoughts the hope that her real forgiveness would redeem him. They walked to the end of the Steine, and in the stillness of the growing heat, surveyed the breadth of the sea around them. She confessed to him that she had never seen the sea before. She was amazed above all by the flatness of it, which seemed to her more than physical, but spiritual, too. It was a landscape which had no human variety to offer; what there was was rather 'mathematical'. She had always 'delighted particularly in your description of it', she said, pausing and staring out, before resuming again in her tone of comical hauteur:

> O'er the glad waters of the dark blue sea,
> Our thoughts as boundless, and our souls as free,
> Far as the breeze can bear, the billows foam
> Survey our empire, and behold our home!

But she found now, she continued in her own familiar voice, on observation, that though the ocean certainly suggested to her the nature of the infinite, the prospect of it seemed rather confining than otherwise. What poor creatures we appear against its scale! how little anything human would avail us, to make an impression upon *that* expanse.

They had reached a quiet stretch of the promenade, and

Polidori, with a smile, by way of contrary persuasion, recited for her:

> There be none of Beauty's daughters
> With a magic like thee,
> And like music on the waters,
> Is thy sweet voice to me:
> When as if its sound were causing
> The charmed ocean's pausing,
> The waves lie still and gleaming
> And the lull'd winds seem dreaming.

It was almost as if the poet were wooing himself. He had once heard Lord Byron console a girl with those lines – it was one of his tricks, to soften the effect of the misery he himself inspired. Byron used to joke that the Greeks had neglected in their roll-call of muses to name the muse of Apology; a creature both practical and tender, she had always served him well. While Eliza closed her eyes to hear him, Polidori added, 'There is nothing, no mountain or sea or sky, that might not be rendered human again, by the poetic imagination.' When she looked up again, her cheeks were wrinkled with wet, and she, feeling her own daring, took his arm and declared, 'I never guessed I was capable of such happiness.' He hadn't the heart then, to reveal himself to her.

At one o'clock they watched a parade of the Prince's regiment, the 10th Hussars, outside the gates of the Pavilion. Their horses were especially fine and marched in bright synchronicity. The sight of the sea, as she remarked, had attuned Eliza to the beauties of repetition. Then a guard discharged them, and the soldiers dispersed to find something and somewhere to drink. Eliza was shocked to see the swarm of dissolute girls who attended them: creatures whose chief attraction seemed to be their shamelessness. Ragged petticoats, loose bodices, exposed the dirty pallor of thighs and bosoms. The sight of them sobered her a little. Sometimes two or three crowded the brisk, indifferent step of a single soldier. What must they have suffered, she asked, to reduce them to this state? What can such men find in the ugliness of their female shame to attract them? Polidori didn't answer. She began to worry that she lacked the free appetite to satisfy a man of Lord Byron's taste; and she imagined herself, stripped bare as these girls, with their black hands and bruised ankles and torn shoes, hanging on his neck, as if every humiliation were only the real language of her desire.

They dined at a chop-house, like master and servant: on livers and bacon and a pint of stout each. Eliza began to enjoy her masquerade. But the beer went to her head, and she worried that the flush of drink on her cheeks ill-suited her ashy complexion. Standing up, she was forced to rest her hands on the table for a minute until her head cleared; and for the first half-hour afterwards, as they looked for somewhere to spend the night, Polidori had to keep Eliza on the wall side of him, to prevent her from straying into the road. She said to him, almost singing, as she bumped from time to time against his shoulder, 'Will you show me what to do? Later, will you show me what to do?' He remembered his own first sexual encounter, the maid washing her hands in the soap bucket afterwards, and Lord Byron's consolation: 'My first taste of passion was rather thrust upon me. But the worst of it was that I longed to repeat – the trial.' He nearly confessed everything to her then. Instead, he said, 'Nothing will astonish you more than how easy and natural everything seems.' She nodded her head, perfectly sober again.

They found a hotel which pleased her at last: the Castle Inn, in whose Assembly Rooms they took their tea. The ceiling above them rose, on classical columns, almost fifty feet in air. Every Wednesday in the summer months a ball was held within it; that night was to be the first of the season. And Eliza was instantly anxious to secure a room for the evening, at whatever cost. She had never been to a ball, but she said instead, 'Do you remember, when we danced at the Duchess of Devonshire's ball – what is it, now, almost four years ago? And you invited me to your rooms, *to see you off*, as you said? You were travelling to Dover in the morning. It seems to me too perfect, the notion of dancing at last the waltz we sat out together.' Polidori still had over ninety pounds in his pocket. They meant almost nothing to him, he could not imagine the stretch of his life beyond their spending. Inquiry revealed that several rooms remained, including a suite, which Polidori accepted. They were led up at once. It had a bedroom with a large four-poster bed, curtained with blue silk; the mattress was covered in white satin. In the sitting room, a chaise longue had been raised onto a dais and draped with brocade. The porter, with a knowing look, said it could be made up to accommodate the young man. The day-bed stood under a gilt mirror, which reflected the French windows opposite. These gave onto a balcony, protected by a fretwork grille; it overlooked the promenade and sea. Polidori, at a signal from Eliza, declared his perfect satisfaction. The porter took his leave, shutting the door behind him, with his hand against his back. The arrangements and the view occupied Eliza and Polidori, in delighting over them, for several minutes before they realized that they were perfectly alone for the first time that day.

Eliza lay on her back on the bed, and Polidori turned from the bedroom window to join her. She had taken off her cap at last; a fan of her pale hair spread across the white satin. She closed her eyes and felt a tremor in her throat of grief or happiness suspended and waiting for release, and then sensed the pressure of Polidori on the edge of the mattress. To think, she thought, that Lord Byron himself is observing me now! To think, what he plans to do with me! And then, to break the awkwardness of their silence, and in a rush of real enthusiasm, she sat up, wide-eyed, and declared, 'I must have a dress for the ball.' She could hear the strains of the orchestra rehearsing below them. Polidori, who had been reaching his hand towards her hair, now retracted it again. 'I should like, more than anything, to dance with you,' she said; and then, conscious of the snub in her remark, repeated, 'I should like it, that is, very much.'

The sun descending on the waters cast its level light into the room. Polidori felt himself entirely at her mercy or pleasure, and answered with real gentleness, in a phrase suggested indeed by his dependence, his consciousness of it, that he put himself entirely at her disposal. It was decided between them that to preserve her disguise Polidori would undertake to purchase her dress, her shoes, and all the necessary accompaniments. Eliza, indulging her own high spirits, gave him very particular instructions. It was rare, she thought, that she could play the *grande dame*, and she borrowed some of her enthusiasm from expressions she had known her sister to employ. Polidori sent out for a measuring-tape. When it arrived, Eliza had to guide his hands, around her waist, her bosoms, along her ankles and arms. She trembled violently as he touched her, and Polidori himself was deathly quiet and slow; they did not dare to kiss yet, and partly enjoyed the agonizing protraction of their enjoyment of each other. Polidori noted carefully, in a little book he had bought to jot down his literary inspirations, the dimensions she required.

And then he was gone, and she had the room to herself. She lay in bed for an hour in the white mist of sunshine, and fell asleep, and awoke with a hot face, just a little burnt in the light. How childish she felt, in her afternoon languor. She was not ungrateful for his absence, for the expectation of his arrival. She felt the pressures of keeping up her role very keenly, and looked forward to the moment when a simpler, more passionate and quieter part would be expected of her. Another form of imposture, no doubt; she did not yet trust the honesty of her pleasure-seeking. She stood up and drank a glass of water from the pitcher set on their night-stand, and then walked barefoot over the rough wool of the carpet to the balcony in their day-room. She looked out, over the Steine, the water; observed the tiny people and boats below her, busy in their unimportant lives. It was only when she noted the heaviness of the sun, taking on colour as it sank in setting, that she began to worry; and once the worries began, they arrived in floods.

First, she thought that Lord Byron had tired of her, had found some other, more willing, sacrifice to his amusement; and there were plenty, she knew, she had seen them herself, in that harbour town, willing to amuse. Then, that Bea and Lady Walmsley had tracked them there, to Brighton – had followed in the calèche and spotted Lord Byron outside the hotel, with a gown draped over his forearm and his intentions clear. That they had persuaded him to 'spare her', that was the word she imagined their using, 'spare the poor girl'. Perhaps, this minute, they were climbing the stairs to her room. She could almost hear the knock at the door and bit-terly regretted that matters, even now, had not gone 'far enough' to commit her to the course of life she was deter-mined to lead. Her *innocence* remained intact. That word itself suggested to her another fear, her sister's warning. (It amazed Eliza afterwards, how easily she had reconciled her doubts to each other.) Perhaps they had discovered at last some proof of his imposture. The real Lord Byron himself might have appeared to denounce the tender and hand-some young man she had kissed outside her father's cottage only two days before.

But even this worry tended only to increase her impa-tience, that whatever would happen *would* happen at last. And she realized, with a perfectly sober and clear view of her-self, that she could not return unchanged to the narrow exis-tence she had been leading: that she needed to break out, finally and irrevocably, from the sweet constriction of her imagined life. For a minute it seemed to her, with the rail of

186

the balcony in her hands, that the easiest course would be to lean out over it until the weight of her head and heart and breasts carried the rest of her with it; and she saw, peering over, the spot of ground where she imagined lying. Saw Lady Walmsley, Beatrice, Lord Byron standing over her body; felt the pity they felt for her. Felt his hand on her face as he stooped to caress her, the hand she had suffered only that afternoon to touch her neck, her hip, the ribs underneath her bosom. And she turned back into the room, exhausted again, by the weight of what she wanted from the world. If only, she thought, Lord Byron would come back, come back soon.

Polidori, by contrast, was rather relieved than otherwise by the solitude of his afternoon. But even in him the sense of expectation began steadily to increase. At first he enjoyed putting on lordly airs and throwing money around. He inquired after the costliest dressmaker in town and was directed to a dark little shop on North Street, where a matronly old lady in a pink bonnet, buying a frock for her youngest daughter's debut, instantly took him in hand. Polidori explained that his sister Frances had lately returned from the continent, only to discover that none of her Italian clothes were suitable for the English climate or English customs. He wished to give her a new gown, to speed her re-introduction into London life. He was presented with a number of materials, gingham and cambric and silk. The feel of them in his fingers offered a secret sensual thrill when he considered the skin against which they would slip and run that evening. Even the mathematical dimensions, as the cloth was cut, suggested vividly to him Eliza's boyish shape, the pressure of her small bosoms, the narrow hand's-breadth of her hips. He settled in the end on a pale green silk from France, patterned with a very small check; and asked, laying a ten-guinea note on the table, for the dress to be made up at once, since urgent business required him to return to London by the morning. Then he set off, under his instructions, to acquire the other necessary props to a lady's appearance, while they busied themselves over the material.

With all his errands run, he had another hour to wait while the dress was being finished, and he spent it on the promenade, looking out to sea. With an opera glass, Eliza might have recognized him from her balcony window: a straight-backed young man with his chin up, resting his weight on a walking stick. A row of temporary stalls had been erected against the barricades laid down to preserve the innocent relations of the water and the land. From one of these, he bought first a glass, and then the rest of the bottle of champagne, which he drank quietly in the equal yellow glow of the setting sun. He was summoning 'the nerve', for what exactly, confession or seduction, his internal silence left pointedly unclear; but the wine, at least, had the effect of cooling his own overheated anticipation. It had been almost a year since he had taken a woman to bed. He had forgotten, he told himself, remembering, the consolation they offered. Lord Byron had once remarked to him that he found something very softening in the presence of a woman, some strange influence, even if one was not in love with her. A caveat that instantly brought to mind the state in which Polidori had discovered Frances, after Lord Byron, deserting them both, it seemed, had departed for Venice. She sat in the garden overlooking the changing colour of her vineyards under the beautiful twilit autumnal Italian heavens and said to her brother, 'I don't want to live; I don't want to live any more. I see no reason why I should.' He reflected, and not for the first time, on how tawdry his own account of the affair appeared beside the quiet enduring gravity of the real thing; and murmured, not without a certain satisfaction, the last lines of his ghostly tale: 'she had already glutted the thirst of a Vampyre'.

He was steady, but perfectly drunk, by the time he collected the dress and returned to the hotel.

*

Eliza was fast asleep in the jagged red light that blew in through the curtained windows. By opening the door, he let in the full force of the orchestra tuning below; and it was this, not his own quiet step, that awoke the girl. 'I was dreaming,' she said when she saw him, and the door behind him had softened the music again, 'that I was only dreaming; that none of it was true.' She stretched like a cat, arching her back, and just as suddenly eased into a ball again. He unwrapped the gown and laid it on the bed beside her. She ran her finger along the cut of it. 'What I mean is, I thought you wouldn't come back. I'm so happy you have.' And then, rousing herself: 'I must try it on at once; such a beautiful green.' She stood up and began to undress, sleepily, like a child; but the unfamiliar fastenings of her costume required Polidori's assistance. She confessed blushing that Willis, Lady Walmsley's driver, had stolen the page's outfit for her. It had taken her over an hour to put on, which is why she'd been late to the coach-station. Together they removed her tunic; and the band of cloth which had wrapped her bosoms to her chest; and her trousers. She was wide awake by this time and stood perfectly naked before him. Her figure, girlish and half-formed, had something sisterly and unembarrassed in it, as if they were only children in summer preparing to swim together. Then she turned towards the mirror and held the dress against her skin. He saw her twice: a green and respectable lady in a silk gown in a gilt frame; and a naked back, the line of it curving between her shoulders, her buttocks, splitting in two and straightening at her knees, which were shaking. He came up behind her and held her to stop her shaking. Her face was already wet when she looked over her shoulder to kiss him.

What followed hurt more than she had ever guessed it would; though she was also surprised to note in herself, until the pain began, the surge of an appetite she couldn't have imagined before, whose sincerity she couldn't doubt or question. Polidori was amazed at the length of her back, which almost equalled his own; a feature he found particularly sensual. When they lay in bed together, their hips and faces touched. The noise of the orchestra had swelled into music below them, and she, throughout, remembered her green silk dress on the floor, and imagined the dances they would never dance. After he had finished, painfully it seemed to her, he held her, spooning; and she could sense his eyes twitching against the scratch of her hair. She still felt the ache in her sexual parts, a half-imagined pain, but it was tolerable; and she also felt that it gave her certain rights over him, over his powers of consolation. The pain seemed to her the price of her new happiness; she was terribly happy. They couldn't catch her now. All that was over, her innocence; and what remained was the endless freedom to corrupt herself further. 'What shall I call you,' she said. 'My lord? my love? I never know what to call you.'

'Call me P,' he said. 'B' or 'P' she couldn't be sure.

Polidori sensed the beginnings of a headache. The glow of the champagne had worn off and left in parting an uncomfortable chill behind his eyes and along his temples, which contrasted sharply with the flushed heat of his cheeks and tongue. Perhaps he was running a fever. He remembered only then what he had half-resolved to tell her *before*, but it was Eliza in the end, who said she had 'a confession to make – now that she was sure of him'. She giggled nervously in the pause that followed; he was relieved to hear her still capable of light-heartedness. 'I was never at the Duchess of Devonshire's ball. You danced with my sister,' she said. 'It was my sister who told me that night you were leaving at dawn, which is why I sneaked out to see you, to see if you were, if you would . . . Which is when I saw a young man I thought was you, and fell in love. But he ignored me. Everyone used to ignore me, until you took notice. And I went away.'

Polidori, almost without thinking, said, 'The young man you saw was me.'

He felt her stiffen in his arms – that slight brittleness

before the collapse of a world. 'What do you mean?' she said, but would not, though he tried to shift her, turn around. And he thought, hopefully, She must have prepared herself for this. One cannot so quickly recognize disillusion when it comes.

'I am the man you saw, that morning, when you fell in love. Lord Byron was in the next room, being . . . consoled by his sister. I was his doctor. My name is Polidori; he used to call me Dory or Polly, which is what you may call me, if you like. Our resemblance has often been remarked upon; we might have been brothers. I had no intention of deceiving you, at first; but you seemed so happy to be deceived.' And then, in a more plaintive tone, which staked some claim to the intimacy that had passed between them: 'I thought you had guessed. I thought it was a game we played, that we played together.'

He did not know what to expect of her, and for a minute, as she kept her silence, he had the leisure to wonder what she would say or do – to hope, in the tender aftermath of what B used to call their 'tooling', that what mattered was something other than Lord Byron's name. That they had fallen in love namelessly. But what she said, or rather shrieked, in the end, almost startled him to anger. Such petulance. She cried, 'This is not what I wanted at all. This is not what I wanted at all.' And when he tried to console her, with one hand tightening around her neck, and the other running through her hair, she almost screamed, 'Will you let go of me now? Let go of me now.' It seemed to him then what an ugly child she was, how brutally he had exposed her. She had brought her knees to her chest and begun to sob, giving way to disappointment as only children can – children dependent on the powers of others to make every-thing right again. Though he knew perfectly well by now that nobody could do that.

And, in fact, Eliza hadn't guessed yet how deep her affliction ran. She had seen in the shabbiness of their adventure the necessary disguise of something tragic and beautiful. Now she realized that it was only the dressing-up of insignificance. Neither of them mattered at all, this was the worst of it. But, with her quick imagination, her healing powers, she had already recast her role: she was the innocent abused, a creature with a pedigree almost as long and honourable as lovers'. And so she shuddered and wept until she grew tired of even that, and relied more simply on her exhaustion to cover up a little longer what she couldn't yet bear to look at plainly.

'What do you mean, Eliza? It's only me.' She heard him insist on the line, like a fly buzzing away and settling for ever on the same spot: 'It's only me.'

'But I don't know you,' she said. 'I don't know any Doctor Polidori.'

He was almost shouting now himself. 'But you fell in love with *me*. With me! Standing in the balcony window, three years ago.' She didn't answer him, and he began at last to repeat himself with the quieter petulance of resignation, 'You fell in love with *me*.'

Afterwards it amazed him, how long they lay there, in the old attitude, with everything changed. The orchestra had begun a waltz, and there was something comical in its three-legged beat, which he hoped might soften her into a more reasonable sense of their position. After all, he was perfectly willing to marry her. 'What would you like me to do?' he said. 'Would you like me to marry you?' He was confident that the trouble with both of them was only solitude and an excess of poetry – its promise of high living. Together they could settle into a happier, hum-drum, nameless sort of life. Polidori had always clung to whatever was being taken from him; and as he felt Eliza slipping away, he said, 'I've fallen in love with you.'

'I would like you to leave me alone,' she answered, like a child, dismissing out of hand what she hadn't asked for. As she lay on the satin sheets (in spite of everything, enjoying

192

their costliness, their coolness) she wanted terribly for her sister to scold her. Only Bea could put her back in her place, as she always did – until Eliza rebelled again. She had been prepared to give up her innocence for *him*, but that was all. She would not yet willingly surrender the grandeur of life. She felt the stickiness leaking between her legs, and it disgusted her; but she didn't yet know there was a trace of blood in it.

Later, as he was dressing, he saw the smear of it, a few spots dabbling the white sheets. She lay on her hip and her bosom with her face in the pillow. He had an image, of her father and sister, of Lady Walmsley with her cloudy hair, coming too late to rescue Eliza, and finding her there, in her own blood, in the bed. He was the vampyre, he understood that for the first time; whatever he touched he corrupted. He had no life of his own. For years he had fed off the blood of everyone around him: Frances, Lord Byron, and now *her*. He was hardly alive at all. He emptied the contents of his purse between her feet and kept back ten pounds for himself, for his homeward journey. He knew what he was going to do, at last. She felt the flutter of the notes on her skin and guessed its cause; only then did the full misery of her position strike her, but by the time she sat up in bed, he was already gone.

CHAPTER EIGHTEEN

YEARS LATER, HIS FATHER MAINTAINED that when Polly came back from Brighton that Thursday morning, he was already very ill. His speech, both slow and abrupt, lacked coherence; and he complained of a headache and retired almost immediately to his old room. On Friday, when they discovered him, the glass by his bed was empty; and the doctor they summoned kindly omitted to examine the dregs within it. For the rest of his life, Gaetano could never hear his son's name, John, without being startled into tears. The family, consequently, tended to avoid any mention of him.

They'd been surprised to see him that morning; he rarely visited. And he looked half-starved. His cheeks had a hollow in them you could fill with a fist. Then there was that slurring in his voice. At the time Gaetano wondered whether his son was merely drunk. Polly asked whether Frances was home – he wanted to sleep again in his old bed. He hadn't, he said, slept in three days; he had only just come back from Brighton on a piece of business which went rather badly. 'Should we wake you for dinner?' his father asked, and Polly answered that he would wake himself.

Frances had taken her son to buy him new shoes. At first it annoyed her, on their return, to have to make do with the sitting room. William wanted his nap, and Esmé refused to leave the poor child alone. Frances tried to make her understand that the boy needed sleep; and the two sisters (so many years apart) made up together a bed on the settee. But once William had been laid upon it, Esmé offered to read to him – which, Frances learned, really meant asking him questions. Esmé had discovered the dictionary. She carried it with her wherever she went. Her conversation had declined, as Gaetano put it, into a series of interrogations, on meaning and spelling – the answers to which, if guilty of the least deviation, set off in Esmé shrieks of delighted scolding. To be fair, she took pity on her nephew William. He was three years old, and couldn't, as she said, be expected to know the difference between *vatic* and *vastative*. So she condescended at last to read to him, as a soporific – a word Esmé had begun generously to employ. She continued in the Vs. By this time it was almost four o'clock. William was sorely in need of his nap; and Frances, irritably, suggested to Esmé that she should wake up their brother, asleep in her bed, and bother *him* with words. He was almost a poet himself, after all.

Polly, in spite of his exhaustion, had lain sleeplessly in his sister's womanly scent, overlaid with William's sweet powdery baby-smells, for almost an hour that morning. He needed to sleep a little; he needed a clear head for what he was going to do. Of all acts a man could undertake, he believed, this above all should be free of slurring, should be rendered perfectly distinct. His headache had almost spent itself, a relief or cessation of pain not unlike restfulness.

A few years ago, shortly after his return from Italy, a carriage he was travelling in had run over a fallen branch, and upset. He had been, for reasons of expense, riding on top; had turned over in his fall and landed violently on the back of his neck. The accident had considerably frightened him. But it left him with no visible injuries, and he had congratulated himself, at the time, on his good luck: on the propitious star, which, for once, had seemed to shine on him. It might, who knew, usher in a more general change in fortune. A month afterwards he began to be plagued by headaches unlike any he had known before. Their pain

suggested to him most forcibly, by way of analogy, the dislocation of a star from its sphere – as if his brain, which had
once rested, in the natural order of things, within his skull,
had shifted slightly, and no amount of correction, no matter how nice, could ever restore it to its former and exact
relation to his body.

There were occasions (although, as he lay in Frances's
smells, this was not one of them) when he blamed the
decline of his hopes and prospects not on the fateful
influence of Lord Byron, but on the simpler injury to his
head. The effects he ascribed to each disaster were the
same: the dislocation, as he poetically conceived it, of a star
from its sphere. As if something, whether biological or psychological, necessary to a man's relation to the world, had
been damaged irreparably in him; as if nothing he could do
or think would ever tally again with the deeds or thoughts of
others; as if, like a vampyre, he was doomed to take nourishment not from what was healthy and natural in the inter-
course of men, but from their blood; as if he could live only
at the terrible cost of the lives around him. In which case
(and the reasoning followed with consoling inevitability),
there was still something left for him to do. But he wanted a
clear head for it; he wanted to sleep.

The bed was still warm with Frances's body; and he
remembered, sometimes, when Lord Byron went riding
after lunch, sneaking into the poet's room to read whatever
B had left on his writing table. There were books, opened at
the spine; correspondences; fresh compositions. Lord
Byron tended to scribble in the small hours, coming home,
a little drunk, too restless for sleep. And part of the charm
for Polly lay in the fact that Byron had often described, in his
own vivid and discursive style, some part of the evening
they had spent together, whether in the rambling hedge-
rows of verse that formed *Childe Harold*, or the wilder uncut
prose of his letters. It was, for Polidori, like discovering, after
an orphaned childhood, that your father had been a king,

that you were a king, now, too. That everything you did, every circumstance of your birth and life, had a wider range of significance, tremendous repercussions. That you were, in fact, the centre of a general interest. It was wonderful for him to see the way the world shifted around you when you lived at the heart of it. And sometimes, as he read, he sat on Lord Byron's bed – and, since it was a cold wet Swiss summer – crawled under his covers, and breathed the air of his sleep. Almost hoping to be discovered at last, and scolded or seduced.

He slept, for an hour or so, until his father woke him with a knock at the door, to see if he wanted to dine with them. It was already two o'clock. Polidori, recognizing the little finalities that were beginning everywhere to crowd around him, made a point of thanking Gaetano with a particular tenderness as he declined; though whether it was afterwards remarked upon, he would never know. The reason, above every sentimental association, that led him to insist on being given his old bedroom, was that he stored his medical equipment there. And as he rose, somewhat refreshed, with his head perfectly clear, to fetch it from the dusty top of the wardrobe pushed into a corner against the chimney-breast, the sight of the black leather portmanteau roused in him memories of the other occasions he had had for using it. That poor boy who was chased under a horse, cracking a rib, for which Dr Taylor had summoned him all the way to Norwich, to assist in re-setting it. Also, to give him the message about Lord B, that he wanted a doctor. Polly remembered hearing, afterwards, about the riots that followed the news of the boy's death. Then there was that terrible run of luck in Venice, when he had killed, in the space of a week, a banker, his son, and the Earl of Guilford, inspiring Lord Byron to quip, that Dr Polidori had no more patients, because his patients were no more. A *good thing* his lordship never tired of repeating, and which, even at this remove, cheered Polidori a little, by the recollection of the poet's careless humour. Yes, he thought, that was the way to *take life* – a phrase that brought with it another little smile.

He was, in fact, far from cheerless, as he sat on his bed and dusted the black leather and began to assemble, with professional care, the necessary vials and powders. The end, at least, was in sight; he had it in his hands. And there was nobody, he had to admit, better placed to administer it. He almost heard, in Byron's characteristic accent, both arch and tender, the poet tell him, smiling, 'Physician, heal thyself.' Yes, he would, and with the usual result. But he was conscious, too, of a deeper source of consolation, of pride, even. Here, at last, was something he had the mettle for; and it pleased him in the end to know that he was going one better than his lordship dared. Wasn't this, after all, the final promise of all Lord Byron's melancholy versifying, the 'sad and sole relief' he had so often sung about – that sweet venom which the Mind, like an encircled scorpion, reserved for itself? Polly had brought with him, to bed, a glass of water; and he now dropped into it a tablet of magnesium, which dwindled in sinking and emitted a stream of variable effervescence. The bubbles gathered at the rim of the glass and broke into air at the surface. They would hide some of the bitterness of the cyanide.

And he remembered, as he stirred the powder in, one night after a party at Coppet, returning arm in arm with Lord Byron along the shores of Lake Leman. De Staël, with that awful frank coquetry of an ugly woman, had been insisting that Lord Byron should attempt a reconciliation with his wife – if only for the sake of their daughter, Ada. Her choice of topic was awkwardly timed. Byron had only that afternoon received a letter from his sister, after a conspicuous silence. It was full of the strangest frights and alarms. In it Augusta seemed to suggest that she had, on the best advice – and he had no doubt *whose* – been persuaded to desist from communicating with him any further. The force of the arguments which had been made to her depended, it seemed, upon the legal consequences of a continued, etc. Byron guessed at once what the poor little Goose was afraid of: that *those*, who knew *everything*, had threatened to take her own children away – for the children's sake. 'My contagion,' Lord Byron said, 'can spread, it seems, yeah, even unto the generations, which are as leaves.'

A hot clear summer night, with the stars very low and crowded in the sky, and the waves persisting faintly in spite of the breathless air pressing upon the waters. 'There is nothing,' Byron cried out, 'that *paragon of womanhood* won't poison. Whatever was once noble and just in her, she has poisoned; whatever was loving in me, she has poisoned; but that her vile *virtue* could infect a creature as dear, as innocent, as my sister . . .' And then, in a different tone: 'The only thing, I confess, which keeps me from blowing my brains out is the thought that it would give pleasure to my mother-in-law.' Polidori listened in silence; he heard, beneath the poet's habitual vaunting, a colder and more forceful misery. So that when Byron bade him good-night at last, he insisted on following him up to bed; he removed the pistol his Lordship kept under the pillow. Byron saw him do it; and as he lay down, turned his eyes up at the young man, and asked, less plaintive than mocking, 'Will you not let me sleep? will you not let me sleep at last?' And, in fact, Polidori sat over him, stroking the curls around the poet's ears, until he could.

How often in the course of his life had Lord Byron threatened to end it! There was the misery of his foot – he used to hope that, in case of a general resurrection, he would rise up with a better *pair of legs* or be sadly left behind in the squeeze into Paradise. The misery of his 'fathering, or rather, *mothering*' as he put it – Mrs B was a vain, ugly, sagacious, adoring mockery of her son. Then the ordinary misery of his youth; it was a kind of game, among his college set, to boast of their intended suicides. The misery of his first literary reception: 'Hours of Idleness' had been fiercely greeted by the *Edinburgh Review*, a lashing to which Lord Byron often referred when consoling Polidori for the abuse heaped upon his own poetical specimens. The restless misery of a young man as he set off for the first time to explore the world, which was followed, on his return, by the settled misery of his marriage. And then the misery of that dark sin which was both the burden of all his verse and the unforgivable hope at the heart of it: the dream of selfless love, pure, free and equal, fraternal and generative at once – which he had found finally in his sister's arms, which had been taken from him, which he had learned to do without. For though he talked of death, and played with pistols, and drank from skulls, something cowardly in Byron persisted in living; he hadn't the courage that Polidori had. Polidori had discovered at last the one thing he would taste first-hand that the poet didn't dare to, though he was sobbing childishly as he raised the glass to his lips. Esmé was banging on the door, and he imagined as he drank Lord Byron himself – as he had three years before at Diodati, after their row over the ghost-story – entering at the fatal minute, his arm stretched forth, his gesture expanding into an embrace.